H

. . . a forbidden love

Dennis E. Hackin

Published by:
Vargas Publishing
P.O. Box 6801

Lubbock, TX 79493
ISBN 10: 0996818626
ISBN 13: 9780996818629

Dedicated To

" V "

Thy Techno Tis Magico

CASSETTE NUMBER ONE JUNE THIRD

Hierarchical network...hierarchical storage management... hierarchical data link control...It was a sunny, crisp autumn afternoon. The coptersedan whirly-twirly'd down from the sky like a hummingbird that had sucked honey out of an opiated flower.

Inside the stainless steel machine Paul Quatro looked through the circular photograde passenger window and thought about his promotion. Techno-Manager at the Department of Technology.

He was a man on the rise.

Mr. Miggs, the real estate salesman, was telling Mary all about the house they were considering buying.

"It's completely computerized! The future is now! Take the advantage!"

Paul didn't like Mr. Miggs. But then, Paul didn't like salesmen. They were everywhere, selling everything.

Ukiah Miggs had done a computer check on Paul and Mary Quatro; they were upwardly mobile. Credit in the computer bank. They were buyers!

Mary was frightened at first as the sky cracked open. She turned to Paul, suddenly childlike.

"Paul, hold me. I'm frightened."

Paul put his arm around Mary and pulled her warm body next to his. They had made love in the morning, and he could still smell the scent of her sex. He put his fingertips to his nostrils.

He said, "It's only the weather dome hatch, dear."

Mary blushed with embarrassment upon hearing her husband's explanation.

Mr. Ukiah Miggs maneuvered the coptersedan through the weather dome entrance. The iron dome door automatically closed, and the stainless steel machine hovered through the perma-frost clouds that clung to the dome's ceiling.

"Twenty-four-hour weather control at your command. Daytime temperature, 78.6 degrees fahrenheit with a nighttime average of 65 degrees. Thirty days of light rain showers and a guarantee that you'll have snow every Christmas."

The salesman had a smug grin on his face as he banked the coptersedan out of the perma-frost clouds.

"Mr. and Mrs. Quatro, welcome to Computer Meadows."

Paul and Mary looked through the circular photograde passenger window. Small beads of perma-frost dripped down the window giving a distorted reflection of the all-new computerized community.

"Logical," Paul thought to himself.

Mary squeezed her husband's arm, whispered, "Fantastical."

Ukiah Miggs turned to Paul and said confidently, "Affordable."

The real estate salesman landed the coptersedan on top of the welcome center. As he led his clients onto the conveyor sidewalk that would glide them to their dream house, he spoke of the marvelous technological advancements Computer Meadows offered.

"Nowhere in the United States does an all-computerized community offer free weather control, robotic garbage disposal, serviceable produce delivery, medical house calls and a full security force."

Paul didn't want to call Mr. Ukiah Miggs a liar, but computer communities were being built in all twenty-five states of the union. The mile and two-mile-high sleeper structures were no longer necessary in a society that was expanding towards new horizons.

"What's that?"

Mary's inquisitive voice always reminded Paul of an innocent little girl. He loved his wife. She made him happy.

Mary pointed at a circular chrome tube with a neon door. Mr. Miggs, always quick to point out a luxury, stopped the conveyor sidewalk in front of the tube.

"No longer will you have to copter to employment; be late for an appointment; miss a shopping date. Every owner at computer Meadows has the advantage of the pipeline."

The salesman opened the neon door, and Mary looked inside the chrome circular tube. There was a sterile ambiance to this new invention.

Paul knew all about pipeing. He had studied the plans over at the department. Yes, the pipeline was a great advancement in transportation. As great as the airplane had once been in the twentieth century. Now, two hundred years later the airplane had become as useless as the once-great horseless carriage.

"In thirty seconds you can pipe anywhere in Washington, D.C.," said Miggs.

Paul didn't like his tone of voice. He was too sure of his statements. All surface, no substance. But then, that was the nature of a salesman, wasn't it?

"How does it work?" asked Mary. Before the salesman could speak, Paul interjected his knowledge.

"Molecular transference from one location to another."

Miggs didn't like Paul Quatro. He knew too much. And anybody who knew more than Mr. Ukiah Miggs was a threat. But, like all good salesmen, he never let his feelings interfere with a sale. He grinned like a middle-aged Cheshire Cat who strategically placed himself underneath the dining room table for scraps.

Paul finished telling Mary the entire readout on the new MTT's Molecular Transference Transporters, which was the official name for the new invention. If Paul felt the pipeline was safe, then Mary felt it was safe. She loved her husband. He made her feel safe.

The conveyor sidewalk carried them past a robot milkman enroute to their deliveries. They were called service organizers. They were programmed to respond to humans in limited service situations.

"Good day, Mr. Miggs," said the robot milkman. His metal lips clicked together as he spoke.

Mr. Miggs would never respond to a robot unless he wanted something, and this day he didn't want milk. Only the bank credit on a sale from a young couple buying their first computer home.

4

Paul noticed a young couple on solarcycles sail by. They were about the same age as Paul and Mary. Young, virile, athletic, healthy, dressed in the latest solarcycle fashion. Synthetic multi-colored shorts and shirts and gym sandals.

Paul didn't like solarcycles. They were bicycles with solar sails, attached to the frame. If you didn't feel like pedaling, the solar sail would inflate and sail you along the boulevard like a sailboat on water.

Although Paul Quatro was a technocrat, he didn't like useless inventions that only cluttered up the citizens' thirst for buying. Yet, he could already see in Mary's eyes that she would have to have a solarcycle if they moved into Computer Meadows. And that meant he would have to get one, too.

Because they were a couple together, sharing activities, making each other happy just for the happiness of being together. They were the essence of the Together Generation: young...upward ...mobile...but most of all, together.

The Together Generation would correct the mistakes made by the academians. The Together Generation would make sure that computers hummed in harmony for all mankind. The Together Generation went beyond the elitists, Paul knew, who had the audacity to believe that they were the right program.

Mr. Miggs stopped the conveyor sidewalk and turned towards the ultra-modern all-computerized house.

"This is the Fountain-of-Youth model."

He could see in the young couple's eyes that they liked the name of the model. This new generation with the lifespan of a hundred and seventy years wanted to stay young forever.

They had no respect for his generation. The It Generation.

Mr. Miggs remembered when he was young, and how different the world was back then. A world that was just coming out of The Great Trauma Shock. A world that was rebuilding. A world that pointed its computer finger at a generation and said, "You're it. Don't look back! Regroup! Rebuild!"

And so Mr. Miggs' generation was it. They took the destructive baton from their parents and completed the dream. But, like all dreams, they can never be completed, and so it is for the next generation to build into that dream and change it into their own dream.

They walked up the plastic sidewalk. The synthetic grass was emerald green in color. Blue oil was sprayed out of the sprinkler system to keep the synthetic grounds fertile. Computer Meadows was a constantly lubricated community.

No rust! No aging! No breakdown!

As Mr. Miggs fumbled to get the right computer card out of his key ring, Paul realized that the music he thought was in his thoughts was actually being played over the community computerfonic system. He noticed small speakers that looked like mechanical birds in the trees.

Mary straightened his tie and looked up at him with happiness in her eyes.

"Oh, darling. Isn't this wonderful?"

Paul had to admit that it was exciting. He disliked the mile-high sleeper structure they were living in. Whenever there was a strong wind, the building swayed like a ship in a storm. How

6

many seagulls flying south for the winter had crashed into their picture windows and broken their necks? The elevators were always crowded. When they had first been married three years earlier, it was the place to habitat. All of their friends had been envious that they'd been the first to hab in the mile-high sleeper.

"Affordable," was the word Mr. Miggs echoed in the coptersedan.

And with Paul's new advancement at the department, he could surely afford to get bank credit for the computerhouse --- Paul Quatro liked being first in his group of technocrats.

He and Mary wanted the lifestyle everybody was talking about in the Together Generation. It could be seen everywhere.

On the public computer screens that advertised every product, available on the free market. The entertainment centers with their two-hundred-foot-high screens and cyclorama visualizations reminding the young, the up, the mobile Together Generation that it was all for the working.

"Each home has its own computer card code," said Ukiah Miggs as he slipped the right computer card into the monitor slit that was located next to the front door.

A soothing computer sound could be heard transmitting the code, and then the door unlocked and Paul and Mary entered their dream house.

"Notice the all-computerized kitchen," said Miggs, as he led Mary by the hand to each ultra-appliance. Paul didn't like other man touching his wife.

"Oh, Paul, look. It has an automat-dietary-nutritional-food-analytical selector!"

Mr. Miggs jumped on the opportunity to sell as soon as he heard Mary's enthusiasm. He quickly spoke up.

"Just what every intelligent householder deserves."

Mary may have seemed innocent, but she did have her degree in Computer Bio-Feedback and she didn't like Mr. Miggs being so condescending.

Ukiah Miggs knew when to retreat with a customer, and he took a step back, allowing the young couple to feel their way around the house.

It was in the bedroom that Paul decided to buy the house. He and Mary had pressed a button on a panel, and the air bed floated down from the ceiling like a magic carpet. It had a sound and sonic motion which they both discovered when Mary laid back and rolled across the bed to get a feel for it.

She looked over at Paul, her long, blonde hair seductively hiding her face. Paul could feel her sex as she coquettishly whispered, "Oh, what fantasies I could show you on this bed." She wiggled her finger, motioning him to come aboard. Paul looked around to see if Mr. Miggs was close by.

Mary realized that sometimes Paul could be a bit of a square-rule, so she turned on the heat.

"Don't be afraid, little human."

She smiled lazily. Her words circulated into his eroscenter. He remembered their lovemaking in the morning. And so Paul Quatro lay down next to his wife and held her in his arms and whispered softly in her ear, "I love our togetherness." They kissed with pure feeling.

8

Mr. Miggs licked his lips as he viewed them from the control computer screen in the master library. He was already counting the commission he would make from these two happily married citizens. In so doing, he would be able to buy that new Vette sportcopter and impress the girls who hung out at the copter dancetorium and who were always looking for a quick nibble, even if it wasn't a young nibble!

As Paul looked over Mary's shoulder, his right eye popped open in shock. The salesman was standing in the bedroom! Mr. Miggs winked and slid noiselessly from the room.

Paul definitely did not like the salesman. But he did like the house. And when Paul liked something, he worked hard to get it. He knew that with his new promotion at the department he would be able to get bank credit. He knew that with the purchase of the Fountain-of-Youth house, he and Mary would be the first of their group to live in an all-computerized house.

He knew he liked being first. He liked the lifestyle. Paul rolled Mary on top of him and stuck his tongue into her warm mouth. They were young. They were upward. They were mobile, and they were turned on to each other's sex.

Mary arched her head back. Paul lifted up and pulled her back down towards him. They rolled across the air bed, and then he looked down at her and smiled.

"Happy anniversary, my sweet love."

Mary smiled back. "Happy anniversary, my love of loves."

Hierarchical storage management...hierarchical data link control ...hierarchical network...hierarchical...The diamond digital computer clock blended Paul's dream into reality as the melodic nocturnal music evaporated into a morning calypso symphony.

Paul lifted up slowly and looked over at Mary. Sound asleep. No matter how many times he set the clock's wake-up music, she still never woke up before him.

Paul turned over and tried to catch some sleep, but it was all in vain. The 3-D circular vid screen was already being extended on its mechanical arm towards their bed. Click! It turned on automatically. The screen flicked on, and the face of a kindly old gentleman dressed in a white nightgown with wings on his shoulders was seen coming out of a cloudburst.

"Good morning, Paul. The time is nine seconds before nine minutes before 9:00 a.m. Thursday, June third. 2145."

Paul rolled over on his back and looked up at the circular vid screen attached to that mechanical arm. It reminded him of a dream he once had where he found himself in a bowl of cherries fighting off a mechanical snake. He rubbed his eyes with both hands and sat up in bed with an early morning yawn.

The vid announcer continued his wake-up call.

"Good morning, Mary. You have an eye appointment with Dr. Lisa Kirk at 11:00 a.m."

The vid announcer was an old friend. Mary turned over and noticed Paul sliding off the air bed. She never could understand why he got up so early.

"Darling, come back to bed."

But her words went unattended. Paul was already putting on his exercise suit and plugging the cord into its computer socket.

10

Exercise suits were the latest in exercise, health and bodily care. They were elastic and wired with ultra transmissions that massaged every muscle in the wearer's body.

Paul liked the new exercise suits because they allowed the non-athletic citizen to feel athletic. He stood on the exercise platform in front of the wall screen that had a 3-D video projection of a road out in the country.

He could press the wind button and a cool breeze would blow on his face. Or he could press any number of buttons that would project any number of outdoor scenes. If you can't go to the Grand Canyon, bring the Grand Canyon to you.

Mary slid out of bed and stood in front of the multi-layered mirror. Her naked body was still firm and supple; her breasts still full of youth. She walked toward the cosmetic room and spoke to Paul before entering.

"Sweets, do you know what day this is?"

Paul didn't hear his wife's question because he had on a set of headphones and was listening to yesterday's briefing from Secretary of Technology Richards.

"The hierarchical network for the Elcon computers are becoming obsolete. We must create a new system."

Paul turned just as Mary entered the cosmetic room. He was always attracted to her sex.

Mary pressed the computer button as she stepped into the sunken shower tub. The glass curtain lowered from the ceiling, and the dozen nozzles began to shoot out an assortment of body nutrients from vitamin E compounds to birth control fluid and hair shampoo.

11

Mary was addicted to the showers. And then the three mechanical metal arms with the sponge hands began to scrub and massage and relieve her body of all the tension she felt. Something was wrong with Paul. They hadn't had sex in over thirty-six hours. It was the first thirty-six-hour period they had ever experienced together when they hadn't had sex. Except, of course, for the times he went away on business trips for the department. Mary felt depressed.

Paul didn't even seem to know what day it was!

The index mechanical arm worked overtime to relieve Mary of her tension. She spread her legs as two of the mechanical arms gently held her in position for the index arm. She was floating in her own doubts. Suddenly, she arched her back and pressed her buttocks and vagina against the sponge. She let out an urgent moan as relief flooded her being.

Still, nothing Mary did or said that morning seemed to make Paul happy. His mind was on something else. Could he have met another woman? Other couples of the Together Generation had experimented with cross habitation. Togetherness could be shared by three just as easily as two. Or four. Or even five. Mary had visualized these experiments in an article in People's Computer while she was at the cosmetic salon waiting to have her hair bent.

But it wasn't an appealing thought to her visualization about her own life. She didn't want to share the only man she ever loved with someone else. She looked over from the automat where she had just pressed a button indicating her wish that Paul's favorite nourishment be prepared.

Paul was seated in the vid nook sipping his morning vitafee and visualizing the morning news on the three-screen multi-national channels.

Mary wondered whether Paul wanted to share her with others as she pressed the automat's service button...President Ricarda has delivered her new three-year Agro-budget to Congress...Premier Vostock of the United Soviet States is vacationing in the South of Georgia with his family...King Bowanda of Uganda has donated three billion bank credits to the citizens of his kingdom to be used for pleasure in the Annual Feast of Happiness...

Paul sipped his hot vitafee and made notes on his computer pad.

The conference this afternoon was of great importance to the nation.

Isn't that what Secretary of Technoiogy, Elliot Richards, said to him before he left the office yesterday?

What Elliot Richards said when it came to the pulse of government was usually right on the button. The Secretary of Technology was an extraordinary man.

Paul had worked for him ever since he got his appointment at the department. The two men thought alike.

If it hadn't been for the Secretary's influence, Paul never would have climbed that upward mobile ladder of success as quickly. He was the youngest undersecretary of Technology in the history of the department. And all because of his mentor, Elliot Richards. A most extraordinary man.

"Lovey, I've prepared your favorite dish."

Paul flicked the multi-national channel without looking up at Mary. He extended his hand to take the warm plate as the vid announcer gave the morning sports result. Paul, like most of the young men of his generation, was a big ball fan. And this was the middle of the big ball season.

Mary's Irish heritage swelled up inside her veins.

"Paul, you've totally forgotten what day this is."

Paul turned and noticed his wife standing next to the refuse disposal, crying.

"You don't love me anymore!"

She wiped her tears with her apron. Paul put his hands on her shoulders and whispered softly.

"Mary, it's June third."

She pulled away from his advances and angrily snapped back like a hurt child.

"Of course, it's June third."

Paul felt miserable. He never liked it when his mind drifted too far away and got lost in his work. It was at those important times that he generally forgot the importance of togetherness with Mary.

"Go back to your big ball scores."

She wasn't letting him off the button.

"The scores aren't important!" he cried. He tried once again to hold her, but she shrugged her shoulders away from his touch.

14

"Mary, happy anniversary."

He hadn't forgotten! Mary turned around, her face wet with tears, and faced her husband of ten years. He had a small gift-wrapped package in his hand that he had been keeping in his coat pocket.

"Paul Quatro. Sometimes…" her hurt was drifting away.

She untied the red ribbon and carefully unwrapped the silver and gold paper. Mary loved getting gifts.

"Oh, what could it be?"

She held the small aluminum case, not wanting to rush the enjoyment of the moment.

"Darling, open it. I have to go to work."

As soon as he said the words, he knew he shouldn't have spoken. It was in her eyes. The joy of receiving a gift had been tarnished by his impatience.

"It's marvelous."

Her disappointment was held in reserve. She liked the delicate platinum, gold, red neon heart-shaped locket computer watch that was attached to an exquisite Indian Ocean pearl necklace.

"I'll wear it forever."

She kissed Paul. They held their embrace, and then Mary quickly forgot her anger. It was so typical of Mary, Paul thought. Angry one minute and then happy and forgiving the next.

"Close your eyes."

He did what she asked. Even though the clock in his hand was ticking away. He couldn't get the conference out of his mind. Everybody from the department would be there. It was difficult sometimes to be in harmony with one's wife and work hard climbing that upward, mobile ladder of success.

"Open your eyes." Mary stood in front of Paul holding onto a nine-foot-tall gift-wrapped narrow box.

"What on Earth?" Paul couldn't imagine what she had gotten him.

"Happy anniversary, lovey!"

Paul quickly tore off the purple-and-yellow gift paper and ripped open the box.

"Great thunder. Computer pogo stilts!" he shouted.

"Just what every Undersecretary of Technology needs!"

She laughed.

"Go ahead outside and test-jump them. Hurry, before you're late for that important conference."

She really did understand his consciousness.

The backyard of the Quatro computer house had the latest in backyard luxury. Pleasure automatic lounge recliners with porta vid screens. A kidney bean-shaped swimming pool with aqua turquoise vita fluid. A low and a high diving board. Synthetically groomed African violets, Hawaiian palms, ultra-turf, just like they used in the big ball stadiums.

"Higher!"

Paul had the computer pogo stilts set at medium height velocity.

"Higher!"

Mary shouted out again for all the neighborhood to hear. Paul looked at the height meter and realized he was too hundred feet above his backyard. He could see Howard and Bernice Bork, his next door neighbors, standing next to Mary. He could see the entire Computer Meadows community. Oh, what a wonderful lifestyle he had!

"Ride 'em, spaceman," yelled Howard, cupping his hands upwards towards Paul.

Howard and Bernice Bork were part of the Together Generation. They had befriended Paul and Mary when they first moved in next door. What a relief to find out you liked your neighbors. They had moved in a month before the Quatros.

At the time, Howard was a junior purchasing agent at Techno, the greatest technological department store in Washington, D.C...in all of the twenty-five states of the union. Bernice always liked to mimic Howard after he had finished some pontification about Techno.

Over the years, Howard Bork, like Paul, worked hard climbing that upward, mobile ladder of success. Howard, too, was part of the Together Generation. Seven years later he was vice president in charge of purchases for the entire Techno department store chain.

"Higher," Bernice yelled.

Bernice was a woman with a genius I.Q. who preferred to shop and have her body massaged every afternoon at the cosmetic salon than utilize that great mind and work for the system. Bernice always figured that a woman's place was to stay as young as possible. She admired Mary's charitable work once a week at the Veteran's Hospital. But that kind of work wasn't for her.

Paul could feel the pogo stilts beginning to shake out of control. He looked on the computer panel for the safety chute, but it was too late. The stilts had swerved off their trajectory, and Paul found himself tumbling down to Earth. He remembered Mary and Bernice screaming, and then he hit the swimming pool like a pelican. Head first.

As he struggled to the surface he kept thinking about the conference…hierarchical network…a new system. He reached the surface and spit out a stream of water.

"Happy anniversary, lovey."

Howard helped Paul out of the pool. The two men had become friends. Their wives liked each other. They made a happy foursome. They took vacations together. The year before, they all went to see the ruins of what had once been the greatest city in the world, New York. They had danced the night away in front of the ancient Empire State Building with irreverent happiness. It was on that vacation that Howard had suggested that they mingle their wives with each other. He had candidly told Paul that Bernice was very attracted to him, and that he had been complimented by that because he had such respect for Paul's mind.

Howard and Bernice always felt they were in the vanguard of the Together Generation when it came to being one step ahead of the group.

18

A computer journalist had even coined phrases for this segment of that generation: they were called "Uppies," or "Upsters," or just plain "Ups," for nothing could affect their positive pursuits with the upward, mobile ladder of success.

They were always first in buying the latest luxury inventions. They were always experimenting with the different combinations of togetherness. Threes! Fours! Fives!

Paul even remembered seeing a vid seg on the morning news about one couple who had found togetherness with a hundred combinations. As fantastic as it seemed, that's what the journalist had uncovered.

But Paul had no desire to mingle the only woman he had ever loved. No, he and Mary had no desire to become "Upsters." They would leave the "Upping" to Howard and Bernice. The two neighbors always took the conveyor sidewalk to the pipeline together each morning on their way to employment.

Paul had been right. The pipeline had replaced the airplane and copters as the main form of transportation.

"Pipeing to" had added thousands of minutes to every citizen's personal time bank. Paul himself was able to pipe to work in less than fifteen seconds.

He knew of experiments that were taking place at the pipeing test grounds in Bethesda, Maryland with a new pipeline that would eventually allow pipeing to other countries. He had evaluated the computer diagrams.

He hated waiting in spaceports. A flight from Washington, D.C. to Paris actually took ninety-seven minutes. With pipeing, he would eventually be able to make the same trip in less than six.

"Who knows, Howard, maybe someday we'll be able to pipe to other planets."

Howard didn't like pipeing. Like a lot of citizens, it made him sick to his stomach. So he was constantly buying an assortment of indigestion medicants that brought temporary, fast relief.

"I'd prefer they invent a pipeing proof tab that would cure my pipesickness."

The two men waited in line at the pipeline.

Paul noticed a forcebot standing guard next to the pipe.

These were robots programmed in security enforcement. Oh, there wasn't what you would call crime in Computer Meadows. On occasion, a robot in the service of the community would de-program, and that could cause some damage.

Last year a mailbot had de-programmed while servicing the Wilsons on Silicon Boulevard, just one street west of Mary and Paul. The robot broke Mr. Wilson's neck and pelvis. He was melted down and fed into a test tube baby orphanage's furnace on the poor side of town.

"Bernice wanted me to remind you that she's made reservations at Circuit's Circus."

Circuit's Circus was Mary's favorite eatery.

"What time?"

Paul was next in line to enter the pipeline.

"7:15 p.m."

The neon door to the chrome circular tube began to slide shut. Paul dusted off a piece of lint that had stuck to his atmospheric suit lapel.

"Good pleasure, Howard."

The neon door's computers locked shut. Paul always felt safe inside the pipe. Unlike being on a sonic stilth flight, where he was at the mercy of the pilobots. How many times had he seen on the computer news the large red card flashing on and off with the word M.A.L.F.U.N.C.T.I.O.N.! Paul would immediately know the news story was about a robot having a bad day.

He heard the metallic sound. It reminded him of a tuning fork. He closed his eyes and allowed his whole body to relax. He felt the electrical current and the heat, and then that instant moment when his whole essence floated: Pipeing felt like sex in a dream. Very stimulating. And then he disappeared.

The neon door opened up, and the young Undersecretary of Technology found himself in the lobby of the Department of Technology.

"Good pleasure, Mr. Quatro."

The newsbot boy handed Paul his mid-morning computer news screen. The eight-by-ten-inch disposable screen unfolded like colorful wings.

"Thanks, Artie."

Paul quickly switched on the screen and visualized the up-to-the-minute news stories that might pertain to the department.

"Hey, Mr. Quatro, who do you take in the Washington/Madrid game?"

Paul looked over at the newsbot boy. He was one of the few robots that had been programmed to understand big ball.

"Washington. All the way."

Paul Quatro was a Technical fanatic, like most Washingtonians. The Washington Technicals had won the world trophy two out of the last three years.

"Don't underestimate those Spaniards." Artie was hooked on big ball, just like Paul.

"I never underestimate the opposition."

Paul disposed of the computer news screen in a waste bin and walked toward the central elevator that would take him to his office on the two hundredth floor. Paul liked getting to the office an hour before the rest of the employees checked in. He didn't have to.

He didn't get paid any more bank credits. The three-hour, three-day work week was hectic for most technocrats, but not for Paul. He enjoyed working. Whereas most of his friends enjoyed four days of pleasure, he actually looked forward to work every Tuesday morning at 11:00 a.m., and then putting in a full four-hour day.

Paul had his motives. That extra hour was what helped impress Elliot Richards in recommending him for promotion every year.

Three days of work equaled four days of pleasure. It was good for the average technocrat but not for Paul Quatro. Not for a man who wanted to be the best of his generation.

"Good morning, P.Q."

Holly James sat behind her computer desk with a set of headphones on, taking dictation from the telecommunicator. She was the only person who called Paul "P.Q." It had an air of friendship without breaking down the employer/employee barrier that was expected of every technocrat and his transcriber.

Holly James was the best transcriber in the entire department. Paul had been lucky to have her transferred into his employment after her previous employer, the Undersecretary of Diagrams, had retired.

"How was the symphony last night?" he asked, peering through the computer cables that had been processed through the telecommunicator.

"Mozart! Lennon! Dylan! Springsteen! Delfonte! The Congos! The Chrome Digits!"

Miss James was an amateur musicologist in her pleasurable time. She loved going and listening to the Washington Philharmonic at the Kennedy Center every season.

Paul always liked to ask Miss James a personal question to start their morning off. It made for a better working relationship. Most technocrats didn't like having personal contacts with workers.

"Secretary Richards requested personal visualization as soon as you finish your computation."

She watched as Paul entered his private sanctorum, as he liked to refer to his office. She liked Paul Quatro. He made her feel young. That's what the Together Generation was all about.

Paul settled back into his computer chair and surveyed his computer desk. It was the ultimate in organization, precision and technology. At his fingertips were six inner departmental vid screens, three multi-national vid monitors, two political vid scanners, and one Wall Street vid requester. He also had a vid-screen telephone with two hundred digitals and his very own private vid screen, a cherished possession in government.

The chair felt powerful. It was! For on the arms of the plush leather-and-chrome creation was enough computer communication to contact every major trader of technological importance in the twenty-five states of the union, the Soviet United States, Europa, Inja, Afrokaniker, South Mexo, Middle Judea, Austral, and all the independent corporate islands.

The remainder of Earth was uninhabitable.

Trade had become the harmony of the world. The glue. The world thirsted for technology, both for service and for pleasure.

The United States was the leading manufacturer of technology.

Over one hundred years ago the Emperor of Inja had made a bold and prophetic statement: "Whoever controls the technology, controls the trade." At the time, his statement had caused an uproar. But he had been right.

For without trade, there would be no World Unity Council. Earth had found out the hard way just two centuries earlier when trauma shock hit. Trauma shock!

Paul had studied Twentieth Century Technology at the Institute. He was an authority.

What he could never understand was the illogical uses of technology by the super power leaders of the time. Why did they desire war? Why did they misuse the power?

He looked at his computer pen and picked it up. He held it like an exclamation mark. He was glad war had been outlawed.

The pulse vibration at his elbow relayed the signal that someone was transmitting. He switched on the vid-screen telephone and pressed the position button which allowed the screen to turn at the same time as the occupant of the chair. A direct line of communication. A handsome and distinguished gentleman's face appeared.

Every hair was in place. He was ageless. Not of the Together Generation but also not of the It Generation. He was betwixt and between, and therefore able to connect the past and the future.

"Good morning, Mr. Secretary."

Paul never called Elliot Richards by his first name until he assessed his mood.

Theirs was the ultimate technocratic relationship in the department.

Everybody knew Paul Quatro was the secretary's heir apparent.

Everybody knew that someday Elliot Richards would run for the Presidency.

A technocrat had never been elected President. The time was nearing.

"Good morning, Paul."

The Secretary of Technology had a commanding voice. It could make you feel important beyond your position, or it could make you feel very, very unessential. Depending on his mood.

Paul felt good when Elliot Richards called him by his first name. "Sir, I have the computations ready for the conference." The Secretary smiled. He liked ultra-efficiency.

Paul Quatro was the best. Hadn't Professor Ludlum personally recommended him?

Hadn't he said that Quatro had the quickest, most retentive mind of any student he had ever taught?

Yes, Elliot Richards liked Paul Quatro. He was beyond doubt. That's why he kept promoting him. Besides the other reason, which nobody ever suspected...

"Plug them into my transcriber and come up to my office.

I want you to fully understand my strategy for today's conference. Oh, and Paul, "Happy anniversary."

"Thank you, Elliot."

Paul switched off the vid telephone.

Someday he would be Secretary of Technology, and Elliot Richards would be the President of the United States. Together they would move mankind towards Utopia.

The conference was the most important one of that calendar year for the department.

All five section chiefs were required to attend. All twelve sub-section managers were required to attend. And attend they did, as their assistants carried their computer satchels full of data.

This was the budget conference. Each department in the Pentagon was required to deliver to the President of the United States a complete computer balance sheet of the year spent and the next year projected.

Elliot Richards ruled the conference like a lion tamer.

Each section chief would demand more bank credits. Each sub-section manager would demand more bank credit as an excuse for not reaching the department projection. Each assistant undersecretary would be forced to defend their section chiefs and sub-section managers or, if politically unwise, allow Elliot Richards to strip them of their position and banish them to a small cubicle in the index sub-section, known as the lowest section in the department.

Paul knew each man seated at the large, oval computerized conference table.

Butlerbots served refreshments during the conference.

If it was a good year, the conference would have the atmosphere of a family holiday feast. But if it had been an unsuccessful year, the conference could be torture for those singled out as mediocre.

Only Elliot Richards knew what kind of conference it was going to be.

He had told Paul during their private strategy meeting of the direction this meeting was going to take.

Paul could feel the tension in the air. Nobody wanted to show their fear. Small talk between section chiefs and subsection managers was always polite. One never knew when a past favor might be needed. Quick glances stole over Paul.

Each man was trying to search out the young Undersecretary to discern the direction of the meeting, but Paul had learned years earlier never to give them an idea.

His loyalty was to Elliot Richards.

The Secretary of Technology waited in his private chambers until he felt the power was totally in his mind. He watched on his private vid screen the reactions of the men and women seated around the oval computer table. And then he entered.

All stood obediently.

The Department of Technology was the most successful department in the Pentagon. It was also the most profitable. Nobody ever questioned the Secretary of Technology when he submitted his tech-budget each year.

"Success is never questioned! Only defeat!"

Paul had made a list of Elliot' s best phrases. He had stored them in his own private computer bank so that they could be studied.

Someday, he knew, he would be in Elliot's seat.

"Examples must be made for the good of the department."

Paul wasn't sure what Elliot meant when he made that statement but, as in the past, he never questioned what he didn't understand in the Secretary's presence.

He would figure out the meaning of all this later, in the privacy of his sanctorum.

The Secretary of Technology kept his sights on Assistant Undersecretary Unger, a brilliant and well-respected mathematician. An abrasive man socially, he had recommended the Eratosthenes Project, and it had failed.

Elliot Richards knew from the beginning that it was pointless.

And now he would make his example for all to remember.

Assistant Undersecretary Unger was sweating profusely. He dabbed his bald forehead with a silk hanky. He was beginning to feel heart palpitations.

"But, Mr. Secretary! The Eratosthenes Project needs more time!"

Paul watched Elliot Richards maneuver the man into a corner he would never get out of.

Although Paul never liked Izod Unger, he never felt comfortable when a man was up against the wall without a chance of escape.

He wondered how he would react if ever placed in such a position.

In a way it was a challenge he subconsciously thought interesting, like a chess master looking at an Othellian move.

He knew what the Secretary of Technology was leading up to. It had nothing to do with the Eratosthenes Project per se. It had to do with evolution. It had to do with the new system. It had to do with the hierarchical network...hierarchical storage management ...hierarchical data link control...It had to do with power!

29

"Your time is up, Mr. Unger. I want your resignation on my desk before you leave this building."

Paul was surprised that Elliot had sentenced Unger to total banishment from the department. He was really making a point for all the others to cherish.

He knew that Elliot was going to remove Unger from his position. He didn't know he was going to banish him.

It was a lesson to be learned.

Paul was immediately reminded that he was never totally briefed on the Secretary of Technology's total strategy.

An Undersecretary could be a weakness just as easily as he could be a strength. Even if he committed total loyalty.

Paul looked over at Elliot Richards. The Secretary of Technology acknowledged his young protégé with an invisible communication.

It wasn't a bodily movement.

It was in his eyes. As if saying to Paul, "So you see, my young friend. You still have much to learn."

Paul allowed in his eyes, as if saying back to him, "You give me great pleasure with your knowledge."

All eyes were on Izod Unger, the recently banished Assistant Undersecretary of Technology, as he was helped from the conference room by two forcebots.

He was clutching his chest. His heart was pounding, and he was having a hard time breathing.

To fall from the top of the mountain takes the breath out of even the greatest climber.

Elliot Richards looked around the oval computer table at his team.

They fought to hold their own insecurities down, each wondering whether there would be other examples made, each not wanting to show the Secretary of Technology they were afraid.

Everyone knew he was a man who despised weakness. In all his years as Secretary of Technology he had never missed a day of work, even though each member of the department was allowed thirty days sick leave per year.

"Izod Unger will be given an all-expense-paid retirement pension for life."

Elliot' s words soothed the immediate fears.

"He will have time to tend his equations. But not at the expense of the department."

Elliot Richards had the total attention of everyone in the conference room. Even the butlerbots were mesmerized by his power.

"We are at the cross circuits of technology!" he continued.

He was standing, his hands raised in front of his chest. In another time he would have been a general. Or the Pope.

"Unemployment is down to 1.5% of the available work force.

An increase of .5% over last year. Production in serviceable technology increased only .8% over last year. Luxury technology is down .2%…a new computer system must be found to increase productivity…"

That was it! A new system must be found. So that was why Unger was banished. The Eratosthenes Project was based on the old system. That was the master plan, and only now was Paul beginning to understand the Secretary of Technology's strategy.

In a world of technological harmony, evolution risked stagnation.

"Keep the opposition on their toes," is what Coach Dobrofsky of the Washington Technicals told his big ball players.

And that was exactly what Elliot Richards was doing. Keeping his team on its toes.

In reality, the only opposition they faced was their own lethargy. The Department of Technology was the most successful in the Pentagon. Elliot Richards was determined to keep it that way.

"Mr. Quatro will explain the hierarchical network."

Elliot Richards sat back in his computer chair and turned the conference over to Paul.

"A communications network will combine all levels of control into one main power source."

The section chiefs and sub-section managers and their assistants and the two remaining assistant undersecretaries of state and their assistants all took out their computer pens and somberly began making notes on little computer pads.

"Maximize the source."

Paul pressed a button on the oval computer table, and a large cyclorama vid screen lit up. Diagrams of the new system were flashed around the room.

"We will re-circuit the entire computer center in the Pentagon."

Everybody listened.

Paul pressed another button, and multi-integral diagrams appeared on the cyclorama vid screen.

"The World Unity council Satellite will be sold to the new system at a 100% profit to the department!"

"Profit!" Everybody looked over to Elliot Richards as he spoke the one word that the world understood.

Paul allowed Elliot Richards' comment to penetrate all in the room.

"The new system will be inaugurated next year on Inaugural Day. That is our priority project for next year's tech budget projection. Each section has been budgeted and will coordinate in my office."

The remainder of the meeting was inconsequential to Paul.

He had been put in charge of the new system. It was the priority project. His career would depend on its success. But, then, he wouldn't have wanted it any other way.

Elliot Richards appointed Section Chief Malone to replace Izod Unger, the banished Assistant Undersecretary. Paul would have to watch him. He was direct competition. Elliot Richards had called the young section chief by his first name. A sign. A signal to Paul that even he could be replaced if he didn't succeed.

The Secretary of Technology banged his gavel, and the conference was over. He had told Paul he had a surprise for him if the conference went well.

Professor Samuel Ludlum was the most respected computer theorist at the Institute of Technology. He had been the professor of Elliot Richards, and also Paul Quatro.

He was one hundred forty-seven years old, with a full head of white hair and all his own teeth. He used a computer cane to get around. Even with advanced computer medicine the body ran down eventually. Professor Ludlum had one bionic eye after a skiing accident in Aspen. It had happened fifty years ago. And he had a bionic right eardrum. Nothing passed his way unnoticed.

It was if a grandfather was having lunch with his son and grandson. The old man had retired to his farm in Virginia a decade earlier. He was content to watch the world from his computerized house and play with his miniature dachshunds. He had three butlerbots to take care of his every need. Still, he missed Washington…missed the Pentagon…missed the department he had formed over eighty years ago.

Samuel Ludlum was the first Secretary of Technology in the department. They had even dedicated the department' s new building to him.

All other secretaries would follow in his shadow.

All except Elliot Richards.

He had taken over the department at a crucial time in history.

The Judea file had been uncovered, and it had caused quite a stir throughout the world.

The conspiracy had been foiled.

Prembrook had been assassinated, the only Secretary of Technology ever to have been killed in the line of duty. Then young Elliot Richards had been the Undersecretary. His appointment by Professor Samuel Ludlum to Secretary of Technology had shocked and stimulated the nation. But that was over a decade ago! As the old man and Elliot Richards spoke, Paul listened. If he pledged total loyalty to Elliot he would surely die for Professor Ludlum.

What would he be if he hadn't gotten a full scholarship to the Institute? He was just another kid with a genius I.Q. There were plenty of those at the test tube orphanage. Most would be adopted into the bureaucracy to live out their lives in harmonious boredom. Paul was lucky, and he knew it. He was part of the Together Generation. Climbing that upward, mobile ladder.

"How did the conference go, Elliot?"

The old man was the only one Paul knew who could call the Secretary of Technology by his first name all the time.

"I dismissed Unger."

The old man leaned forward, questioning, yet offering solace.

"It is never easy to banish."

Paul immediately understood that Professor Ludlum had been. briefed about the conference. And why shouldn't Elliot include him? Hadn't the old man been his mentor?

"How is Pauline?" Elliot wanted to stay away from the conference as conversation.

The old man smiled. Grandchild next month."

"My daughter gives me my ninth."

"You are a lucky man, Sam."

Paul could tell that Elliot had strong affection for the Professor. The three men continued their lunch in the private dining hall at the Department of Technology. On two occasions several dignitaries walked over to give greetings to Professor Ludlum. He was a legendary figure in Washington. In the world!

"I spoke with President Ricarda," said Professor Ludlum.

Long an honored guest at the White House, he was accustomed to V.I.P. treatment.

"And what did she say about running for re-election?"

Paul could feel Elliot pressing for an answer during the conversation. He realized that he was witnessing the priority for the entire gathering.

"She hasn't made up her mind."

The old man placed his hand on Elliot's.

"Be patient. Time is on our side."

Another strategy was being planned, and it had nothing to do with the Department of Technology.

Paul, like a dutiful son, sat quietly and listened. They allowed him at the table because they wanted to use him in their strategy. But he was not allowed to help create that strategy.

Paul only wanted to climb that upward, mobile ladder of success. He didn't care how he got up that ladder as long as it was through hard work and loyalty to those by whom he had profited.

That was the one, great flaw of the Together Generation, thought Professor Ludlum to himself. They didn't question the consequences of their profit.

The old man stirred as the two other men stood.

"Paul, you must bring Mary out to the farm," he said, reaching to embrace him.

The limo-copter twirled gently to the ground beside them, ready to take him back to the farm.

He would not allow a pipeline to be installed at his farm, even though Elliot Richards had offered to have the department pay for the installation. The old man felt too many people would disturb his privacy.

There was truth in his words. He was a man of great truth.

Elliot and Paul watched the limo-copter lift up and climb through the weather dome above the Department of Technology. They stood on the escalator as it accelerated upward to the main arcade. Both men were lost in personal thought.

Elliot Richards wanted to be President of the United States. It was the next logical step for him. And logic was Elliot Richards' greatest weapon.

Paul was already thinking about the new system, how he would coordinate the transference. He didn't notice Elliot Richards disappear into his private elevator until he caught a last glance of his face just before the elevator door closed. There was something in his eyes which Paul couldn't understand. So often he would look at the Secretary of Technology and try to figure out what he'd do next. He could never figure it out. Which was what made working for him so exciting. You could never tell what he might do next.

Paul was busy behind his computer desk going over a diagram that had been submitted to the Department of Technology from a toy inventor in Toronto. It was a computerized doll that would grow from a test tube embryo in a synthetic womb to a full-grown adult, and eventually pass into old age in perfect synch with the purchaser. The inventor had named his creation the LifeLong Doll.

It never ceased to amaze Paul that his position in the department brought him into contact with the greatest technological advancements in the world, and also some of the most inefficient, innocuous, frivolous, irresponsible, useless inventions known to mankind.

As he looked at the embryo-diagram enclosed in the package, he got a cold, lonely sensation in his stomach. He held up the purex test tube and could see the small embryo doll. He flash-visualized back to the test tube orphanage. Who were his parents? He stared at the invention for an endless moment, and then his loneliness turned to anger, something that didn't often happen to Paul Quatro.

"Who needs a doll that only reminds the purchaser of his own aging? Surely it performs no serviceable function, like a robot does. The only pleasure one could get from this…this artifact is a vicarious, oblique, surrogate relationship that doesn't exist in the purchaser's own real life."

Paul spoke into his telecommunicator as he made his final assessment. "No. Absolutely not."

He would send an inner departmental transmission to all section analyzers informing them that if the inventor of the LifeLong Doll ever submitted another toy to him with such irresponsible usage he would place his (or her!) name on the inoperable list.

No inventor wanted to be on the "I" list. It was a black list that prevented the inventor from selling inventions to the Department of Technology, which was one long way to bankruptcy.

"Sir. Lord Lothar has arrived."

Paul could see in Miss James' face that excitement which he loved. Why shouldn't she be excited? Lord Lothar was the greatest whiz kid inventor of the Together Generation. The public was spellbound by his achievements. He switched off the vid phone and got up from his chair

The two men hugged.

"Lothar! You pinhead genius!"

"Paul, you eight-fingered technocrat!"

The two laughed at their sarcastic remarks towards each other.

"Do I smell the scent of rosebud perfume, my pampered

maniac?"

Paul and Lothar sat in the lounge section of Paul 's large office.

"The better to catch butterflies with!"

Lothar dabbed his nostrils with an opiated hanky. The hankies were very popular with the scientist, as well as other inventors who spent long hours in sterile laboratories dreaming up fantastic new technologies for their race, and maybe others.

"Care for a whiff?"

Paul tensed for a moment and then grinned.

"You know I don't believe in opiates."

"Of course. Paul the pure. But you weren't always so chemical free"

Lothar knew Paul's secret. "I was lost in a dream once..."

Paul thought back to his adolescent years at the orphanage. He and Lothar were the best of friends. They had been bunkmates all through their tweens and into their teens. Lothar the Pinhead Genius and Paul the Dream.

Together they terrorized the orphanage with their pranks and escapades. Because they both scored in the top one percent of their test maneuvers they were given the softest rebukes for bad behavior: extra duty in the garbage disposal included sorting solubles from squish.

"And then you re-programmed the logistical tutor robot's equilibrium, and he began to disassemble himself in front of Professor Manzarek as he peeled a synthetic orange!" Paul couldn't stop laughing.

"What about the time you snuck into the girls' shower and hid in the towel dispenser taking insta-photos!"

"I made profit"

"We'd both have made profit!"

Lothar dabbed his nostrils once again with the opiated hanky. Paul hadn't seen Lothar in over six months, but in that time he noticed a change in his old bunkmate. Oh, not so much in his appearance. The whiz kid inventor still dressed flamboyantly in the most colorful atmospheric suits from Europa. No, the change was in his eyes. They seemed to be on fire. Could he have become addicted to the opiated hankies?

"What new invention do you bring me today, Lord Lothar?"

Paul teasingly inserted the Lord as a playful jibe at Lothar's increasing fame. The whiz kid had created quite a stir in the scientific community when he married Lady Zoella of Inja. In so doing he was allowed the title Lord. Lady Zoella's father was Prince Sanjab, third in line to the Inja throne.

An inventor had never married into a royal family before.

There weren't that many royal families left on Earth. What caused a stir was Lady Zoella's age. She was only eleven years old at the time of their honeymoon.

Lothar was a known womanizer in Washington. He had peculiar taste for sure, but Paul never really knew how peculiar until that night in December, ten years ago, when Lothar took Paul to The Illusion, a notorious robot brothel. Lothar had roared with laughter when Paul got sick to his stomach that night, so sick he had to excuse himself from the coitus delectable, Robotic Erotica. The following month Paul married Mary, and the two men never spoke of the evening again.

Lothar divorced Lady Zoella two years after their marriage. He retained the title Lord and continued to dazzle the technological world with his inventions. The pipeline was Lothar's last great contribution to society. There had been rumors he was working on an invention that would surpass even that brilliant actualization of visualization.

"A cocktail that allows the drinker to disappear from the party without being noticed."

"What?" Paul was puzzled by his friend's remark.

Lothar removed a jewel-encrusted pillbox from his secret breast pocket. He spun the small computer combination and then picked a sparkling pink-colored crystal out of the box.

"The invisible tab," Lothar whispered, as if revealing the secret of eternal life. He dropped the glittering bauble into Paul 's hand.

"Invisible tab?" Paul looked at the mysterious tab in awe. Was he holding a time bomb that would blow him to kingdom come?

"But what purpose will it contribute to society?"

"Purpose! Paul! Have you forgotten your dreams?"

Lothar was a true Upster. He was as Up as any Upster in the Together Generation. His activities were followed in all the society computers. In fact, Computer Journalist had labeled Lord Lothar the "Grand Potentate of 'Up'!"

He squinted playfully at Paul.

"Think of the fun you'll have getting out of those boring conferences. You'll drop a tab and just disappear in front of those stuffed trousered technocrats."

"Those stuffed trousered technocrats allow you great profit."

"Without me they'd be purchasing second-rate techno-garbage."

Paul couldn't believe this was the great invention Lothar had been working on. Not Lothar, the one genius who designed technology that had a specific purpose. That's what Lord Lothar was known for in the scientific community of inventors.

Weren't most inventors eccentric? The Together Generation had produced a certain lifestyle that allowed eccentricity to those who worked towards that upward, mobile cachet-ridden goal: success. Lothar's inventions furthered mankind toward Utopia.

"Is this your great invention?"

Paul loved Lothar. They were like brothers. He hated to see him drown in his own genius as others before him had. Lothar's smile disappeared for the first time since he entered Paul's office.

"No," he cried out, dabbing his nostrils again with the opiated hanky.

"I'm afraid I've bankrupted my mind of late."

"Don't talk that way."

"It's true, and you know it."

"Your greatest years are ahead of you."

Paul didn't want to believe his friend's genius had dried up, and he would live out the rest of his life on past laurels, no matter how great those past laurels might be.

The Together Generation's goal was to take mankind into utopia. They needed Lord Lothar if they were to get there.

"Oh, don't worry about me. It's only a temporary lapse. We all go through it."

He took out another hanky, this one with a chromatic laboratory scent. The whiz kid inventor of the Together Generation dabbed both nostrils. His eyes began to tear, and he jerked his head back as if he was getting a jolt from the hanky. Paul wondered what chemicals had been mixed into the fiber.

"I never should have recommended Zelman's invention," thought Paul, grabbing the opiated hanky out of Lothar's soft hand.

"Don't be angry at Zelman. He's a spirited synthesist."

"The only reason I voted for the opiated hanky was because I thought it would be used strictly for the prescribed ailments," moaned Paul.

Lothar's grin was devious. "Whoever would've thought!"

He flipped the invisible tab in the air and caught it in his mouth. It dissolved quickly, sliding down his throat like honey.

"Lothar, I want to have a serious talk with you about your problem," said Paul.

But the whiz kid inventor disappeared right in front of his eyes. All Paul could hear was laughter, and before he could stand up, he realized Lothar had placed a synthetic apple on top of his head. It dropped to the floor as soon as he stood up.

"Lothar. Stop this foolishness."

"You ain't seen nothin' yet!"

With those words, the door to Paul's inner sanctorum slammed shut.

"Lothar!" Paul opened the door to Miss James's office and shouted for her to come quickly. She dashed out of the vestibule, mouth agape, as both she and Paul watched, incredulous, as the reception door opened and closed by itself.

Miss James looked at her boss. "P.Q.?"

Paul felt as foolish as she felt bewildered. He shrugged his shoulders and smiled sheepishly. He didn't want to say anything negative about his friend, Lothar, so instead he sent her on an irrelevant errand to pick up a transcript cassette, one which he'd already reviewed for the research section in the Computer Times. When she came back, he said Lord Lothar had left. She asked him how the meeting went, and Paul said, "Interesting, as always."

What an understatement that was! Paul set back in his chair feeling untracked. Elliot Richards' words came into his mind:

"A technocrat can never allow foreign interference to distract him from his first priority, which is to get the job done!"

Paul repeated the phrase to himself a dozen times. It seemed to soothe his mind. Still it didn't remove the image of his best

45

friend dabbing his nostrils with an opiated hanky. He made a note on his computer pad to have a review of the Zelman Tissue, as it was officially called. Apparently, legislation was too lax on this product.

What had been intended as an inexpensive disposable tissue to cure minor ailments from the common cold to arthritis had been turned into a luxury item for extrasensory entertainment.

Luxury items came with specific instructions, both for safety reasons and to heighten enjoyment. Abuse of a luxury item could be dangerous.

Paul put in a transmission to Zelman at his laboratory, but the synthesist's transcriber said he was off on holiday in the jungles of South Mexo. Paul knew about Zelman and his holidays. He was constantly bringing back strange plants and extracting exotic chemicals from them. "All in the interest of science," he said. "In the interest of society." "For Utopia!"

Paul could see his own reflection in the Wall Street Requester screen. At one time he thought being an Upster would be the "up thing" to be. Howard and Bernice were constantly talking "Up" slang and doing "Uppie" antics, but after a while it seemed to Paul that being "Up" in the Together Generation wasn't the only way to be. The Together Generation encompassed all varieties of upward, mobile, success-oriented climbers. The truth was that just being in the Together Generation made one an "Upper" if not totally an "Upster."

Zelman, Lothar and Paul had all started out from the test tube orphanage. Zelman was always tagging along after Paul and Lothar. He was a short, pudgy-faced kid who everybody thought was going to grow up and become a computer cuisine artist. He was always cooking something in the orphanage kitchen when he wasn't tagging along with Paul and Lothar.

"Whoever would have thought."

Lothar's words ricocheted through Paul's thoughts.

Paul the technocrat. Lothar the inventor. Zelman the synthesist. Each had helped the other to attain prominence.

Paul's status within the Department of Technology had enabled him to make sure the right people saw his two friends' products. And because Paul was able to bring first-rate technology to the department, his standing among his peers and superiors increased.

He was sure Elliot Richards respected him for this reason, as well as other reasons. Paul knew he had a natural ability to understand the most intricate technical device and then incorporate it into society's needs and desires.

He rested his elbow on the armrest of his chair. Yes, at one time he had been Paul the Dreamer. Yes, at one time he did experiment with chemicals. They all had.

Zelman was just beginning his interest in chemistry. They all took the course together. Professor Pizz had a terrible twitch in his face, and it had been hard to concentrate. Paul and Lothar were constantly making their own faces twitch when they were called upon to answer a question. It caught everybody's funny bone -- everyone's, that is, except Professor Pizz's and Zelman's.

Lothar and Paul could never understand how Zelman could say Professor Pizz was the best teacher he 'd ever had. Of course they'd never had Professor Pizz as a counselor.

Zelman said the poor man turned him on to the wonders of chemistry. Paul and Lothar later learned Professor Pizz also turned Zelman onto "D," a chemical they'd named after the wonderful dreams it produced. Lothar had enjoyed "D," but his mind wasn't totally suited to dreaming out. And Zelman liked "D," too, but he was learning to be a synthesist and never learned to love just one chemical. Paul almost got lost that one summer doing "D" and dreaming out.

And then Professor Pizz was hired by a multi-national corporation, and he moved to Afrikaniker. That was the end of "D." Zelman never got the formula, and the one time he attempted to make it they all came down with a terrible case of diarrhea. Paul had decided then and there that "D" was best left in the laboratory.

What good would a chemical do if it took you away from reality's task? It wasn't worth the risk to find out.

Maybe when the Together Generation had succeeded in reaching Utopia. Maybe then they could have time for "D." For dreaming out.

Paul suddenly felt the transmission impulse surge through his elbow. He pressed the armrest vid telephone button and looked up at the screen. Holly James relayed the transmission:

"A Doctor Nikcah from Reagan Memorial Hospital."

Paul didn't know a Dr. Nikcah.

"What is this in regards to?"

He placed the opiated hanky in the top drawer of his desk, next to the invisible tab.

"He said it was an emergency transmission."

48

"Put him through."

Paul closed his top drawer slowly.

"Mr. Quatro!"

"Yes, Doctor."

Paul listened to the Doctor's antiseptic voice.

"Sir, I am sorry to report that your wife, Mary, has been disassembled in a pipeline malfunction."

"Disassembled? Is she hurt?"

His logic was illogical.

"We have recovered seventeen percent of her molecular structure."

"Not enough for rejuvenation?"

Paul's voice quavered.

"Mary is dead, sir."

"Dead?"

"Yes, Mr. Quatro. Your wife is dead."

M.A.L.F.U.N.C.T.I.O.N.

M.A.L.F.U.N.C.T.I.O.N.

M.A.L.F.U.N.C.T.I.O.N.

"Death becomes a visitor."

It was a simple, private funeral. Mary's mother and father, good, decent people from Pennsylvania, had arrived the night before. Never having had his own mother and father, Paul never fully understood the attraction. Yet, he knew he was missing a response every time he saw Mary with her parents. Jaspar Daven was a retired municipal judge. Arlene, his wife of forty-five years, was a computer librarian.

"The Lord giveth and the Lord taketh."

Paul looked up at the eighty-foot vid screen that reached above the altar of the computer cathedral. The vid priest was dressed in black, and he was reading from a computer Bible. Mary would have liked the ceremony, Paul thought to himself.

"My baby is gone," cried Arlene Daven. Jaspar put his arms around his wife, and they held each other up.

"Who will hold me up now that I'm all alone?"

Paul's soul cried out, but no one heard. He caught Arlene and Jaspar looking at him. They blame me for her death, he thought as he said goodbye to them. They knew he'd recommended the pipeline to the Department of Technology.

"Come to Pennsylvania and stay with us, Paul," Arlene whispered as she kissed Paul's hand.

"She was a good girl."

Jaspar shook his hand, then wiped his tears away with the sleeve of his jacket.

Paul knew he would never see Jaspar or Arlene again.

He knew, too, that Mary would have understood.

The mortician handed Paul a small urn that contained Mary's ashes.

"That will be $4,000 bank credits." The mortician held out his hand, and Paul took the computer pen he offered. He signed the form.

"Hey!" cried the mortician, as Paul gamely tucked the pen into his breast pocket.

"That's my pen!"

Jolted out of his misery, Paul flinched.

"Why so it is. I'm sorry. . ."

"Yes, yes. I'm sorry, too."

The mortician held his hand out for the pen, grabbed it, then turned and pranced off into the hollow of the computer cathedral.

Paul was all alone. He looked back up at the vid priest staring down at him from the eighty-foot screen behind the altar. Then they turned off the transmission, and Paul was left in the dark.

The heat was oppressive. The sky was a haunting purple filled with vibrating, scudding computer clouds. They hid the sad face belonging to the Man In The Moon. Naked men and women were falling off the laughing cliff of society, slithering at the bottom of the pit in a putrified cauldron of technological squish percolating and erupting electrical impulses staining their once virginal computer reflexes...tongues licking crevices of burnt flesh-filled holes of blinking computer screens...screaming out transmissions...emitting tarnished circuits with a headless ringmaster punching in the clowns programming.,,gulping down static information of neutered equations.

"Paul, I'm falling out!"

"Mary, take my hand!"

He could see her slipping towards the edge of the laughing cliff. Two forcebots held his arms as he screamed out. They stood under a dead antennae tree next to the conveyor sidewalk. Heaps of humanity was methodically being maneuvered toward the cliff.

"Paul! Don't leave me!"

"Mary, I love you . . ."

"Paul, I'm falling to pieces."

He struggled free of his captors and leapt onto the conveyor belt, stumbling over the heaps of maggot-infested computer parts. Flesh, arms, eyeballs were crushed underneath his shoes. A dead LifeLong Doll torn in half, the grinding echo driving him mad as he neared the laughing cliff. Mary teetering on the edge, her naked body already yellowing...her hair beginning to fall out...her fingers turning into skeletal forks...

"Mary, don't leave me!"

He could see a robot kneel in front of his wife and stick its cold, metal tongue between her legs and begin to lick her vagina.

Blood on metal. Other robots lined up for the free taste.

"It hurts, Paul!"

They were sticking their metal fingers inside her, ripping each other apart as they fought over the flesh. Disassembling technological logic as it slipped over the laughing cliff.

"Mary!"

She was slithering over the side. They had surgically removed her heart, and three technobots were kicking it around like a big ball warm-up exercise.

"Paul! I don't want to die!"

He picked up a computer pogo stilt and smashed into the robots kicking Mary's heart. Their heads and arms and torsos bludgeoned until there was just the buzzzzzzing of their circuits leaping around like snakes without heads.

Rattlers without bodies. He leaped over the last heap of technological garbage and grabbed her hand. It separated from her wrist, and she fell off the laughing cliff.

"I love you, Paulllllllll!" He held her hand.

"Maryyyyyyyyyy. Forgive me!"

Paul jolted out of his nightmare drenched in tormented sweat. But there was no more Mary. The only sound he could hear was the low whirring of the harmonious computer that ran his all-computerized house. It was as if the house were breathing a low moan of sorrow in response to Mary's death.

Paul and his computer house mourned the passing of a loved one in similar fashion. All of Mary' s luxury appliances were

53

buried inside their stainless steel cabinets, not to be beckoned, for there were no more parties or barbecues or social gatherings.

Music was banished, for it only reminded him of her happiness, a happiness that had been so unfairly disassembled. Lights were no longer turned on when needed. For he moved in a dimly-shadowed fog of consciousness. Computer dust began to accumulate over all the furniture, shelves, cassettes and clothes.

Paul just sat in his computer library, an old atmospheric button-down sweater draped over his slumping shoulders, a three-day growth of beard on his face, his eyes bloodshot and sunken into a dismal, haunting stare.

It had been three days since his beloved Mary had been laid to rest in the Arlington Computer Cemetery vault.

He had not responded to the endless vid phone calls. Nor had he bothered to get up and answer knocks on his door. The shutters were blinded, and the door was bolted.

Tomorrow was Tuesday, and Paul would have to make a decision as to whether or not he'd call in sick at the office. But for now he sat quietly in his cushioned library chair, looking into a blank vid screen.

He heard the knock at the door and put it out of his mind like all the other knocks. But this one wouldn't go away. He could faintly hear his name being called.

"Paul…Paul…Paul…"

He thought he might be dreaming. Maybe it was all a bad dream.

Could it be Mary calling out to wake him up? To get dressed? It was Monday. They would go on a picnic. Yes…that was it.

Mary wasn't dead. He'd been having a terrible dream!

"Paul, wake up!"

That was it. He'd been having a nightmare. Wait till he told Mary this one! She would hold him. Bathe his face with kisses. Run her warm fingers through his hair.

"Mary, I'll get the door." He didn't want to alarm her. He would tell her about his bad dream after he got rid of this person at the door.

"Paul...open up..."

"Mary, go back to bed. I'll get it!"

He ran through the dark hallway, into the living room.

Everything was so dim. He had forgotten why. He only knew that as soon as he opened the front door he would awake and everything would be as it was. Mary was asleep. She would wake up. He would greet whoever was at the door and then go back to bed to hold Mary and make love.

"Paul...open up!"

Yes, he would open the door, and everything would be right.

He clutched the doorknob, his heart pounding.

"Mary!"

The pudgy-faced man stood in the doorway holding back tears for his dear, beloved friend. When he looked at Paul, he could see immediately that he was near total collapse.

"Paul, I just got back into the city."

He hugged his old friend.

"She's dead, Zelman! Mary's dead!"

He looked over Monty Zelman's shoulder and into the loving eyes of Lord Lothar. His two friends had come to save him.

At that moment, Paul Quatro fainted.

The three old friends from the test tube orphanage sat in Paul's living room sipping cups of hot vitafee. Tears streamed down their faces as they reminisced about their childhoods.

Paul and Lothar listened and watched as Zelman demonstrated some of his magic tricks. He made a computer pen disappear out of his hand and then reappear behind Paul's ear.

Zelman had just returned from a holiday in the United Soviet States. Mary brought a tray of sweet dots and sat next to Paul.

Lothar and Mary eyed each other. The night before they had had their conversation, and still there was tension between them.

"Zelman, tell Mary about the Cossack."

She wanted to avoid Lothar's eyes. She was drawn to them and didn't know why.

"I had been coptered to a small community in the western part of St. Gorbachev. My translator wanted to purchase a black market vid phone, so he left me alone in the computer tavern. Seated next to me was an old Cossack. Although I don't speak

Cossack and he didn't speak English, we seemed to communicate perfectly."

"Psychic responses," commented Mary, as she sipped some of Paul's vitafee.

"Yes, exactly. He knew what I was looking for," said Zelman.

"Which was a perverted time!" Lothar's eyebrows bristled in the direction of his pudgy friend.

"Some of us are serious about our work!" Zelman was always recoiling into a defensive position whenever Lothar teased him about his strange pursuits in the name of synthecism.

"Lothar, let Zelman speak." Paul was inevitably defending Zelman from Lothar's cavalier jabs.

"He's a big boy, Paul. He can take it!" gurgled Lothar.

"Yes, I can. So shut up, you pinhead genius!"

They all laughed. Paul caught Mary eyeing Lothar.

"So the Cossack takes me outside and we walk across the blacktop and enter a rather ancient plastic and aluminum hovel. It's hard to believe there are still people living in electrically-powered houses."

Zelman dabbed his nostrils with an opiated hanky, and his whole face winced from the chemical response.

"Let me have a whiff!"

Lothar took the hanky from Zelman, who continued with his visualization.

"He took out this tin container wrapped in an oil rag which he had hidden behind a brick in the fireplace of his dining room."

"What was inside the tin container?" Mary was impatient with Zelman's slow storytelling.

"Mary, give our synthetist a chance to tell his story."

"Thank you, Paul, but Mary's right. I sometimes linger on a thought like an agro tractor plowing mud furrows."

Zelman was the only one who ever really laughed at his own jokes.

"Goddammit, what was in the tin can?"

Lothar stood up and lit a vitamin B smokette. He passed the white-and-red ribboned health tube to Mary. Their fingertips touched, causing a spark.

"The Cossack took out a strange root and handed it to me."

Paul watched Mary inhale the vitamin B smokette. She held the smoke for a long time inside her lungs. Then she passed the vitamin B smokette to Paul.

"He said the root had the power of immortality."

Blue smoke twirled around their heads, forming fantastic dragons and gargoyles.

"Immortality!" Lothar's voice was full of questions.

"Immortality!" Paul's whisper was full of excitement.

Mary smiled to herself as she watched Paul and his friends together. They were so different, yet they loved each other so much. She was happy her husband had friends who kept his intellect alive. She knew her husband's desires. And they did not always include her.

"The Cossack produced a birth certificate that showed he was over three hundred years old."

"Three hundred years old!" Paul let out a high-pitched whistle.

"Have you analyzed the chemical compounds?"

Lothar the inventor had been hooked by Zelman.

Mary sometimes wondered if it was not Zelman who controlled the group. But she knew, too, that each man held a certain power over the other two, and that together these three could lead the Together Generation to Utopia.

The vitamin B smokette was beginning to take effect.

Paul wasn't a big user, although he highly approved of vitamins. His head began to feel light.

"Immortality, Mary."

He could see her staring at Lothar. Zelman was laughing. They were all so young. It was June third. They were celebrating Paul and Mary' s fifth wedding anniversary.

"Mary!"

He could see Zelman taking out the strange root from a day-glo pouch he carried strapped to his shoulder.

The root looked like two Siamese twin embryos twisted together in a battle for supremacy. Zelman's face was full of perspiration as he held it in his hand.

"Immortality."

"Utopia."

Zelman let everyone hold it. It was as if they were shaking hands with God. The root was so powerful that whoever held it could feel their entire cellular structure tingle with energy.

Suddenly, Mary dropped the root on the floor.

For a moment all three men looked at her as if an omen had been cast upon her destiny. She laughed and took another inhalation of the vitamin smoke.
"Mary, pick up the root," Paul shouted.

He was angry at her. But Mary didn't want to pick it up.

"No, it frightens me."

"Mary, pick up the root."

Paul found himself in a state of confusion. Scolding her. But she wouldn't pick up the root.

"Pick it up before it's too late."

She wouldn't pick it up.

"Pick it up, goddammit!"

He started to shake her, but she wouldn't pick it up.

"Paul, wake up."

Paul pushed Zelman's hand away.

"Pick it up, Mary."

"Relax."

Lothar 's voice echoed through Paul's brain.

"We're here to see you through this nightmare."

The sedative was wearing off.

"How long have I been under the influence?"

He sat up in the airbed. Zelman and Lothar helped him to his feet. He had been asleep for twelve hours.

They escorted him into the cosmetic room. Zelman turned on the computer faucets. Lothar placed a hot tranquilizer towel over Paul's face.

He felt the wetness, then he removed the towel. He squinted at himself in the mirror. He looked, to himself, like an old man.

He began to cry. His two friends supported him as they helped him sit down on the computer toilet.

"I was dreaming."

"Paul the Dreamer."

Zelman remembered that summer Paul told his two friends about the dream. About the root. They all remembered the gathering.

Zelman, in particular, remembered it because the Root of Immortality, as it was later called in the Synthetic Journals, was his greatest contribution to the Together Generation.

What Zelman had been able to extract from that root, and then incorporate into his own synthetics, would allow each member of the Together Generation an average age of one hundred and seventy years; for some as much as two hundred and fifty years, depending upon how well they'd kept themselves over the decades.

It was Zelman's hope that with enough research he might someday be able to combine the chemical contents of the Root of Immortality with other synthetic and organic chemicals that could truly give immortality to the Together Generation.

Zelman, the synthetist, was a revered man in the Together Generation community. It was said he could walk into any home in the union and get a free meal and a warm bed, not to mention sexual pleasure if he so desired.

And Zelman, the eccentric, did have his desires. If Lothar was the Grand Potentate of Up, then Zelman was its High Puba.

"Here. Drink this."

Paul took the cup of warm chicken soup from Zelman's pudgy, pink hand and sipped.

"What day is it?"

"February fourteenth."

Paul looked up at Lothar and then over to Zelman.

"Valentines' Day!"

He buried his face in his hands and sobbed.

Lothar looked at Zelman and told him he knew the surgeon director of the West Point Sanitarium. He said he would give him a transmission and they could get Paul admitted immediately.

The sanitarium was housed in what used to be the Army's military academy. Since the Armed Forces had been outlawed, along with war in general, the academy was no longer needed for what the government had termed "negative training."

"Yes, maybe that will be the best thing for him."

Zelman looked down at Paul as he slumped on the computer toilet.

Lothar turned to make the call from the cosmetic vid phone. Paul struggled to his feet to stop him.

"Mustn't make that call."

"But you need cerebral exploration."

"No, you listen to Lothar, Paul, he only wants to help you."

Paul pushed his hand through his uncombed hair. He had to fight to get back his logic. What was it that Elliot Richards always said?

"When the going gets tough, the technocrats get logical!"

Paul knew he had to pull himself together. Mary would want him to. He had to show her he was strong. He had to carry on. He had to be logical.

"Paul. You need help."

He knew his friends meant well.

"If I went to a sanitarium, it would ruin my career."

Zelman and Lothar looked at each other and then back at Paul.

"He's right!" said Lothar, agreeing not only out of concern for Paul but also for himself.

He knew how important Paul was to his own career, too. Especially now that he had inventor's blockage. Zelman knew also that no matter how great one's contribution had been to the Together Generation, the pressure to top your past laurels was a painful reality and burden they all shared.

"Yes, Paul," conceded Zelman.

"You have to pull your logic together."

Paul extended his hand. All three men clutched their hands together. It had been their secret handshake at the test tube orphanage.

"For Utopia!" the three friends whispered in unison.

That night Paul drank as much black, hot vitafee and ate as much nourishment as he could. He didn't know where he was getting the strength to put himself back together, but he knew he had to.

He was a technocrat. He was the Undersecretary of Technology. He was Paul the Pure. If he wanted to continue up that upward, mobile ladder of success, he must get back on his feet before Tuesday morning when he would be reporting to work.

Zelman had collapsed on the couch to get some sleep.

He had given himself a strange injection of vitamin X.

He said it was the only way he could get to sleep without having bad dreams.

He offered Paul some, but the Undersecretary of Technology didn't feel like sleeping.

He wanted to get back to work. It would be the only way he'd be able to bury his pain.

As Paul and Lothar sat quietly in the computer nook sipping vitafee, Paul asked Lothar what he and Mary had talked about that night before Zelman showed them the Root of Immortality.

Lothar lifted up his tired head and spoke softly.

"I told Mary I loved her."

"And what did she say to you?"

"'That she loved you, Paul."

The two friends sat together, holding hands. Both had tears in their eyes. Both had lost someone they loved.

Paul would never forget what his two friends had given him that night. And they in turn would never forget Paul's friendship.

But there would come a time when friendship would have nothing to do with their respective destinies. Only their deaths.

"She's a stilth stewardess for Europa Express. She's flown all over the uncontaminated world. She was married to Ronnie Chrome, the all-star big baller for the Kansas City Cutters. He was a great jammer until they severed his spinal cord. I believe it was the playoff game with Notre Dame. A late blow with a scalpel! The whistle had blown. Paul, are you listening to me?" Howard Bork sounded annoyed.

Paul looked up from his Computer News Screen. He and Howard were riding the conveyor sidewalk to the pipeline on their way to employment.

"It was the eastern regional game, not the playoffs."

Paul had the ability to hear subliminal conversation while he was concentrating on important visualizations.

"What do you think?" said Howard.

"About the Kansas City Cutters?"

"No, about mingling with Bernice's cousin."

It had been four weeks since Mary's passing.

Everybody had been amazed by Paul's inner logic. They knew that he was working overtime so as to forget the pain. He hadn't missed a day's work.

If at times his mind wandered into that dimly-lit passage of unattentive logic, no one was aware of it except Elliot Richards, who was keeping a close visualization on Paul.

"Howard, I'm not ready to mingle."

"Paul, it's not healthy to mourn."

One of the unspoken Upster rules was to remain happy, even when one lost a loved one. Mourning, in specific, was frowned upon.

"It's not positive to be alone," he continued.

Another unspoken rule was that it was not Up to be alone.

If necessary, one could make a transmission to the escort center. A citizen who could mingle and therefore prevent loneliness would be sent over immediately.

"Howard, I'm still sorting out Mary' s belongings."

"Listen, Paul. Do me and Bernice a favor and have dinner with us."

Paul looked at his next door neighbor. Howard was the only man apart from those from the test tube orphanage he had ever felt close to.

He was pretentious at times and could be overly aggressive while watching big ball games on the home screen, but he was a hard worker who was contributing to the system. And he had a great sense of humor.

"Yes!" Paul stepped into the pipe and half-heartedly waved good day to Howard.

As soon as the neon door closed Paul tensed up. Ever since Mary's malfunction he found it difficult to pipe.

He fought to push down his own fear of being disassembled.

By the time he stepped out of the pipe and into the lobby of the Department of Technology he was drenched with sweat.

It took him several seconds to regain his composure.

"Good pleasure, Mr. Quatro!"

Artie, the newsbot boy, handed Paul his mid-morning Computer News Screen. Paul pressed the button and scanned the visualizations.

"Hey, Mr. Quatro. Who do you take in the Washington-Middle Judea game?"

Paul didn't answer the robot. He turned and started down to the escalators. Artie leaned his metal head out the newsstand window and shouted out as if Paul had made a responsive comment.

"Don't underestimate those Jews!"

He laughed and returned to his metal chair behind the newsstand stall. Artie was hooked on big ball. It was all in the programming.

Paul could feel everybody looking at him, waiting to see if he was going to crack.

Others had.

Why not the Undersecretary of Technology? But he was going to show them what he was made of. They would remember Paul Quatro and how tough his logic was.

"A packed decimal numeric representation in which the low order nibble of the priority byte will contain the value indicator housing both the positive and the negative responders."

Paul traced the diagram with his computer pen. All the section chiefs and the three assistant undersecretaries of technology waited for Paul's approval, especially John Malone, the newest assistant undersecretary, the man who had succeeded Izod Unger, the banished technocrat.

Malone was constantly crowding Paul, pushing him, forcing him to make quick decisions, hoping he would make a mistake. Especially during the weeks following Mary's death.

Elliot Richards visualized his Undersecretary's conference. He was high up in his private office, but he was only a fingertip away from his screens.

Everybody knew he was watching them. There was no privacy in the Department of Technology. There was a feeling of family.

"You left out the size of the back-up selector."

"If you'll scan to diagram seven, you'll see it in the fourth paragraph."

John Malone had caught the Undersecretary with another omission. Omissions had been occurring on a regular basis.

Oh, nothing important. Always small, incidental omissions, but omissions, nonetheless.

Paul scanned to diagram seven and noticed that what he thought was an omission on John Malone's part was actually one of his own.

"Yes, I see!"

Paul knew Elliot Richards was visualizing him. He could feel his eyes behind his back. He knew the Secretary of Technology abhorred weakness.

He was aware that the Secretary had shown great favor toward John Malone. Hadn't he invited the young assistant undersecretary to dine with him on two occasions?

Paul could feel the circuits of his mind crackling. He fought to regain his logical balance.

"Gentlemen, the Secretary of Technology and I expect you to have the complete diagram printouts for the new system ready for inspection at the test grounds no later than June third!"

He gritted his teeth as soon as he spoke the ill-fated date.

"I meant September third!"

Once again he made a mistake.

Could he be faulted for remembering June third? Paul asked himself. "Yes!" In the back of his mind he visualized the Secretary of Technology screaming.

The thought of that date untracked Paul. Mary's face began to flash-visualize around the room. He began to feel dizzy and short of breath.

"Mr. Undersecretary, are you all right?"

John Malone 's devious face penetrated Paul's visualization. He gripped his logic with both hands, clutching the armrest on his computer chair.

How long had he lapsed out of conscious control?

A split one hundredth of a second?

Could it have been seconds?

Paul's logic began to race. He had to regain control of the conference. He knew Elliot Richards was just a fingertip away from the screen at all times.

"Mr. Malone, this is the first time you have been an Assistant Undersecretary, and I suggest you concern yourself with the facts!"

Paul could see the young Assistant Undersecretary didn't like being confronted with his inexperience. Paul had found a weakness, and he would have to exploit it to his advantage.

"Yes, Sir. I will scan only the facts!"

The other section chiefs watched the power game.

They didn't want to get involved.

If John Malone was going to succeed Paul Quatro as Undersecretary of State, then he would have to do it on his own.

Until Paul was near defeat, they could not show their allegiance. For the time being they would obey Paul. He had been supportive of them.

Of course, if the Secretary of Technology showed continuous favor towards John Malone over Paul, they would have no choice…

The politics of advancement was a subtle, inner-departmental game only the most logical could ever attempt to play. No one needed the approval of the Secretary himself because, as everyone knew, he loved to play the game.

Paul knew.

Paul had seen how section chiefs were promoted to Assistant Undersecretary; believing they had the Secretary of Technology's approval they went for Paul's chair. But, always in the past, they had been banished for this. Had he not played the game and won?

So Elliot was testing Paul to the maximum of his logic. In a way it made Paul gain greater logical strength.

It took his mind off Mary. It took his mind off everything outside the department.

He was spending as many as five hours a day working. It was almost unheard of for anybody to put so much time in.

Rumors started to spread that the Undersecretary of Technology was working an outrageous and demanding schedule: four days a week.

One free day for three work days allowed him only three days of pleasure. But what did a man in mourning need in a day of pleasure?

Others had been demoted for working a free day.

It was frowned upon and perceived as counterproductive to the harmony of the work force.

Elliot Richards stared intensely into the vid-screen image of Paul seated alone in his office.

He analyzed Paul's eyes. He put the image through a psycho projector and waited for the evaluation report. He had to know whether Paul was going to make it.

There was no time for sentiment. No time for past loyalties.

If Paul couldn't make the logical leap, he would be replaced by John Malone.

"Millicent just stilthed in from Brittany."

Howard wiped the cream off his lips with a cellophane napkin and winked at Paul seated across the dining room table.

"It's not my normal flight."

She had the voice of a parrot.

"Tell Paul what you told Howard and me about your holiday to Middle Judea," said Bernice.

"Bernice!"

Howard gawked at his wife.

"Well, you know it's only been in the last fifty years that Middle Judea has been decontaminated. They have an enormous mutant population which they put to good use in service," said Millicent, dabbing at her lips with a cello-phane napkin.

"Why don't they purchase robots?" asked Howard.

"Howard, let Millicent tell her visualization!"

73

Bernice sounded mildly irritated.

Paul looked across the table at Millicent Chrome.

The stilth stewardess was considered attractive, intelligent and available for mingling. She had been married to Ronnie Chrome, the Kansas City Cutter all-star big-ball jammer.

Howard had mentioned something about Ronnie Chrome being hurt in a game and that he was sitting out this season because he had had his spinal cord severed.

He never mentioned why they had gotten an annulment.

Divorce had been outlawed over a hundred and fifty years ago. It was considered morally wrong and physically unhealthy to divorce.

If a couple found they'd made a mistake following their marriage, they had the right to file for an annulment. No one would consider it morally wrong.

A person could only get nine annulments in a lifetime, so one had to be careful when one was selecting a marriage partner. The Together Generation was very intolerant of irresponsible selecting.

"I took a walk to the wailing wall and started to take some insta photos when I felt a tug on my skirt," said Millicent.

"I looked down and realized it was a mutant. Or should I say a family of mutants? The father had an insta camera in his three-fingered hand, and he asked me to take a picture of him with his family."

"Can you imagine a mutant wanting his photo taken?" Bernice was appalled at the thought.

She turned and motioned to her homebot that he could serve the fifth of the eight-course dinner.

"Bernice, you shouldn't be so appalled. Mutants are citizens -- even if they're ugly!"

Howard roared with delight at his own snobbishness.

The Together Generation hated anything that was ugly.

They were the perfected generation. Their lungs had not been contaminated with radiation.

For the Together Generation had been born under the security of atmospheric domes that protected every community no matter how large or small.

Atmospheric clothes with decontaminator units were worn at all times, a carry-over from past generations. Actually, Earth's atmosphere was ninety percent decontaminated from radiation.

Trauma shock had so penetrated the remainder of Earth's survivors that upon rebuilding the civilization which had so nearly been destroyed, the primal fear of contamination was built into the chromosomes of humankind.

"Bernice and Howard told me your wife is dead."

Millicent Chrome was not known for etiquette. Even the non-mourning Together Generation liked to exhibit respect for the personal tragedies of others.

75

Paul felt helpless with her sterile compassion. He looked over at Howard and Bernice, both of whom were embarrassed of Millicent's manners.

"Millicent!"

"That's all right, Howard."

Paul set his computer knife and fork down on the plate.

"I didn't mean any harm."

Millicent was playing games.

Howard quickly put Millicent in her place.

"Of course you didn't, Millicent. You're harmless."

An awkward moment passed as a homebot accidentally spilled peas on Howard's lap.

"Damrnit, you illogically-programrned heap of twisted circuits!"

Howard stood up quickly, and the green peas bounced across the glass floorboards.

"Don't blame Rob. I told him to serve the peas."

Bernice had a strong vibration for her robot.

"Bernice, how many times do I have to tell you not to call our robot Rob!"

It was against the law to give a home service robot a name, although in a recent survey it was found that over fifty percent of the homes with homebots had surreptitiously given these metal helpers a name.

"Why can't you give him credit for contributing to the harmony of our home?"

Bernice ran out of the dining room weeping.

Paul looked over at the robot. He could see Rob had a strong impulse for Bernice.

There hadn't been a survey conducted yet to find out how many marriages had been annulled due to one marriage partner's falling in love with his or her homebot.

Paul mused to himself, it must not be an uncommon occurrence.

"Bernice!"

Howard turned and looked over at Paul.

"You see what I have to put up with?"

He hurried out of the dining room after Bernice, who had retired to their bedroom. She was draped across the air bed, weeping.

"Marriage does have its failures."

Millicent pulled out a vitamin C smokette, and Rob the homebot immediately lit it for her.

"That will be all, thank you."

She exhaled smoke like a dragon, not even glancing at Rob. She had a smugness about her that repulsed Paul.

"As you command."

Rob turned and retreated. into the kitchen.

"Shall we adjourn to the couch?"

Paul found himself obeying this obnoxious woman.

"Sit closer. Don't be a stranger!"

She had saliva on the sides of her mouth. Her voice was full of sexual visualizations.

Her flimsy atmospheric see-through inchy skirt left no doubt in Paul's mind that Millicent wanted something very specific.

"Do you mingle?"

She knew nothing of coyness. She was blatantly aggressive in her desire.

Paul, by nature, was shy.

"As you know, I am only recently widowed."

"Are you saying you haven't mingled since your wife's death?"

Her words were like a poison gas slithering up his nostrils.

"No. I have my work."

"Work!" She threw her head back and laughed like a wild animal. The sound of it gave Paul a chill.

She leaned closer into Paul 's body, pressing her thigh against his leg.

The smoke from her C-smokette was making his eyes burn.

"You have a strong scent, Paul."

She licked the saliva from the sides of her mouth and smiled seductively.

"Howard was telling me you were married to Ronnie Chrome, the all-star big baller."

Paul was feeling very uncomfortable.

Oh, would Lothar and Zelman have a laugh if they could see him now!

"Ronnie Chrome has small balls."

"He does?"

Paul was surprised by her hostile comment about her former husband.

"But...I thought..."

"You thought just because he was an athlete he was a great mingler."

Paul nodded.

"Yes! I've recently even scanned a study that concluded the majority of big ballers were parasexual specimens."

Millicent looked bored.

"Ronnie was in the minority."

"Is that why you got an annulment?"

"How would you like to be married to someone who only had sex three times a week? And during spring training I was lucky if we had it once every ten days!"

Paul's interest was pricking up.

He was making an uncomfortable situation into a frolic of intellectual amusement! The first one he'd had since Mary.

"How many annulments have you had?"

"Four!"

Millicent snuffed out her smokette.

She unzipped her atmospheric blouse and exposed her voluptuous naked, red-nippled breasts. She grabbed Paul around the neck with her right hand and pulled his head into her flesh.

With her other hand she grabbed the zipper of his atmospheric slacks and started to unzip them.

"Let's mingle!"

She knew what she wanted.

Paul struggled to catch his breath.

She was extremely strong. Her breasts had been doused with a strong, sweet perfume, and he began to feel nauseous.

"Millicent."

His words were muffled.

She wouldn't let his head go. He could feel her cold hands slipping inside his slacks in search of his root.

He struggled, not wanting to physically hurt her. He just wanted to extricate himself from her python grip.

"No!" He pushed her off the couch, and she landed on her back, her inchy skirt pulled up over her navel.

Paul could see her sex. He turned his head away.

Millicent hadn't worn any atmospheric panties. She had dyed her sex-hair orange, and it was a weird sight.

Paul straightened his bolo tie.

"I must be going."

"What's wrong? Can't you get it up?"

Millicent hated rejection. Ronnie was constantly rejecting her. She hated men who rejected her advances.

Paul quickly put on his atmospheric trenchcoat and fedora hood.

"You technocrats are all alike!"

She was out of control.

The mascara was dripping down her tear-stained face, making her look like a Halloween night witch.

"My wife just died."

Paul ached with personal visualization.

As he turned to leave Howard and Bernice's all-computerized house, he noticed Rob the robot looking at him through a crack in the kitchen door. In a way, Paul felt the robot had more compassion for his loss than Millicent Chrome did.

"I've had a thousand real men."

Paul closed the door on her declaration. He walked across the synthetic lawn to his own house.

He stopped and caught his composure.

How many times had Mary and he stood out on their front lawn late at night and looked up at the weather dome sky, the perma-frost clouds clinging to the metal arc? One hundred nights out of the year were star-filled projections.

"Mary," he whispered. "I miss you."

He entered his computerized house. It was deathly quiet.

He hadn't cleaned the computer vents; he hadn't re-serviced the computer center.

The house sounded like it was getting a small case of asthma in its respirator system. Dust was accumulating everywhere.

More often than not, Paul found himself falling asleep in his cushioned, library computer chair.

He hated sleeping in his air bed alone. It felt so unnatural to sleep alone. Hadn't Lothar been his bunkmate all through his tweens and teens?

Paul couldn't wait to get to work the next day and forget about Mary.

The Putney Inventors Convention was held each year at the Putney, Vermont underground tunnel -- a reconverted nuke bomb shelter that had been remodeled and equipped with computers of the latest technology.

The town of Putney used it year-round as a community pleasure center, making use of the underground hot springs that had been converted into a large Jacuzzi health pool.

The auditorium was large enough for ten thousand seated people, although the seats had long ago been taken out.

The living quarters had been turned into hotel suites for overnight guests of the community members.

There were two shopping arcades with the latest technological products sold year-round.

It was a mammoth grotto capable of supporting an entire community's survival. But that was two centuries ago.

There were many of this kind, today. Most had been decayed into oblivion. Some had been discovered by small children intrigued with a world outside their domed city.

Children always seemed to find tunnels and such things. Somehow, they always knew how to get outside.

Often, they came down with respiratory coughs due to the contaminated world atmosphere. Each year the number of respiratory coughs increased.

The atmosphere was almost healed.

At one time, the town of Putney had a population of twenty thousand.

The entire twenty-five states of the union accounted for one quarter of the one hundred million people who lived at large in the world.

The Putney Inventor's Convention was not the largest of its kind. That prize went to the Afrikaniker Exposition, which was held every three years in Kongola.

Nor did the Putney Convention have the largest selection of inventions. That honor went to the Hiroshima Techno Fair.

No, the Putney Inventor's Convention was known for cachet. It was the most influential, the most prestigious of all the expositions of its kind.

The Convention was also Elliot Richards' brainchild.

He had grown up in Putney and wanted to give something back to the people who had been so charitable to him during his childhood.

When he became Secretary of Technology, he had the annual Department Inventor's Contest select the best new inventors in five categories. The chosen few were then transported from Washington, D.C. to the Putney underground tunnel, and the festivities began.

What had begun as an inter-departmental banquet grew to be a three-day technological extravaganza, complete with marching bands, baton twirlers, boxerbot fights, plenty of food, wine and mingling, if you decided not to bring along your marriage partner.

It was at the Putney Inventor's Convention that Lothar won his first Gold Wrench and was declared Inventor of the Year.

He would go on to win the Gold Wrench five more times.

In-between his wins, Zelman won three Gold Wrenches.

Elliot Richards was the judge, and he was treated like a mythical shogun.

Besides the world's leading inventors, the most powerful manufacturers of technology also attended, along with the technological distributors.

Computer press from all over the world converged on the Convention, as did the vid announcers.

Interviews with the citizens' favorite inventors were as important, if not more competitive, than big-ball playoffs. Inventors of technology were media stars, emulated by boys and girls everywhere, their lives scrutinized and copied.

None more so than Lord Lothar, the inventor of the pipeline, holder of six hundred patents, the man everybody called "The Grand Potentate of Up."

Men and women swooned over him. Little boys wanted to be him when they grew up. Little girls wanted to marry him.

And Zelman, the man who discovered and invented what was called the Root of Immortality, was considered the High Puba of the Together Generation, the sultan of sytheticism.

Everybody was asking the same questions.

Would they top their last great contributions to the system?

What new inventions would they unveil to the public?

And who would win the big prize? Inventor of the Year...the Golden Wrench.

Paul hadn't thought about attending the Putney Inventor's Convention until he heard Miss Holly James tell him she'd heard Elliot Richards had personally invited John Malone to be his guest at the Convention.

Paul had been putting all his logic into the new system. There had been problems, and with each problem he felt the ever-present eyes of Elliot Richards boring holes in his back.

John Malone was becoming bolder in his tactics, and Paul sensed the threat. If the new system failed, he would be blamed.

Yet, Paul's logic kept him balanced. The pain of Mary' s death had been harnessed, the energy of his grief forged into a lethal weapon.

He only hoped the time he lost during the first two months of his confused visualization could be made up in time for the projected year deadline, set for January first.

He had six months to complete the new system, install it and demonstrate its flawless capacities. He didn't want to give up three precious days of work on the new system, yet he knew he couldn't let John Malone get too close to Elliot Richards.

Lately, Elliot had seemed distant to Paul. Was it his own visualization? Or was the Secretary of Technology teetering away?

The day before Paul was to pipe to the convention he got a call from Lothar at his office.

Lothar had just purchased an old Commando copter and had revved it up to max speed. Lothar had a large collection of antique copters.

He was heading out to pick up Zelman and a few other fun-loving Upsters for a copter ride to the Convention. He'd saved a seat for Paul.

Although Paul had lost trust in pipeing since Mary's death, the thought of a two-hour copter ride seemed ludicrous.

When he hesitated, Lothar called him every name in the Upster Lexicon, ending with, "Old man, get your head out of the screen."

That did it.

Paul accepted the invitation.

What he didn't expect was the copter to be full of nubile nymphets. Lothar said they were young students to whom he was teaching the intricate secrets of technology.

Paul kidded him about becoming a "tutor," and Zelman put his arm around two fleshy young things and said he was ready to enroll.

Paul found himself seated next to a sixteen-year-old high school senior studying Computer Home Making.

Every time he asked her an intelligent question she giggled and blushed.

Her name was Dallas, and she couldn't keep her hands off Paul's inner thighs. Every time he tried to lean back in his chair and read a computer magazine, he would find her hand rendezvousing between his legs.

When he turned his head to look back at Zelman, all he could see was the High Puba's pudgy pink buttocks undulating and

a girl's high heel shoe with sparkling rainbow spurs kicking into his flesh.

He turned his head away from the debauchery and was confronted by a soft, wet kiss from Dallas. He turned his head away and she stuck her young, fresh tongue into his ear.

For a moment he thought he was going deaf.

Then the copter started to do a nose dive.

"Help!"

Paul heard a girl's scream coming from the cockpit. He fought with all his strength to break past the G-load.

He climbed over Zelman and his two nymphets, who by now had rolled down the aisle to the front of the copter in a ball of arms and legs.

He fought to open the cockpit door.

They were seconds away from crashing.

His fear gave him strength to rip the door off its hinges.

He climbed into the cockpit. What he saw shocked him for an instant.

Lothar and his twelve-year-old nymphet were having sex in the pilot seat. They had gotten into such an erotic, perverted passion that Lothar had forgotten he was piloting the copter!

"Lothar! Pull out!"

His shout was like a bolt of lightning through the genius pinhead's brain. Another second and they would have been smashed to smithereens.

Later that night, the three of them convulsed on the floor of Paul's suite at the Putney underground tunnel. It was the first time since Mary died that Paul had laughed.

God, that felt good, he thought to himself.

The five invention categories were medical, scientific, educational, luxury and commerce.

The judges were all from the town of Putney. They were all close personal friends of Elliot Richards.

Although he didn't judge the five categories, it was generally agreed by all that his opinion was requested before the winners were announced.

His was the ultimate judgment.

He chose the Inventor of the Year.

For two days and two nights the Putney Inventors Convention vibrated with the most outrageous, fun-filled mingling in all the technological communities. The conference was legendary.

Lord Lothar was constantly besieged by the vid announcers for on-screen interviews.

He was so opiated that half the time he didn't make any sense. But then, he was an inventor, and most people didn't understand the language of an inventor. Their knowledge was so intimidating.

Zelman, the synthetist, was asked many questions, but he, too, was throbbing to a different dimension having recently returned from a holiday at a mysterious island he would only refer to as "Zoomsville."

The island couldn't be found on any map, but Zelman had a pouch full of roots which did strange things to his mind.

Whenever the interviewers would ask him a question, he would say, "I've already answered that," thus leaving the interviewer in a static state of confusion. Most hadn't had the opportunity to talk to the High Puba of the Together Generation before, and they weren't prepared to get air for an answer.

He wore his traditional panda-bear grin with pride, though. All in all, he unnerved the interviewers to no end.

Paul was interviewed by only one well-known computer publication. It was read by a small clique of techno-intellects who wielded great influence in government.

They always wanted to keep their fingertips on those men and women in the Department of Technology who they felt were true contributors to the system.

Paul Quatro had been watched for over a decade.

These power brokers were aware of the upcoming election. They knew of Elliot Richards' intentions.

These few people belonged to the three political parties. Two of the parties were in search of a contender who would unseat President Ricarda and send her back to her husband, a retired banker and well-known bon-vivant.

After the interview, Paul scheduled a luncheon with Professor Ludlum at the Putney Bar and Computer Grill.

When he arrived he found the old man seated with a raven-haired woman in her late teens. Paul estimated she was about nineteen going on twenty. They were playing chess and munching on fresh synthetic strawberries.

"Paul, my dear boy. How are you?"

Paul sensed immediately that Professor Ludlum didn't want him to stay for their scheduled lunch.

"Just fine, Professor."

Paul stood next to the table, as it only had two chairs. The young woman who had taken his chair made no indication she was going to leave.

"Miss Vickers, I'd like you to meet Paul Quatro."

"It's an honor to meet the Undersecretary of Technology," said Miss Vickers.

Not many people knew Paul. He wasn't a public figure.

Nobody in the department was well-known, really, except Elliot Richards. Paul was impressed with her knowledge, and his ego felt soothed, stroked, and delightfully inflated as a result.

"Miss Vickers has entered her invention in the medical category," cooed the Professor. His voice sounded like milk.

Paul noticed Miss Vickers' knee touching Professor Ludlum's knee. Was an old man being seduced into helping a young inventor's chances? Paul tried to figure her out.

"What did you invent, Miss Vickers?" he queried.

Professor Ludlum realized Paul's suspicion. It was understandable, of course.

A trusted student protecting an honored old man from making a fool of himself. The Professor smiled to himself.

Everybody knew about his bionic right eye, and his bionic eardrums, but nobody except Elliot Richards knew about his bionic penis. His whole body would die before that jewel's glow dimmed.

"A cure for adolescent atmospheric contamination cough."

Paul was impressed.

Not that he thought she had actually discovered the cure. For every year there were a handful of inventors in the medical category who said they had the adolescent atmospheric contamination cough cure: from syrups to tongue suppressors and foot massagers.

"I hope you win."

Pofessor Ludlum still had not asked Miss Vickers to excuse herself from the table which would allow Paul to sit down. And Paul had decided not to pull up a vacant chair from the nearby table.

"How does it work?"

Paul was intrigued with this beautiful young woman.

"A lung implant filternet that is dissolved in an adrenalin solution."

Miss Vickers placed her hand on Professor Ludlum's wrinkled fingers.

"Internal filtration."

Paul found that an intriguing idea. If it worked.

"Paul, what do you have planned this afternoon?"

Professor Ludlum was a man of delicate maneuvers.

He did not want to be rude to his former student, nor did he want to ask Miss Vickers to leave. Paul picked up the subtle message.

"I have to prepare my speech for tonight's department banquet. If you'll excuse me. It was a pleasure meeting you, Miss Vickers. Professor, do enjoy your pleasure."

The Professor appreciated Paul's logic.

"We will!"

Miss Vickers' voice was reassuring.

She was really hooked into the old man's brain. Why shouldn't she be? She was a genius, and he was the maker of geniuses.

He was the greatest Professor at the Institute of Technology, the best ever employed, the first Secretary of Technology.

His credentials were so powerful no one in the world could or would debate him. He could only be turned on by virgin intellect seeking new questions to old answers.

Miss Vickers will help the world attain Utopia, Paul thought to himself as he walked away. That is, if she has the cure.

He looked back before turning the corner. Professor Ludlum and Miss Vickers were kissing.

For a moment Professor Ludlum looked like a young man.

Maybe it was the distance, Paul thought.

The power of love was an awesome energy that had never been harnessed into society.

It is not needed in the present technology, Paul thought, as he strolled down the quaint Putney streets, looking at the provincial products glistening in the small shop windows.

But someday, when the world had been led into the visualization of Utopia, love would be the frosting on the new sanity. Paul wondered if he would ever find love again.

His heart ached with loneliness each night as he entered his all-computerized house.

He stopped and quickly took a step inside a communications booth. He pretended to be making a long distance transmission.

What he actually was doing was watching Elliot Richards and John Malone across the street as they spoke to a group of well-wishers.

The Secretary of Technology was the most famous man ever to have come out of Putney, Vermont. He had a difficult time strolling around town without being greeted. In turn, he introduced each person to John Malone as he was approached.

"His new protégé."

Paul gritted his teeth at the visualization.

Was it not just last year that he, Paul Quatro, had walked with Elliot Richards down that same street? Had been introduced to the same townspeople?

Paul eyed the young Assistant Undersecretary as he shook hands and smiled.

He was certainly full of confidence!

He seemed so secure! Immortal as only youthful power could be.

And then Elliot took John Malone by the arm, and they entered a private door, vanishing from sight.

"What number do you wish to transmit?"

Paul was awakened to the realization he had accidentally put his fingertip down on the vid-phone digital panel. He had pressed Operator.

He looked at the shebot operator's metal face and slammed his fist down on the No Charge button.

The screen went blank.

Cylinder compressors, piston rejectors, elevator ingestors, atmospheric decontaminators, receptacles, disposables, removables, all-computerized tools for the all-computerized world.

Shebots, hebots, pilobots, monobots, aerobots, visualbots, butlerbots, elastobots, aquabots, homebots, forcebots, agrobots

One inventor had the audacity to exhibit a sexobot. He had been banished immediately from the convention.

Forks, knives, scissors, scoopers, beaters, pounders, plungers, strainers, stretchers, cutters, stringers, flatteners, sprayers, puffers, pullers, peelers, dicers, scrappers, soakers, dyers, needlers, dryers, threaders, feelers, splicers, wedgers, blowers, flamers, all-computerized kitchen utensils.

One inventor attempted to place a computerized enema juicer in the utensil category, and it went up to the committee for a vote.

He was told to enter his invention in the medical category if he could come up with a proper definition of its medical purpose.

Oinkers, burpers, criers, laughers, ticklers, huggers, biters, shouters, stampers, kickers, scratchers, spitters, expelers of every imaginable excretion, sleepers, dreamers, players, studiers, obeyers, forgetters, reminders, suppliers, realizers, organizers, jumpers, back flippers, front flippers, twisters, bouncers, cuddlers, computerized dolls for every purpose in the all-computerized family.

Toy inventors were the least respected in the technological community of inventors.

The marching bands paraded up and down the convention floor.

Revelers, pedestrians, fans, buyers, showcasers, technocrats, autograph seekers, vid interviewers, announcers, public relations forecasters, inventors, and children were lined up in front of the portable automats waiting to get a quick nibble of nourishment before the judging began.

There was an ecstatic nervous energy in the air.

Paul was seated in the private glass-enclosed vid-view box, high above the convention floor. He was able to scan the entire auditorium from the forty vid-screen wall just in front of him.

Or, he could lean his head around and observe with his own visualization, depending on how he felt.

Lothar and Zelman were to meet him for a pre-judging drink. They were already twenty minutes late.

Paul hated it when people weren't punctual.

Suddenly, he felt a strong hand clap down on his shoulder.

He turned around to face Elliot Richards. Paul wondered how long Elliot had been standing behind him, observing his actions.

Would the Secretary of Technology think it a weakness that Paul didn't recognize someone was in the room immediately? His sixth sense should have told him something!

Flash visions were quickly gathering into a foundation of thought.

"Elliot!"

As soon as he said the Secretary's first name, Paul realized he'd made a mistake. How many times had he told himself never to mention the Secretary's first name until he'd had a chance to analyze his mood.

"Mr. Quatro, I'd like you to meet the five honorable judges of Putney."

Elliot's voice had a tint of anger mixed into that firm, verbal boom.

Paul immediately stood up and found himself shaking hands with five extremely old men and women. Their faces were wrinkled beyond senility, yet their voices were as clear and sane as anyone of the Together Generation.

In all of his times at the Putney Inventors Convention, Paul had never been introduced to the judges.

As he was greeting each judge, he thought that maybe his first assessment of Elliot Richards' tone of voice had been wrong.

Was he not being introduced to the honorable judges? How many technocrats in the department had ever been given that honor?

Then John Malone entered the vid-view box, and all five judges immediately surrounded the young Assistant Undersecretary.

Paul realized immediately they had already been introduced to him, that he knew each one by name.

"Paul, have your transcriber make an appointment for you to meet with me first thing Tuesday morning."

"Is there anything wrong, Mr. Secretary?"

Nothing Paul said seemed to come out right. Calling Elliot "Mr. Secretary" was so condescending he could see how it revolted the man immediately.

The Secretary of Technology didn't even bother to respond. He looked directly at Paul for a split two hundredth of a second and then turned to the honorable judges and to John Malone.

"Gentlemen, shall we enter my private vid-view box?"

He escorted the group into the next box. John Malone turned around before closing the door behind him and expelled a sarcastic laugh.

Paul didn 't know how long he stood in his vid-view box alone.

His hands felt cold. He was short of breath.

His old atmospheric contamination cough started acting up again. He remembered visualizing Miss Vickers and hoping she really did have the cure for such an ailment.

"Dammit. Where are Lothar and Zelman," Paul wanted to shout. He had never felt anxiety in his whole life and now, ever since Mary had gone, he was feeling it every day.

He didn't want to set up a meeting with a private medicine man and ask for a prescription. He knew it would be reported back to Elliot Richards and used against him. He couldn't afford that.

He would have to gut out his logic. He would show everybody in the Department of Technology what logic he was made of.

The new system had to succeed.

"Have your transcriber make an appointment for you to meet with me first thing Tuesday morning."

Elliot's voice came back to haunt Paul.

"What did he want?" Paul's logic began to bounce off his illogical visualization.

He could feel everybody in the convention staring up at his private vid-view box wondering what was wrong with him.

What was wrong with the Undersecretary of Technology? Had he lost it?

Why couldn't they understand he'd lost the only woman he'd ever loved!

"Because they've never been in love," a little voice echoed back.

Paul whirled around and faced Lothar, who was holding a minirotogyro that was blowing rainbow bubbles into the air.

"I thought I was all alone!"

Paul was beginning to experience a hefty dose of anxiety.

He couldn't believe he'd spoken out loud. He didn't remember the reflex. He had to get hold of himself.

"That's your problem, Paul. You're all alone."

Zelman stepped out from behind Lothar. He had his arm around the sexobot that had been disqualified from the convention.

She was an erotic metal contraption that had been programmed to the owner's personal sexual fantasies.

"Where did you get that?"

Paul was amazed at what was happening to his two friends.

No more than his two friends were concerned about his logical well-being.

Zelman told him the inventor sold cheap.

Zelman introduced Paul to the sexobot, who placed her metal arms around Paul's neck and whispered a perversion in his ear.

He blushed, and Lothar and Zelman roared with laughter.

"Hold your tongues. Secretary Richards is in the next vid-view box."

Paul pressed a button, and the venetian blinds closed the room off from all outside visualization.

"She'll service his needs!"

Zelman slipped his hand inside her inchy skirt, and the sexobot made a technological moaning sound.

Paul jerked Zelman away from the sexobot and admonished him for his public perversion.

"Are you out of your logic?"

"Relax, Paul. We're here to have experiences!"

Lothar placed his hand around Paul's neck and began to massage it. Just the way he had when they'd been bunkmates back in the

test tube orphanage.

"Why didn't you both enter inventions this year?"

Paul was becoming increasingly disappointed with his friends' immoral actions.

"We wanted to give the other inventors a chance!" crowed Lothar.

Paul didn't think Lothar's words were very convincing. He knew Lord Edwin Lothar...the genius pinhead.

The Grand Potentate of Up had hit the old inventor's wall.

Inventor's blockage was not uncommon in the technological community.

"No visualization, no invention."

Paul's words stung Lothar's pride. The genius pinhead belligerently stopped massaging Paul's neck.

Zelman quickly connected his two circuits into the conversation:

"To contribute or not to contribute is not the contribution!"

Paul and Lothar turned around to respond to Zelman's polemics. What Paul witnessed at that moment totally untracked his respect for the master synthetist.

The sexobot was on her metal knees pulling Zelman's atmospheric tuxedo trousers down to his knees. She was pressing her red-colored metal lips around his fleshy pink penis.

Paul was repulsed by the visualization.

"I'm going home!" Paul huffed.

Lothar began to roar with laughter, and Paul accidentally pushed him as he bumped his shoulder to get out of the room.

Lothar stumbled into the sexobot and knocked her forward into Zelman's undulations.

The sexually aroused, pink, fleshy fellow let out a horrendous pain-wracked cry.

"OUCHHHHHHHHHHHH!"

Paul and Lothar could see Zelman's pink, fleshy penis wiggling and throbbing in the sexobot's clenched metal lips.

Not every invention submitted at the convention had been thoroughly tested. Zelman had learned a bloody lesson.

"Is there a doctor in the convention?"

Paul patched into the loudspeaker intercom vid monitor.

Luckily for Zelman there were over one hundred certified doctors in over one hundred certifiable practices. One was an expert micro-seamster surgeon from the Sorbonne.

Zelman would have to stay off his sex for a month of Sundays, but he was reassured that he would be able to perform his most perverted visualizations within a year's time.

Paul caught the first pipeline available and piped back to his lonely, all-computerized house in Computer Meadows.

He didn't even wait for Elliot Richards' presentation of the Golden Wrench to the greatest inventor at the convention.

If Elliot asked him later on about his absence, Paul would explain he had wanted to get back to work on the new system.

Surely the Secretary of Technology wouldn't castigate him for wanting to succeed.

Paul sat all alone in his plush library computer chair.

He could hear the all-computerized house computer wheezing as he coughed into a medicant tissue. Neither one was feeling well.

Neither had taken good care of the other. Computer dust was all over the house, clogging up the respirator filters.

Later on that night, Howard and Bernice walked by.

"I fear Paul is sliding down the ladder of success," said Bernice.

Her tone was gloomy.

Howard felt sad to hear his wife make such a negative comment about his friend. For even though he and Paul were close, Howard and Bernice were Upsters, and it was against their constitution to think of negative thoughts.

"It's not 'Up' to be down," Howard said.

He and Bernice stood in front of Paul's house. They noticed the once emerald green synthetic grass hadn't been oiled in over a month. It was turning lime yellow.

"Howard, isn't there anything we can do to get him 'Up?'"

Bernice lit Howard's vitamin A smokette first.

They both inhaled deeply, letting the vitamin-packed smoke penetrate the depths of their lungs. They exhaled in unison.

Howard snapped his fingers.

"I have an idea!"

An ingenius glow surrounded his face.

"What is it?"

Bernice was feeling the effects of the smokette.

"You'll find out."

Howard started to walk back to his own house. Bernice ran after him, hoping he'd tell her his secret.

Paul dreaded his Tuesday morning meeting with Elliot Richards. He so much wanted to start out the first day of the work week on a positive digit.

He had taken a mouthful of Atmospheric Lung Contamination Decontaminator cough dots, but nothing seemed to stop his coughing.

"Good morning, Mr. Quatro."

"Good morning, Wallace."

"Mr. Richards said for you to go right in."

Paul walked past Elliot's transcriber. Wallace had always given off positive vibrations before, but not this morning.

Paul felt the chill as he entered Elliot's holy sanctorum, as Paul had nicknamed the Secretary's office. It was the largest, had the best view, was located on the top floor, had its own personal luxuries like the most advanced computer chair and desk in all of the Pentagon.

For a moment Paul stood in the doorway and watched Elliot Richards speak with a dozen different technologists over a-dozen vid screens.

He was a symphony conductor and it was a sight to behold. How he positioned, maneuvered, escaped, charged, parlayed, congratulated, reprimanded and finally combined the vid conference into one circuit of thought: his!

Paul hoped when he became the Secretary of Technology he would be able to conduct himself with such techno mastery.

As Elliot Richards switched off the dozen vid screens and started to turn around in his computerized chair, Paul had an after-visualization.

Will I become Secretary of Technology? A cold ripple of insecurity rumbled down his spine.

"Mr. Quatro, don't just stand there. Step forward!"

It was starting.

The Secretary's voice was commanding and without a shred of warmth.

Paul responded like a new recruit on the job. He hastened forward and in the process dropped his computer briefcase. The lock broke open, and all of his cassettes spilled out across the floor.

Paul scrambled to put them back in the case and take his seat without any further delay.

But, somehow, the cassettes wouldn't fit back into his computer briefcase as easily as they had before he'd left for work that morning.

He could feel Elliot's cold eyes staring down at him with complete disrespect.

"I've asked John Malone to sit in on this meeting."

Paul couldn't believe what he was hearing.

He crammed the last cassette into the computer briefcase and forced the combination lock to bolt shut. He would figure a way to open it after the meeting.

He looked up and noticed that John Malone was just stepping out from behind Elliot Richards' high-backed computer chair.

He had been standing there all along!

"It's your office."

Paul didn't mean to sound quite so disappointed. Nor did he want to concede his own power to John Malone. But he could feel his foundation crumbling beneath his aching logic.

"I have been scanning the new system diagrams and have uncovered several data omissions."

The Secretary was putting his 5-D scanner computer bifocals on as he pressed his diagram vid screen.

Paul was seated in front of the desk staring up at John Malone, who was standing next to Elliot Richards like an attack dogbot.

"What omissions are those, Mr. Secretary?"

Paul would conduct himself with the utmost professional logic.

This would be no time for personality conflicts.

"Logic works" was a motto every technocrat learned when he first entered the department. And Paul was going to have to live by that motto throughout the meeting.

"John has a list of six omissions in the hierarchical data link controller."

"I felt it was my duty to report these omissions to the Secretary."

John Malone was making his move. If he could convince Elliot Richards that Paul was a liability to the completion of the new system, then he would be elevated and Paul would be demoted, or even banished from the department!

For the next sixty-three minutes, Paul Quatro made his logic work.

He countered every charge.

He turned omissions into submissions yet to be decided upon.

He parried when John Malone thrusted.

He retreated when overrun with data he did not have at his fingertips.

He jammed when John Malone showed his lack of departmental requisites.

By the middle of the meeting, Paul was beginning to regain his strength.

Like a wounded big-ball player called off the bench in the ninth quarter, he got his second breath and then moved in for the kill.

"So you see, Mr. Secretary, the five omissions are not really omissions."

Paul rested his case as he stood in front of Elliot Richards.

Both men turned and looked at the Assistant Undersecretary of Technology.

John Malone was sitting down at the desk, his face drenched in perspiration, his haughty immortality gasping with the dread of defeat.

"What do you have to say for yourself, Mr. Malone?"

The Secretary of Technology was extremely disappointed in his new protégé. Paul could feel it in his cortex throb.

"I...I...only want to protect the integrity of the new system, Elliot!"

As soon as John Malone called the Secretary by his first name, he knew he'd made a magnificent blunder.

Paul seized this opportunity to murder with kindness.

"I'm sure Mr. Malone's motives were honorable, Mr. Secretary," he said, slightly underscoring the words "Mr." and "Secretary."

He'd decided not to go in for the kill.

And why should he? His accuser had fallen short of victory, and Paul did not need to rub that in.

In so doing, Paul successfully reminded Elliot Richards who his one, true protégé was.

"Mr. Assistant Undersecretary, I would like to be alone with Paul Quatro!"

John Malone skulked meekly out the door.

If he'd had a tail, it would have been between his legs.

Paul hadn't felt so secure with Elliot since the day before Mary died.

"He has a bright future!"

Paul was surprised at Elliot's comment. Surely it did not come from a man totally disappointed with a promising protégé. "Yes, he is very conscientious."

Paul's renewed security was quickly put on notice.

His cough began to act up.

"Try one of these!"

Elliot Richards handed Paul a small, synthetic, wire-meshed tablet coated with an adrenalin solution.

"I have my own cough dots," Paul begged away from the Secretary's offer of assistance.

"This will get rid of your atmospheric decontaminated lung cough!"

"Nothing can cure my cough!"

"Ohh, but you're wrong. This little tablet was the winner of the Golden Wrench award."

"Miss Vickers!" whispered Paul.

His throat was raw from coughing.

"She won?"

"Yes. She perfected the cure with a lung filternet coated in an adrenalin solution."

So the old man had chosen right.

Paul swallowed the synthetic wire-meshed tablet coated in adrenalin, and within fourteen seconds it stopped his cough. His lungs tickled as the pill unraveled itself.

"Paul, I want to speak with you about a very private matter."

For the first time in a meeting, Paul detected friendship in Elliot's voice.

For the next twenty minutes, Elliot Richards explained to Paul that he was going to run for the Presidency of all twenty-five United States of America, and that the union party, the unofficial party of technology, had chosen him as their candidate.

"That is a great honor, Elliot."

Paul felt secure enough to call the Secretary by his first name. At least for the time being.

"I will be spending a good portion of my time on the campaign vid screens. I must be reassured that you will be able to complete the new system in time for the next year projection date. Paul, my whole campaign is going to hinge on its success."

Paul felt as if Elliot Richards was threatening him.

He had never felt threatened by the man during his whole career.

But there it was: a threat. If Paul did not succeed in delivering the new system on time, he would be replaced.

It was all laid out in front of him.

"Sir, I won't let you down."

"It's not me, Paul. It's the department that's counting on you."

Call it what you want, Mr. Secretary, Paul thought to himself. But you are threatening me, and I know why.

Paul stood up and extended his hand. Elliot Richards grabbed it and squeezed hard.

"Utopia can be for us!"

He let go of Paul's hand and turned his computerized chair around, leaving Paul to exit by himself.

The thought of reaching Utopia in his lifetime was what every member of the Together Generation visualized.

Paul Quatro was connected to the man who could make it happen...if only he was elected President.

Paul knew Elliot Richards would show the senate what technology could really do for society...if only he were elected.

He took the escalator down to his office instead of the elevator. The escalator would allow him several more seconds to visualize the meeting.

He had always respected Elliot Richards.

He had never questioned his decisions.

Nor had he faltered in their execution. What Paul wrestled with was the illogicality behind the threat Elliot had posed towards him.

But by the time he'd reached his office and read through Holly James's transmissions he'd put the whole thing in perspective:

Elliot Richards was running for the highest rung on the upward and mobile ladder of success.

The Presidency! And with that office came certain problems.

Elliot Richards was human, just like everybody else.

He had his own anxieties; his own insecurities. It was just that he masked them better than anyone else.

In a way, knowing that little secret made Paul feel better about himself. There was no shame in feeling anxiety as long as that vibration didn't untrack one's high standard of actualization.

"I must be reassured you will be able to complete the new system in time."

Paul would hear that threat echo through his mind many times before he unveiled his "new system."

As he looked through the transmissions, he noticed one from John Malone.

"Would the Undersecretary transmit at his leisure?"

Paul nodded his understanding.

This Assistant Under-secretary was a cagey foe. Paul knew he'd try to smooth over the mistakes he'd made during the meeting.

"If at first you don't succeed with your opposition, try, try again!"

So, John Malone was transcribing Elliot' s phrases just as Paul had done, not so long ago.

Paul responded to all his incoming transmissions except for John Malone's.

He would let the young Assistant Under-secretary choke on his own twisted logic for a while.

Let him feel that shortness of breath!

Let him look over his shoulder to see who was scanning his every visualization!

Let him sink into the abyss of misjudgment like all the other assistants who had attempted to kidnap Paul's position in the past!

He was proud of his modus operandi: cool, efficient, well-mannered, unruffled, seasoned, a true technocrat.

Until recently he'd always had the soft love from his wife to fall back on when in doubt.

Since her death he'd discovered he could withstand the pressures of climbing that ladder without her.

But he also knew that if he was going to make it to the top he was going to need the companionship, the partnership, the communication, the trust and the co-habitation of a wife.

For Paul knew he was a true member of the Together Generation. To live alone was unnatural.

Paul knew he wasn't like his two friends, Lothar and Zelman.

No, Lord Lothar could have a combination of Togetherness matched only by a handful of technological men and women, but not by Paul.

Nor could Paul allow his life to become as perverted as Monty Zelman's.

Zelman's perversions were destroying his ability to contribute to the Together Generation' s betterment!

Paul knew what he needed was a woman who could understand his needs as he climbed that ladder of success.

He needed a woman who was secure in her own identity, a woman who was not afraid to express her true love to him, nor receive love from him.

Would he ever fall in love again and meet such a woman?

Paul opened the door to his all-computerized house with a sigh.

CASSETTE NUMBER TWO

Love in Mondo Techno

Upon entering the house, the coldness in Paul's soul quickly returned.

The excitement of the day's events couldn't be shared with anyone. Climbing up that upward mobile ladder of success was meaningless and debilitating without a wife to talk to. Being alone left Paul feeling as if his heart was empty.

Tears had long ago been replaced with a melancholy which he shared with no one. The anguish that tormented his dreams was banished by the insomnia which would not tolerate such negative visualization.

He had learned to function on three and a half hours of semi-consciousness.

His diet consisted of vitamins, an assortment of herbs, minerals, and certain synthetics that gave him the necessary energy to compete with complete logic.

He hung up his atmospheric trenchcoat and fedora hood and stepped into the living room.

The wheezing of the all-computerized house was getting worse.

A ray of light from the streetlamp outside filtered through the venetian blinds and coordinated the shadows into an intriguing design.

Paul locked into his auto consciousness. He couldn't remember one night from another.

He had thought of selling the house recently, but that would completely sever all his memories of Mary. He wasn't ready yet.

He stuck his hand into his atmospheric suit pocket and searched for Miss Vickers' contaminated lung cough filternet tablets.

Suddenly, the lights sprayed out. Paul shielded his eyes from the sudden glow.

"Surprise!"

Bernice let out a screech which reminded Paul of one of the cheerleaders at the Putney Inventor's Convention.

"And from Techno, the greatest technological department store in all twenty-five states of the union comes the latest home helper to hit the market spot! It's fantastic! It's remarkable! It's revolutionary! It's the one...the only...the...H-wall!"

Howard finished his sales pitch just as Paul refocused his eyes upon the strange, stainless steel twelve-foot-by-four-foot technological wall. It had been placed on a circular platform with three step pods positioned against the living room partition.

"Howard just loves to advertise."

Bernice quickly mimicked her husband's pitch.

"Techno, the greatest department store chain in the universe!"

Howard did not like his wife to make fun of his professional modus operandi.

"Howard...Bernice..."

Paul hadn't had any guests over since Lothar and Zelman helped him through his near-nervous breakdown.

"Go ahead and try on the glove."

Howard handed Paul the all-computerized leather and chrome glove, completely equipped with a control panel in the fingertips.

Paul was puzzled. Why were Bernice and Howard bugging him?

He appreciated their concern, but..."I appreciate your kindness, but I'd really like to be left alone."

"Paul, just put on the glove."

Howard helped him on with the glove.

"What is this?"

The glove felt alive, but he didn't know why.

"Press the button that's located on the thumb."

Howard could see Paul's confusion, so he pressed the button for him.

As soon as the On button was activated, the H-wall began to give off a powerful metallic vibration. The vibration was much stronger than the pipeline's vibe.

"Isn't this exciting?"

Bernice was trying to reassure Paul.

Paul had never felt anything like it.

The glove was both terrifying and glorious.

It had a certain power, but for what?

"Press the lavender button!"

Howard was reading the instructions from the computer pamphlet.

Paul looked at the fingertips of the glove.

Each one had a different colored button: lavender, blue, red, and the yellow "Off" button for the baby finger. The white "On" button was for the thumb.

Paul pressed the lavender button and felt a surge of energy go through his arm.

His attention focused on the H-wall.

The wall began to generate a loud vibration.

The intensity frightened him.

"What's happening?" Paul shouted to Howard.

"I don't know!" answered Howard.

Bernice clutched her husband's arm and screamed.

"I thought you knew how it worked!"

"I do," bellowed Howard, "but I've never seen it work!"

Bernice rolled her eyes in disbelief.

Paul wanted desperately to remove the glove.

Then a bluish-red glow in the center of the H-wall began to wink, like a time slit from another dimension.

An energy mass appeared on the first step pod.

It had a globular shape.

The mass leaped onto the second step pod and took the shape of a humanoid without a facial expression.

Finally, it leaped onto the third step pod and produced itself into its own holographic character image.

"Sir, my name is Pi. I am a gentleman's hologram. My duties are household computerized service."

Pi was a cherubic, rosy-cheeked holographic character dressed in a form-fitting butler's uniform. He had a bit of a Brittany accent.

"The P models are the finest chefs this side of Europa," crowed Howard with pride.

"Sir, I am capable of preparing over sixteen hundred different dishes at any given moment."

"Paul, when you're done with Pi, send him over!" said Bernice.

"Bernice, you still haven't learned how to program our own homebot!"

Paul was becoming intrigued with the H-wall.

"I didn't realize the private sector was into mass merchandising holographic characters."

"I ordered two hundred H-walls last week, and we were sold out the first day we had them in the main store."

Howard was positively glowing.

"It's the latest! It's the greatest!" Her sarcasm was playful.

Howard cut Bernice off.

"Press the button again, Paul."

"Yes, Paul, press the button."

Bernice regained her composure as Paul selected the blue fingertip button.

Once again he felt a bolt of energy fire up his arm. This time it was stronger than Pi's.

He looked over at the H-wall and watched the holographic transference from inside the wall through the time slit dimension as it reproduced its form onto the three step pods.

By the time the blue energy mass reached the third step, Paul, Howard and Bernice were introduced to Delti, a holographic strongman character.
He was wearing a form-fitting jumpsuit that accentuated his muscles. His face looked as if it had been chiseled out of pure energy, then buffed with sexual vitality.

"My name is Delti. My duties are household computerized maintenance."

He stood next to Pi, his whole body vibrating with power.

Howard read out loud to the group from his computer pamphlet: "The D model holographic character can do the work of five service robots. He can lift solar panels by himself."

"By himself!" Paul and Bernice spoke in unison.

Solar panels weighed over five hundred pounds apiece. It took two service robots just to balance them off the roof!

"He specs out at six hundred pounds maximum lift-up weight. He's knowledgeable in pool maintenance, filter brushing, synthetic oil lubricating, kitchen repair and refitting maintenance, and he knows every aspect of the central computer control panel system."

Paul was impressed.

"That's more capability than any service robot on the market!"

Howard agreed.

"I have a hunch that the holographic character will replace the service robot as the primary home helper."

Bernice was becoming impatient. She wanted to know what the last button would produce.

"Press the red button, Paul!"

Paul pressed the red button on the index glove finger.

He felt a different form of energy. It wasn't as powerful as Delti's, nor was it so voluminous. It had a certain sensuality to it.

Paul watched as the reddish-pink holographic energy transferred out of the dimension slit and began its three step pod formation.

Paul could feel the energy circulate up his arm. By the time the third holographic character had appeared on the third step pod, the energy had touched his heart.

"My name is Heleon!"

She was unlike any other female essence he had ever experienced.

Her skin had a milky rose color tint. She had short, reddish hair and a figure that had been simmered to perfection. There was a childlike sensuality in her whispery voice.

"My duties are personal maintenance, sir!"

The way she looked at Paul made him feel uncomfortable. He wasn't sure why.

Howard found the paragraph to go with Heleon's earthy debut: "H models are trained in the computer library sciences. Whatever your mood, she will regulate the home entertainment on your vid screens."

"Sir, I am an expert in programming."

Her voice had texture, a certain resonance that reminded Paul of something…

"Is it warm in here?"

He felt flushed.

"Sir, the temperature is 78.6 degrees Fahrenheit."

"Thank you, Pi."

Paul nodded at the little hologram.

"Would you like a change, sir?"

"No, that won't be necessary, Delti. But thank you."

A long, awkward silence followed.

Paul didn't know what to do.

He held the glove in his hand, and it felt natural.

"Well," said Howard, "Bernice and I should be going."

"Howard!"

Paul didn't know how to express his feelings.

"Good pleasure, Paul."

Bernice kissed him on the side of his face.

"Bernice!"

Paul watched as his next door neighbors excused themselves.

He walked them to the front door.

"I don't know if I can accept such a gift."

"Paul, you'd be doing me a big favor if you try it out. Who is more suited to judge a new appliance for technology than you?"

Paul watched Howard and Bernice walk across his dried-up synthetic lawn.

He hadn't realized the once emerald green color had faded so badly. He would have to start lubricating it out of its now lime-yellow hue.

He closed the door and walked back into his living room.

Pi, the cherubic butler; Delti, the all-purpose computer maintenance strong-man helper; and Heleon, the personal entertainment programmer stood in a row on the third step pod.

They awaited his commands.

Paul was sure this wouldn't work out, but he would try the technological home helper wall...as a personal favor to Howard.

He'd even throw in a free evaluation for his old friend before sending it back!

Howard and Bernice Bork sat in their kitchen vid nook sipping a late night cup of vitafee.

"Did you see his face when those holographic characters appeared? Technoooooooo! Bernice, I'm telling you that these H-walls are going to be the biggest sellers since..."

Howard turned and glared at Rob, their home-service robot. He was standing in the doorway waiting to bid his owners good evening before shutting down. Bernice interceded on his behalf.

"Yes, Rob...b'bot!"

She knew Howard would scold her for calling the robot by name.

"Will there be any other commands for me to obey before I shut down for the evening?"

He had a tentative tone to his vocal responder.

"Mr. Bork and I will turn off the lights."

Bernice had a tender vibe for her "Rob," and he for her.

Howard watched the metal man walk into his stainless steel closet which was located in the kitchen hallway next to the pantry.

"Mark my words, Bernice. These new H-walls will someday replace robot-service helpers."

Bernice found that hard to believe.

Her Rob had become her best friend ever since Mary Quatro had died. Howard was always at work, or else bolted to his computer chair in the vid-screen library, watching his sacred big-ball matches.

Howard continued to sip his vitafee and expound on the campaign strategy to market the H-walls.

Bernice wasn't really visualizing his chatter.

She kept drifting her visualization towards Rob, who by now was standing inside the stainless steel closet, his power shut off.

She knew how much he disliked being shut down.

How many times had she cried on his metal shoulder?

How many times had she listened to his own mixed circuitry?

How many times had they done more than listen to each other's loneliness?

Although Rob was not equipped in the practical application of sex -- as had been the sexobots -- he was able to find ways to comfort Bernice.

She, in turn, brought a vibration not yet programmed into his system. He found this invigorating.

The two of them knew that if Howard ever found out he would have Rob disassembled, and Bernice would be brought up on charges of abhorrent disillusionment.

If she were found guilty, Bernice would never be allowed to remarry.

A horrifying thought!

She would have no options but to commit herself to a technological nunnery.

She'd visualized an article in one of those trashy computer news screens entitled National Visualizer which told of a respectable woman who had been discovered by her husband to have been having an affair with a pilobot she'd met on a flight from Cincinnati to Ontario.

The woman had been found immorally guilty and sent to a technological nunnery located in Sioux City, Iowa, which was as far away from habitable civilization as one could get before entering the uninhabitable part of North America.

"I'm going to bed, darling." Howard kissed his wife on the forehead.

"I'll be alone in a ticking second."

She watched him place his empty cup of vitafee in the sink and walk out of the kitchen.

She waited to make sure he had enough time to walk across the house to their bedroom which was on the far side of the house.

Then Bernice stood up and quietly walked into the kitchen hallway.

She stood next to the stainless steel closet that housed her Rob.

She placed her hand on the warm door and whispered, "Good night, Rob."

She pressed her cheek against the warm door. She could hear a low, robotic circuit throb.

Her robot was asleep. She wondered if he was dreaming about her, as she did of him . . .

Paul was reading his morning Vid Screen News as he glided across Computer Meadows on the boulevard conveyor belt.

Howard pushed his way through the crowd to catch up with his next door neighbor.

"Well? How does it work?"

Paul looked up from the news and was confused.

"The H-wall, Paul!"

"Howard, I just got it last night!"

"What?"

Howard couldn't believe Paul's nonchalance.

Here he'd given Paul the most revolutionary home helper since the robot, and he was treating it like a computerized tweezer for nostril hair!

What Howard didn't know was that Paul had awoken that morning, just as he had since Mary' s death, and slowly stepped into the shower tub where he washed away the night's insomnia.

He had then made himself a cup of vitafee and patched into the morning news.

He didn't like to spend mornings in his all-computerized house now that Mary was gone. The light reminded him that once he'd been happy before dear Mary was taken from him by a technical malfunction.

Then as Paul turned the front doorknob, he looked back at the computer glove as it rested on the third step pod in front of the H-wall.

It seemed as if a magnet drew him back into the house towards the glove.

He picked it up and put it on his right hand. The energy response was incredible.

His head cleared up immediately as the static tension borne of another bad night was eliminated from his awareness.

He pressed the On button and felt the powerful energy vibration of the H-wall in front of him.

In true technocratic form, Paul immediately looked around and found the computer pamphlet.

The night before he was too exhausted to be inquisitive, but as soon as Howard and Bernice had gone home he'd turned on the Off button to watch the three holographic characters re-enter the slit dimension of the wall.

First Pi presented himself in the morning, followed by Delti.

Paul hesitated a moment before pressing Heleon's red button on the glove's index finger. Then he pressed it, as if a subconscious command had been given.

All three holographic characters stood at attention on the third step pod, awaiting their orders.

When Pi noticed Paul visualizing the instructions in the computer pamphlet, he stepped forward and cleared his vocal energy to speak.

"Sir, may I suggest you recommend the maintenance you wish performed and leave the actualization to us."

Pi stepped back, next to Delti, not sure whether he had spoken out of turn and would therefore be reprimanded by his new controller.

Delti gave the cherubic hologram a harsh glance.

"Yes, that is an excellent idea."

Paul put down the glove and the computer pamphlet and walked to the front door.

Pi, Delti and Heleon watched him with great interest as he buttoned up his atmospheric trenchcoat and placed his atmospheric fedora hood on.

"Sir, your briefcase!"

Heleon was standing next to him holding his computer briefcase.

He hadn't really seen her walk over. Had she dematerialized and rematerialized within the second?

"I'll let you know, Howard."

The neon door to the pipeline slid shut.

Just before he heard the tuning fork vibration of the pipeline pipeing him to employment, Paul realized he hadn't given the holographic characters their maintenance orders.

What did it matter, though, he thought to himself.

Without commands, a robot could not accomplish a task.

So what if the house didn't get organized?

He had more important actualizations on his visualization than his all-computerized house in Computer Meadows, which was really only a sad reminder of a happy lifestyle once lived.

"Responsibility. The new system must be responsible to the needs of each department in government...flexibility! The new system must be able to evolve with the enormous actualization of each service it is called upon to maintain...compatibility! Control etiquette! Delivery systems and software interfaces must be compatible with each country's organizational requirements."

Paul finished his transmission into Holly James's transcriber.

She finished the last of the transcription which she would relay onto the master transcriber and then forward onto the specified assistant undersecretaries, the section chiefs, and the sub-section managers.

Paul gathered up his computer notes and started to stack them on his computer desk.

Ms. James quickly took off her headphones and walked over to Paul.

She took the computer pads out of his hand.

132

"P.Q., I'll take care of that, or you're going to be late."

"Late?"

"For the President's forecast!"

Paul breathed a startled sigh of relief.

He was forever grateful to Holly James for keeping him apprised of his schedule when he was so absent-minded about these things.

Holly marveled at the inner logic of this man. In some ways he reminded her of her first husband.

An absent- minded professor on the go. Always trying to move up that ladder of success.

But that first husband hadn't been in Paul Quatro's league! No, Frederick had been a butcher in a synthetic automat market.

They'd been married a year when she received the notice via the computer message vid screen:

"We are sorry to inform you that your husband, Frederick Maxim, fell asleep at his cutting machine and accidentally leaned forward, enabling his atmospheric shirt collar to get caught in the clawer. He was pulled into the cutter, which diced him into little pieces which were then wrapped in five syntho boxes. We have not yet traced the whereabouts of these boxes, and we hope they are not being sold on the Open Market.

However, if that is the actualization, we can only assume he has been devoured into society. At least his remains will not go unused. Sincerely."

Holly dabbed her eyes with a frilly hanky. Although she had been married six more times, she would always remember "Freddie," as she'd fondly called him, with special affection.

And, she remarked to herself, that was why she felt such compassion for Paul.

He'd lost someone, too, and she knew that pain.

So when he made omissions, she always made sure to correct him.

Although Holly James was fifty years older than Paul and at the present time unbethrothed, she knew deep down in her private visualizations that she and Paul would never have a personal connection.

Nonetheless, she felt emotion for her employer, and that was more than most transcribers could say about their superiors within the Department of Technology.

Paul had not wanted to sit next to John Malone at the President's forecast, but the young Assistant Undersecretary had arrived at the White House Oval Room several seconds before him, and he had no alternative since all other chairs but his had been taken.

"We live in a time when the decontaminated habitable sectors of earth need the most creative optimism governments can organize. For, without optimism, the citizens of the world would have no need to explore new avenues of evolution. My administration…I pledge…"

"Isn't she a bag of gas?"

John Malone whispered snidely into Paul.'s ear.

The Assistant Undersecretary was trying to get on his good side, trying to be one of Paul's allies, trying to show Paul he could play big ball.

Paul didn't respond to John Malone's remark. He was too interested in what the President actually had to say.
"And I forecast that the economy of the nation shall exceed last year's high yield of sixteen percent over prime value of the work forces actualization to the contribution in all fields of personal services. Technology, imported and exported, is this administration's highest priority!"

Paul had voted for Andrea Eberhardt Ricarda in the last election.

She was a stately woman who had started out as a high-tech fashion model in the software business.

He had once seen some rare vid snapshots of the President modeling computer shoes.

She was wearing only the shoes while she balanced on a beach ball.

They were provocative poses, though, for that time in history.

Her opponent later tried to use those poses against her when she ran for the Presidency.

But the public found her beauty so enthralling they didn't judge the photographs as morally unjust.

Hadn't she tried to make a proper living at a time when unemployment was at an all-time high of 22%?

President Ricarda was from the It Generation.

She had been orphaned like many others and left out on the plains to fend for herself. She knew what it was like to live from hand to mouth, where only the strongest survived.

The terrible atmospheric decontamination storms which were constantly stalking the remaining populace had claimed many lives.

The It Generation had rebuilt the world and helped implement order and logic back into society.

President Ricarda called herself a Humanist. If she didn't always agree with the course technology was taking, at least she did not discourage it.

"I have been reassured by Secretary of Technology Richards that the new system will be implemented on the projected date. I believe Mr. Quatro, the Undersecretary of Technology, is here to support that visualization."

Paul realized everybody was staring at him. He felt himself freezing his posture as best he could without being self-conscious.

"Of course, if the new system is not successful, my administration will have to reassess the Department of Technology's purpose of contribution to society."

So that was it! She was putting Elliot Richards on notice!

If he was going to run against her for the Presidency, he would have to know the consequences.

The power base of the department was on the line.

Elliot Richards' entire career would be impaired if he lost the election.

Andrea Eberhardt Ricarda was as tough as she was beautiful.

Paul liked her. He felt secure in her presence.

Many in the media had nicknamed her "The Mother."

To many Together Generation members who were born in a test tube, she represented the maternal connection they'd never experienced at the test tube orphanage.

"Elliot will disconnect her in the next election."

John Malone walked alongside Paul toward the White House pipeline.

He annoyed Paul to no end.

The young Assistant Undersecretary was only ten years younger than Paul Quatro, but in Paul's visualization they were from separate generations.

"Never underestimate the opposition."

Paul did not like John Malone's attempt at getting familiar.

"Surely you don't believe she can defeat Elliot!"

John Malone was incredulous.

"Mr. Malone, I suggest you stick to the facts and leave politics to the politicians."

He didn't want the Assistant Undersecretary of Technology to get connected with him.

How many other assistants had tried that tactic and then attempted to assassinate him when he wasn't visualizing?

No, if John Malone wanted to defeat him, he would have to do it face to face. Open visualization!

John Malone watched Paul enter the pipeline. He would have the Undersecretary of Technology's position one way or another!

It didn't matter to him.

A new generation was beginning to establish their own doctrines, a generation which would eventually be called the "Force Generation."

The Together Generation worked in harmony to climb that upward, mobile ladder of success.

The Force Generation wanted everything! Immediately! Don't wait!

They knew nothing of patience…did not visualize Utopia as a goal, but sought power and the control of it.

"Good day, Mr. Undersecretary."

John Malone watched the pipeline neon door slide shut.

His time would arrive.

Men like Paul Quatro would have no place in the realm of power.

He would make sure of it.

It had been a strenuous day in the department.

Paul could not remember when he'd felt so exhausted.

It wasn't just the work, it was the pressure of competition. He was four months away from unveiling the new system.

Elliot Richards had called a vid conference for the media this afternoon. The Secretary of Technology had announced his candidacy for the Presidency of the United States of America.

Only minutes before the announcement, Paul had been with the Secretary in person to inform him of the President's forecast.

Somehow during the meeting Paul got the feeling Elliot Richards had already been informed.

Then, by chance, Paul glanced in the direction of a computer pad which lay within easy visualization on the Secretary's desk.

John Malone's transmission sat there, caught, like a small animal.

"Aha!" growled Paul to himself.

He clenched his fists in anger.

His feelings did not go unnoticed by the Secretary.

"Is something wrong, Paul?"

"No," said Paul.

He wished Elliot the largest landslide in the history of the electorate.

By the time he got off the conveyor belt sidewalk in front of his all-computerized house, he was desperately tired.

He needed to sleep.

As he walked up the plastic pathway to the front door, he didn't notice the sprinkler system spraying the yellow-lime synthetic lawn with blue lubricant.

Nor was he aware of the lights which twinkled with welcoming warmth from his house.

As he put his hand to the front door, it opened automatically.

"Good evening, sir."

Pi stood at relaxed attention, smiling. He helped Paul off with his coat.

"Here, let me take that from you."

Heleon took hold of his computer briefcase.

"Did you have a formidable day, sir?"

Delti was carrying a length of solar pipe over his shoulder as he walked past Paul and out the front door. The strongman' s face was smudged from working outside all day.

"Sir, I hope you like your vitatinis dry."

Pi was efficiently courteous as he escorted Paul into the house.

Heleon followed.

Paul felt caught off guard by their attentiveness.

"Yes, of course, Pi. That will be fine."

"Sir, I've prepared a warm bath for you."

Heleon bowed her head.

Something stirred in Paul. He hadn't had a warm bath after work since Mary had passed away.

"I didn't know if you use Relaxo or Contempofluids, so I mixed the combination. If I did wrong, I can change the fluids."

She waited.

She had the most sensual tone of voice he'd ever heard.

"The combo is just fine, Heleon."

She handed him the vitatini.

"Would sir be prepared to dine at 8:00 p.m.?"

Pi was well-trained in manners and etiquette.

"Eight p.m...yes, of course."

Paul had not been taken care of in such a long time that he forgot the visual pleasure.

And then he noticed Heleon was leading him towards the bedroom.

"I've prepared synthetic beef wellington, computerized hot-house miniature peas and potatoes in a carrot sauce, and a fresh, green salad. I didn't have much to work with in the automat freezer," Pi called out as Paul slipped down the hall with Heleon.

His voice sounded like bells.

"I look forward to your meal presentation," Paul shouted back to Pi, who had already disappeared into the kitchen.

"He was worried you'd be disappointed in his selection," confided Heleon.

They passed the computer library.

Paul noticed the door was open and all his cassettes were on the floor, their vid-screen panels pulled out. Heleon seemed to read his mind.

"I'm reorganizing your cassettes in alphabetical order by subject and date of reference."

"I haven't been as organized as I could have been lately, I know," said Paul.

"And Delti is overhauling your whole computer system!"

Heleon sounded proud.

"I'm sure it needs an overhaul," said Paul, as Heleon guided him into the bedroom and sat him down on his air bed.

Before he could say anything, she started to untangle his bolo tie and unbutton his three-piece atmospheric shirt.

He stopped her by grabbing onto her hand.

The touch was electrifying.

He had never felt anything so magnetic, so alive.

"I can undress myself," he said gently.

As soon as he had spoken he could see he had hurt her vibes ...or whatever her responsible mechanism was labeled.

"Did I do it wrong?"

"No," said Paul, "It's just that I prefer to do it myself."

"As you so desire, sir."

Heleon excused herself and backed out of the bedroom.

Paul sat quietly on the bed, savoring the solitude, sipping his perfectly dry vitatini.

As he eased himself into the warm bath that awaited him, the sauna steam engulfed his consciousness.

He closed his eyes and listened to the soft, symphonic music that played over the computerfonic system.

Heleon's selection was proper for such a moment.

"Sir! Dinner will be served in fifteen minutes!"

Paul's eyes snapped open. He had no idea how long he'd been asleep.

Heleon was kneeling next to the tub, her hand on his neck. She was massaging him gently.

143

"Heleon?"

"Sir, dinner…"

Paul felt self-conscious in her presence.

"Yes, I'll be just a moment."

Heleon stood up and took his atmospheric robe off the hanger.

She waited for him to get out of the tub so she could swathe him in it, as if he were a child.

"Heleon, I'd like to be left alone."

Once again, as soon as he rejected her help, Heleon seemed consumed with hurt, as if she thought she'd done something wrong but knew she hadn't and therefore couldn't understand why she was being rejected.

"Yes, sir."

She replaced the robe on its hanger and quickly left the cosmetic room.

Paul sat at the head of his dining room table, slowly cutting into the warm, synthetic beef wellington. Each piece was delicious.

It had been so long since he'd had a home automated meal.

He chewed softly.

Pi, Heleon and Delti stood at the opposite end of the table watching their controller, arms to their sides, chins square, eyes forward. They had been taught to stand in service this way at the Learning Garden.

Pi so much wanted to know if the controller was enjoying his service, but he had been trained never to impose his own vanity upon those he maintained.

When Paul stopped and looked at the miniature hot house potato at the end of his fork, Pi wasn't sure whether to take that as a sign of disflavor or as a split visualization.

When Paul took the small potato from the fork and rolled it around in his mouth before chewing, Pi was further confused.

Was the controller enjoying his meal?

Paul was savoring each bite.

He glanced across the table at the holographic characters between taking bites of his peas and potatoes.

As he sipped his vitavino he peered over the brim of the crystal goblet and caught Heleon's eyes.

He found it hard not to visualize her, as if she had a magic power.

The Afrikaniker drum music which was playing over the computerfonic system excited his visualizations as he ate.

The rhythm danced along with his heartbeat!

"Would sir desire another slice of beef?"

Pi took a step forward to make his request official, as he had been trained to do at the Learning Garden. He had been taught, too, it was acceptable for a butler hologram to draw upon his controller's instincts.

Delti found Pi's actions rather condescending. Surely a D model hologram would never stoop to such pandering.

The strongman holographic character was an absolutist. If there was maintenance to be done, he never hesitated to complete the task, no matter what the controller's instincts might be.

D models had been taught at the Learning Garden that controllers did not always have the time for total maintenance visualization.

Therefore, it was the responsibility of the D model to maintain at all times.

"No, Pi. I'm content with the portion set upon my plate."

Pi immediately took a step back, resuming his place next to Delti.

"As you so desire, sir."

Pi so much wanted to please the controller. It was his nature to want to deliver exemplary maintenance.

Heleon watched Paul chew his nourishment. His jaw, his chin, his lips, his tongue...all moving with one purpose.

She found the experience of watching him exhilarating.

At the Learning Garden the clinicticians never showed them such honesty of purpose. When they taught "purpose" they did so with such coldness that at times, Heleon thought the essence of the lesson was obscured.

Upon graduation from the Learning Garden, Heleon felt frightened.

She remembered Doctor Rick holding her hands and consoling her. What a dear fellow the good Doctor had been! She wondered if she'd visualize his presence ever again.

She took a step forward, and she inhaled deeply. She was nervous as she addressed her controller.

"Would sir prefer a different musical cassette?"

Her voice drifted across the long table and curled its vibration into his nostrils.

Paul stopped chewing the last pea in his mouth, then quickly gulped it down.

"Yes!"

Before he could state his choice, she spoke.

"Duke Ellington, 1940."

She had plucked the visualization right out of his cortex.

It happened so fast he wasn't sure whether or not he'd spoken his selection out loud.

She repeated his choice.

He lifted up his vitavino crystal goblet to take a sip, savoring for a split second the shimmering emerald trans lucence as it played in the light.

When he glanced back at Heleon, she was gone. Only Pi and Delti stood at attention, arms to their sides, chins square, eyes forward.

Paul felt uncomfortable with the way they stood at the end of the table, waiting to actualize his every desire. Funny, it had never bothered him to have a service robot standing at attention waiting for a command.

Somehow, these holographic characters brought out a different visualization.

He didn't remember seeing Heleon return to her place next to Delti at the far end of the table, but there she was.

Then he heard Duke Ellington singing, "I've Never Felt This Way Before," as the rich sound infiltrated his sensorial circuitry.

Heleon's face was so innocent.

He dabbed his lips with the cellophane napkin and patted his stomach.

"A most delicious meal, Pi!"

The P model holographic character heaved a sigh of relief.

"Yes, sir. Thank you, sir! Would sir care for an after-dinner drink in the living room?"

"Yes, I'd like that."

Before Paul had gotten up from his chair, Delti had cleared the table, Pi had pulled his chair back and Heleon had extended her hand to escort him into the living room. Everything was done gracefully, as a team.

The energy that flowed among them felt harmonious, an energy one didn't feel with service robots.

As Paul sat on the cushioned couch sipping his after-dinner vitapertif, he thought about the limitations of robots.

Somehow, no one had ever invented a program that coordinated more than two robots to do one task at a time. Yet, in a matter of seconds, Paul had witnessed three holographic characters assessing an actualization and coordinating its completion in unison.

As Paul took the last sip of his vitapertif, Delti, Pi and Heleon stood on the third step pod next to the H-wall in the living room and watched.

To each, Paul represented something different.

Paul was glad Duke Ellington had survived trauma shock.

He placed both his hands on his knees and straightened his back. He hadn't felt so at home in his all-computerized house since Mary had been alive.

"Delti, I want to commend you for vacuuming up the computer dust."
Paul stood up and faced the strongman.

"A simple maintenance, sir."

The D model did not find the controller's comment complimentary. Any holo- graphic model could perform such a maintenance.

D models had been taught at the Learning Garden that their purpose was to be performed to perfection. Always, a D model was to be beyond reproach.

Paul sensed a certain arrogance in Delti's deep, textured voice; nothing that was going to be uncomfortable, really, but a certain edge.

Perhaps the tone wasn't arrogance, Paul thought to himself.

These holographic characters would have to be examined before he could give Howard a viable evaluation.

They were definitely not like robots. They didn't seem programmed the way robots did yet they were a technological creation and were therefore programmed every bit as much as robots were.

Years ago when Paul had been promoted to his position as Undersecretary of Technology, he had analyzed holographic diagrams.

He was a sub-section manager at the time, but that was so long ago he'd forgotten the exact calibrations.

He made a visualization note to himself as he put the computer glove on. He would get the transcript cassette on holographic characters when he had the time.

"Good night, sir."

"Good night, Pi," said Paul, as he pressed the lavender fingertip button which controlled the cherubic butler.

Pi dematerialized back into the wall, a soft cloud of light that faded quickly from view.

"Good night, sir, said Delti.

"Good night, Delti."

Paul pressed the blue fingertip button. The strongman dematerialized into the wall.

Only Heleon remained. Paul was glad they were alone.

She could sense he wanted to communicate.

"Does sir desire my maintenance?"

She waited anxiously to see if he pressed the red index fingertip button. She had never felt such an energy response to any of her clinicticians at the Learning Garden.

"You seem to have a foundation in Musicology."

"Yes, sir. I have a visualized catalogue of over eighty-eight thousand compositions. And I can hum, whistle or snap with my fingertips an additional fourteen thousand non-composed folk ballads that have been passed down through the ages."

Paul was impressed.

He knew of no service robot that had been programmed in Musicology that could store such a wealth of information.

"Would sir desire me to sing him a favorite song?"

H models had been thoroughly taught the art of pleasure-giving at the Learning Garden.

Heleon did so much want to give pleasure to Paul. Giving pleasure was her purpose!

"Not tonight, Heleon."

As soon as he rejected her offer, he could see that heartfelt, sad-eyed look that was beginning to be familiar to him whenever he rejected her offers to help.

"Is sir not pleased with Heleon?"

She was a child! A child who needed reassurance, who seemed to be subconsciously pleading for attention.

Paul didn 't know how to explain his feelings, because Paul didn't know what he felt for Heleon.

She was a technological appliance that had been created for home maintenance. He was a technocrat and a human being.

"You have fulfilled your actualization by my visualizations," he said not too sternly.

The two of them stood in front of the H-wall, awkward in their communication.

She understood their purpose. He didn't.

"Good night, sir."

"Good night, Heleon."

Paul pressed the red index fingertip button and watched her dematerialize back into the technological H-wall.

He didn't really want her to go, but he didn't feel comfortable enough with her to continue the conversation.

He placed the computer glove on the third step pod and walked across the living room towards his bedroom. The lights turned off automatically.

Delti's computer maintenance was ultra-efficient. In a matter of weeks he would have the central computer panel overhauled and running harmoniously.

Paul visualized the impending order with satisfaction as he entered the bedroom.

His eyes fell upon the synthetic rosebud lying on his air pillow.

"Heleon!" he whispered to himself.

She sensed his needs!

He saw she had laid out a fresh pair of atmospheric pajamas. As he crawled into bed he could scent and feel the new linens she had fitted.

Just before the lights automatically turned off, Paul glanced again at the synthetic rosebud, which he 'd placed on the reading table next to his air bed.

As his eyelids began to close, he could feel the warm vibration of the air bed carrying him away. . .

He would sleep like a baby in an incubator. He would have only good dreams. He would never battle insomnia again.

Then, the ancient, musical lullaby of his test tube orphanage days began a friendly visit to his subconscious.

"Heleon!"

He visualized her kindness, and then he fell into a deep sleep…swaying palm trees dancing to the ocean breeze…a sparkling rainbow across the horizon…bare breasted Gauguin girls frolicking in the decontaminated aqua blue sea…yellow canaries…green parrots…white seagulls…harmonizing in the jungle.

He was walking along a sandy beach, naked, his sex feeling hard and purposeful…he stroked himself, and it felt right…the muscles in his body primed…his lips moist…and then he saw her in the distance…she was like a simmering mirage of heat.

He quickened his pace. She was naked…holding her breasts, lifting them up, then lowering her hands to her sides and moving like a panther in pursuit…he licked his lips…his sex getting harder and harder…ready to explode…he ran towards her…she stopped…he ran faster…she squatted down…her fingers began to explore…he could see she was holding a fig…spreading it apart…the thick jelly oozing out, dripping down her legs…sticking to her fingertips.

His lungs were burning from running so fast. He wanted to lick her fingertips. She lowered herself onto her hands and knees and turned her buttocks in his direction. Slowly, she began to sway her sex to the motion of the ocean breeze, but no matter how fast he ran towards her, he couldn't reach her. She took her left

154

hand and began to shove the fig up into her sex. The jelly was oozing out…his lungs were ready to burst…his sex was like a red-hot iron rod pulled from a burning blast furnace.

He wanted to stick his tongue between the fig and lick out the oozing jelly…and he felt electrifying currents running through his sex as he stroked his hardness again and again. She rolled over onto her back and lifted up her legs…she opened her mouth…she wanted to be filled with his electric cream…it squirted out…and she bathed her body in its warmth…rubbing· the white ooze all over her lips…her tongue licking his pleasure.

"Paul!"

He could hear her calling his name.

"Paul!"

Her voice was tender.

"Paul! Wake up!"

He didn't want the dream to end.

"Sir!"

He rolled over on his back and stared up at Heleon.

He felt the sticky pajamas against his legs. He visualized the wet dream he had, apparently, just actualized.

"Heleon! How did you get here!"

Paul quickly pulled the blanket up to his chin and felt embarrassed.

"You put the glove on auto-respond before you went to bed."

Her tone was honest.

Paul couldn't recall that actualization.

"I didn't know there even was an auto-responder button."

"Oh, it's not a button, sir. It's a responder pad in the palm of the control glove."

His pajama bottoms were soaked.

"I don't remember pressing it."

"It is activated by your subconscious visualization."

Paul was amazed at the intricacies of the computer glove.

He had studied many reports submitted to the department from different inventor clinics across the land, all of which outlined in theory how the subconscious could actually control certain technological appliances.

This was the first one he knew of that actualized such a visualization.

He sat up in his air bed, suddenly aware he had not been keeping up with the technical transmissions submissions recently.

"I have drawn your bath, sir!"

Heleon had his maroon atmospheric bathrobe in her hands, ready for him to slip into.

But Paul didn't move. He didn't want her to see his sticky-wet pajama bottoms.

"Heleon, I do appreciate your attentiveness to my maintenance."

"It pleases me to know that, sir."

"But I need a few more moments in bed."

He hoped she would get the message and leave him to his own maintenance.

But she didn't.

She continued to wait obediently by the side of his bed, the maroon bathrobe in her hands. Paul glared at her.

"Alone."

"Please forgive my over-maintenance."

Heleon laid his robe down at the foot of the air bed and immediately left the room. If she'd had wings, Paul would have sworn they were broken.

Heleon dashed to the kitchen and threw herself into Pi's comforting arms. Her tears rippled like energy streams over his shoulder as he baked whole wheat vitabuns in the automat.

"I'm a failure," she wailed.

"No, you're not."

Pi turned the whole wheat vitabuns over with the computer spatula. Closing the pyrex automat door, he watched them rise between hugging sessions with Heleon.

"Sir responds negatively to all of my personal maintenance!"

"Give the controller time, Heleon."

Pi was sympathetic to Heleon 's upsetting energy.

He, too, had felt a loss of self.-energy when the controller had not immediately responded to his beef wellington.

"Remember what the clinicticians taught us at the Learning Garden?"

He dabbed her energy tears with his apron.

"Maintenance is a gift, not a chore."

Heleon struggled to remember other important doctrines.

"For those who maintain!" pronounced Delti as he walked by carrying a coil of circuitry wire over his shoulder.

He was rewiring all the circuitry in the house. Computer dust had clogged the circuits, and a major overhaul had become necessary.

"To maintain is to be maintained," she responded against Delti's negative energy.

But Delti didn't recognize her energy at all as the back door slammed shut with his exit. Pi and Heleon didn't connect very well with Delti.

"He's a real drain, you know?" giggled Heleon, thrilled with her own honesty.

"Yes," nodded Pi.

"I believe he is."

"Good morning!"

Both Pi and Heleon turned as Paul entered the kitchen and sat down in the vid nook. Both quickly regained their technological composure.

"Good morning, sir!" they pronounced in unplanned unison.

Pi proudly served a computer basket piled high with hot vitabuns.

Heleon poured Paul a cup of steaming vitafee and turned on the multi-national vid channels.

She stood next to his chair and watched him visualize the morning news. President Ricarda was giving a speech.

"I have transmitted my proposal to Congress, asking them for additional bank credit to the Explorer's Club.

In so doing, I have recommended a new team of explorers for training which will enable them to foray into the uninhabitable territories of Earth, so they may search out new frontiers where domed settlements can be constructed. Our population is growing at a rate of .09% every year.

We cannot wait until it is too late to further our habitable boundaries."

"Excellent proposal!" said Heleon.

Paul was caught off guard by her innocent enthusiasm.

He laughed, not out of malice but because her responses lacked all pretense; she had no hidden agendas. He couldn't say that about anyone at the Department of Technology.

"Sir, if you'll excuse me."

Her expression didn't hide her embarrassment. She left the kitchen quickly.

"Did I say something wrong?"

Paul turned to Pi as the cherubic butler scooped two piping-hot vitabuns out of the computer basket and plopped them onto his plate.

"Might I speak freely?"

Pi was not totally secure in his own position with the controller, but he felt it his duty to interpret Heleon's condition before it became damaging to the harmony of the household commununication.

"By all means, Pi!"

Paul bit into the hot, tasty bun.

The crust was nice and chewy, the way he liked.

"To give maintenance is to maintain the maintenance of maintaining."

It was hard for Paul to visualize Pi's logic. By the time Pi had finished his dissertation, Paul was thoroughly lost.

"As you can visualize, sir, you have not allowed Heleon to maintain her maintenance with regards to your maintenance."

"Ohhhhh," said Paul, clapping a hand to his forehead. "I understand."

He realized he would have to grant Heleon more actualizations with him!

She needed to give to him in order to feel she was maintaining her maintenance!

He looked at Pi.

"Thank you, Pi," he said.

He meant it from the bottom of his heart.

"You're quite welcome, sir!"

Pi watched as Paul chewed the second whole wheat vitabun.

The controller was deep in a visualization, and Pi didn't want to disturb him.

As Paul left for work, Heleon was waiting by the front door with his computer briefcase. Pi watched from the kitchen. He did so want them to connect!

"Sir, do have a profitable day."

He noticed she was being very conservative with her visualization.

"Thank you, Heleon, for your maintenance."

He took the briefcase from her, and their hands touched for a split second.

Communication welled between them.

For an eternal moment they searched each other's visualization. Then he pulled away.

"Sir!" she called out.

"Yes?"

He turned.

"Your fedora hood!"

She handed him his atmospheric hat. He appreciated her professionalism.

"You give good maintenance!" he called to her as he made his way down the plastic pathway.

Heleon's energy gyrated pink blush. She watched him saunter off towards the boulevard conveyor belt sidewalk. He was greeted by Howard Bork.

"Good pleasure, Paul."

"Good pleasure, Howard."

They glided out of Heleon's sight, but Paul Quatro was not out of her visualization.

"Heleon, the library cassettes need to be maintained!"

Heleon turned around and observed Delti carrying an aluminum toolbox over one shoulder, and a length of respirator pipe in his other hand.

"I know my maintenance, Delti."

She didn't like the strongman's vibrations. He was too aggressive for her pulse.

Delti found the H model, Heleon, to be inconsistent with her maintenance.

At the Learning Garden D models had very little contact with the H models, who were housed separately and taught differently.

D models were always impressed upon by their clinicticians that they were responsible for the entire maintenance of an action.

Unlike other models who were specialists, D models could do the whole maintenance if called upon.

It gave the D models an impulse of power the other models did not possess.

"Delti, my automat percolator is not functioning properly. Might you have a moment of maintenance to spare for it?"

Pi's happy face was momentarily clouded with concern for his maintenance.

"You've criss-crossed the circuit connectors," grumbled Delti, as he reconnected the circuitry and continued on his way.

Pi didn't like his tone of impulse when he expressed himself disdainfully like that.

"P models! What had become of modern visualization!"

Let that D model attempt Middle Judea lamb stew! Then let's see how maintained he is! visualized Pi to himself.

Delti stomped out of the kitchen and into the backyard, where he was actively refitting the swimming pool respirator pipes.

Suddenly, Rob the robot walked up to him.

"Hello. I'm Rob," said the tentative robot.

Delti glared up at the metal man, his circuits on full alert.

"I didn't know robots had names."

Rob was confused.

What was this energy form? Surely it wasn't human! Or was it?

His computer panel attempted to analyze Delti but with no positive results.

Service robots had not yet been programmed to holograms, nor would they ever be.

He had no answer to Delti's question, only a programmed response to an incoming impulse.

"What name have you been programmed to respond to?"

"I am Delti, and I do not respond through programming."

The robot found this impossible to understand.

He continued, in his own, limited programming, to try to communicate.

"Would you have a cup of computer lubricant I can borrow?"

"Why don't you have your own?"

Delti was maintained to maximum maintenance at all times. He frowned upon those who did not reach up to his maintenance level.

"I forgot to place the order in the transcriber."

Rob was beginning to feel uncomfortable in this energy's presence.

And then Pi interceded on his behalf and saved him from short-circuiting.

"I have an extra cup of lubricant if you'll follow me."

The holographic butler took the metal man by the elbow joint and escorted him into the kitchen.

Delti found Pi's energy to be soft.

He wiped the energy sweat from his forehead and went back to refitting the respirator pipe in the swimming pool.

"Why is Delti so anti-robotic?" asked Rob, as he sipped a cup of warmed ComputoFluid.

Pi attempted to explain the logic of holographic characters as he kneaded the synthetic dough for his pie crust. He was preparing a rare, Alabama peach cobbler for his controller.

"D model holographic characters tend to have a kinetic edge to their energy pulse. They throb to a different beat."

The robot listened through his audio responders, but he couldn't find a circuit which would visualize his actualization of what Pi was expressing.

Nonetheless, Rob was very appreciative of his warm vibration.

Although he was not programmed to understand what holograms were, he began to put two circuits together as Pi continued his interpretation of the essence of holograms.

He had overheard a conversation between Mr. Bork and Bernice at one time.

Mr. Bork had described the new product with great enthusiasm. He had said it would revolutionize the home-service market.

"As soon as my lubricant arrives, I'll return this cup!" said Rob, standing to go.

"Hello."

Heleon entered the kitchen and greeted them both warmly.

Pi introduced her to Rob, and they spoke for several moments.

She wanted to know about Paul's neighbor.

166

"Mr. Bork is married to Bernice. They live next door. Mr. Quatro and his wife, Mary, were best friends. They actualized together!"

Heleon was surprised to find out Paul had been married.

"Paul...I mean, Mr. Quatro...is married?"

Pi was just as surprised.

"We've never met the controller's wife!"

Heleon's eyes were hurt pools.

"She's been disassembled!" exclaimed Rob.

Pi and Heleon looked at Rob and then at each other before speaking in unison: "Disassembled!"

"A pipeline malfunction," explained Rob.

"Oh!"

Heleon felt relieved that her controller's wife was no longer with them. Still, she felt a strange sadness that confused her.

The two holograms watched the robot clank out of the kitchen.

They both commented on their feelings about robots to each other.

"I find him to be a cordial appliance," said Pi, as he finished kneading his dough.

"I wonder what it's like to be trapped inside a program?" mused Heleon.

She couldn't visualize such an actualization.

As she walked back through the living room, she passed the H-wall.

It had never occurred to her that she, too, was trapped.

"Technology is the savior of civilization. Without it, there would be no civilization."

Paul Quatro sat up in the balcony of the Pentagon's media vid room and listened to Elliot Richards address his campaign speech to the workers of the new system over the giant vid screen.

"No technology, no work! No work, no pleasure!"

The Secretary of Technology was stirring up audiences all across the nation's vid screens.

"Three for four...never more!"

Paul had to smile to himself. The Secretary's phrases were becoming campaign slogans.

"I visualize a world harmony for all to actualize!" Elliot Richards was a natural communicator.

He even had the workers applauding!

The service robots were clapping, too! Their metal hands clanked with goodwill as they stood at the back of the media vid room.

"What a technocrat!" said a booming voice behind him.

Paul turned around to see who it was. Lord Lothar leaned back in his seat, smiling, his arm around a beautiful Afrikaniker computer cover girl.

"Lothar! What on Earth!"

Then Paul noticed Zelman skipping down the aisle towards them.

He was wearing a South Mexo atmospheric robe and weed sandals. He carried a thirteen-year- old native girl who was dressed in a provocatively inchy skirt on his back.

"Me and Zelman were in the neighborhood, and we couldn't pass up an opportunity to visit our favorite friend!"

Lothar ruffled up Paul's well-trimmed hair.

"Hark! I am the ark!" shouted Zelman.

The pudgy syntheticist plopped down in the seat next to Paul, the native girl stretched out on his lap, kissing his neck.

Paul didn't understand South Mexo as a language, but he got the visualization when she began actualizing Zelman's perverse desires.

"Stop that!" he barked.

The girl, frightened, leaped out of Zelman's lap and ran back up the aisle away from them.

"Now what have you gone and done?"

Zelman was perturbed.

"What have I done!"

Paul whispered under his breath, incredulous.

"Keep your voice down, Zelman!"

Zelman 's implication he had done something wrong outraged him.

"Relax, Paul, or you 'll blow a fuse."

Lothar kissed Paul on the cheek.

Paul pushed his face away and wiped the wet from his cheek. Lothar and Zelman couldn't stop laughing, which only infuriated Paul more.

If he didn't act quickly Elliot Richards would look up and see this horrible commotion.

This was the last visualization he wanted. Paul leaped to his feet.

"I'm leaving!"

He grabbed the Afrikaniker cover girl's hand and walked quickly up the aisle towards the balcony exit door.

The ebony beauty looked over her shoulder at Lothar with a puzzled expression. She wasn 't sure what was happening.

Lothar and Zelman followed them.

When Paul reached the hallway elevator and pushed the floor selector, he was no longer mad at his friends.

He observed them as they scurried towards him, surprised and concerned about his behavior.

Lord Edwin Lothar, handsome and brilliant, surely was the Grand Potentate of the Up Generation.

Sure, he had inventor's blockage, but he would work through it!

And Zelman...overweight, out of shape, even though he seemed a blob sometimes, he smiled!

How could anyone be angry at someone who smiled?

The three stood next to the elevator roaring with laughter.

Ona, the Afrikaniker cover girl, stood several steps away and watched them slap each other on the back, bump each other's shoulders in fun, and ruffle each other's hair with boyish enthusiasm.

It amazed her that such honored members of the Together Generation could visualize such embryonic actualization.

She remained cool as she stood there, watching, but she burned with desire for Lothar.

Most women of substance found him irresistible.

"Tonight! 7:00 p.m.!"

Lothar was insistent.

"One for all and all for all!"

Zelman was a terrible poet…the worst Paul had ever heard, but he was sincere.

Paul stepped into the elevator and smiled at his two friends.

Had they not been with him all through his terrible tragedy?

The least he could do was accept their dinner invitation. They only wanted him to be happy.

That would be fun, said Paul to himself as the elevator jetted upward towards his office.

It had been three weeks since the H-wall had been installed in his living room.

Each morning Howard Bork asked for an evaluation.

Each morning Paul said he hadn't completed his studies.

Like a true technocrat Paul never rushed into making a decision about a device until he had totally analyzed its affects. To analyze affects took total visualization, and actualization, too.

Actually, Paul had had plenty of time to actualize the H-wall.

He wasn't in any rush, though.

Not that Howard was going to take it back or anything…Paul had finally been able to admit to himself he didn't want to send the wall back.

Pi's cuisine was better than Mary's if he cared to admit it.

Delti had not only overhauled the entire computer system in the house, but he was also in the process of upgrading its efficiency.

The computer no longer wheezed, and Paul, as a result, no longer coughed from all that dust.

As he stepped off the boulevard conveyor sidewalk, he visualized Heleon waiting for him at the front door, waiting to maintain his comfort.

He had to admit Mary never actually maintained him quite this way.

But then, she'd been the wife of a technocrat! She'd been human! Not a hologram!

Still, he hadn't thought of Mary all week. Here it was Thursday, and he'd had a whole clear, carefree week without grief!

"It's time to get up!" he sang to himself, smiling softly.

What did Lothar say, "It's time to get Up!"

It was an old Upster slogan.

"It's time to get Up!" he sang out loud.

Every time he said it he wanted to get more "Up!"

All those past Thursdays he had suffered…dreaded the return home…knowing he would have to wallow in heartache until the next Tuesday when he could escape the misery of remembering through the hard work of actualization.

173

"Good evening, sir!"

Heleon took his computer briefcase.

"Did sir have a profitable day?"

Pi hung Paul's atmospheric trenchcoat in the hall computer closet.

"It was gratifying," said Paul, accepting a nice, cold vitatini from Heleon.

"Dry enough, sir?"

Paul sipped it and smiled at her. She smiled back.

"I've completed the computer library organization and scheduled a concert for you after dinner," said Heleon, eyes shining. He could see she was very happy.

"I've prepared lizard under glass."

Pi was proud of the dish, even though he had never prepared lizard before, not even at the Learning Garden.

"I got the recipe out of the Computer Times Cookbook."

Paul looked at his companions reluctantly.

"I'd planned to dine out tonight with friends."

Their disappointed faces made him wince.

"Yes, of course, sir. I shall freeze the lizard, or pipe it over to the test tube orphanage, as per your instructions for leftovers."

Pi turned, his face tranquil, and glided back into the kitchen.

Paul and Heleon stood quietly in the hallway. She so much wanted to present him with her concert.

"You can give the concert tomorrow night!"

Paul tried to console her.

"As you desire, sir."

Heleon tried, unsuccessfully, to mask her disappointment.

"Sir, would you take a visualization over here?"

Delti's voice intruded on their silent communication.

Paul looked over at the strongman holographic character standing in the living room.

"I'll draw you a bath, sir."

She excused herself and walked past Delti who was waiting for Paul. As Heleon passed, Delti eyed her intently.

"Yes, Delti, what is it?" said Paul.

"I have drawn up a diagram for the installation of a hydrophonic botanical hot house garden that can be built in the backyard if sir approves."

He handed Paul the computer diagram notepad.

"Very interesting, Delti!"

But Paul's visualization was not on the botanical hot house.

"With the extra efficiency from the central computer there is enough juice to support the additional function."

Delti felt confident his proposal would be accepted.

"I'd like some time to go over this," said Paul, as he walked away from the strongman.

"Sir, it's perfect, believe me!"

Delti found Paul's actualization a personal rebuff to his impulses.

"Thank you, Delti."

Paul left Delti alone next to the H-wall.

The D model holographic character was hyper-energizing.

He clenched his fist and felt the power build up until he thought he would explode, until he finally released it and allowed it to neutralize.

Delti was finding Paul Quatro inefficient.

He found maintaining the all-computerized house boring.

Any model could do what he was doing.

It took but a fraction of his skills to maintain such a lower-level technological application.

Paul didn't have time for a bath.

He felt, in fact, a bit impatient, so he stood in the shower and allowed the mechanical arms with the sponge hands to clean his body.

She was waiting for him as he stepped out of the shower, a full-length tranquilizer towel in her hands.

It was too late for him to close the glass door.

She scanned his face, stared at his sex and then wrapped the warm towel around his body.

She began to dry him, patting his body softly with the warm, soothing towel.

"Where are you visualizing?" she asked him, her voice purring against his ears.

She was like an inquisitive child.

"In town."

He could feel her hands through the towel.

They were sensual beyond belief!

"With who?"

She dried between his legs. He was afraid his penis would harden, that she would wrap the towel around it with her hand.

"Friends."

He controlled his voice from breaking, then turned around and pulled the towel out of her hands.

"Heleon, would you get out my tangerine suit?"

He could feel his penis rising through the towel, and he didn't want her to see it.

"Yes, sir."

She turned and went into the bedroom.

She always felt fulfilled when Paul asked her for maintenance.

It took Paul five minutes of visualization on computer diagram manuals before his penis backed down. Computer diagram manuals were the most boring things a technocrat could ever visualize.

Heleon opened his walk-in clothes closet and scanned Paul's atmospheric suits. Most were conservative: three, four or five-piece suits, although at the end of the rack she could see three colorful sports suits.

As she looked for the tangerine suit she thought of Paul 's sex.

She had never seen it before.

Back at the L·earning Garden she had taken a course in human anatomy, but the instructor had never actualized that visualization for her!

It looked friendly!

She wanted to hold it. Perhaps it would be a pet. But she had such confusing impulses.

"The tangerine suit!"

She turned around as soon as she heard him speak.

He took the suit from her hand.

"Heleon, would you ask Pi to prepare a tray of pre-dinner Taste Buds."

He was learning how to maneuver Heleon away whenever he wanted to be alone. He wasn't always successful, but he was learning.

"Sir?"

She didn't respond immediately to his request. He stood with the towel wrapped around his waist.

" Yes, Heleon?"

Just standing near her brought sexual impulses to his loins.

"What's it like in town?"

She had a way of making him feel wanted.

"Pedestrians, flashing neon, chatter, all-night entertainment."

Obviously, she didn't understand the visualization, but the images produced a yearning she wanted to actualize for herself.

He noticed she was deep in visualization, and he began to feel his penis harden.

"Heleon, the Taste Buds…"

"Yes, I'll tell Pi immediately."

She was gone before he realized it.

Sometimes it seemed as if the holograms just dematerialized in front of him. Other times they walked away normally.

He heard the front door chimes and knew Lothar and Zelman had arrived.

He dressed quickly.

"Well, hello…Who are you?"

Lothar scanned Heleon from head to toe. He liked what he visualized.

"I am Heleon."

"Hello. I'm Zelman."

The syntheticist pushed Lothar past Heleon.

"And I'm hungry."

A tall, statuesque bleached raspberry blonde pushed Zelman out of the way.

Her name was Velma Vinestreet. She was Zelman's latest diversion.

Behind her was Ona, the Afrikaniker computer cover girl, and Yolanda Keefhotter…a rather gaudily-attired Uppie whom Lothar and Zelman brought along for Paul's pleasure.

Lord Edwin Lothar didn't follow the Upsters into the living room where Pi had begun to serve a tray of multi-nutritional Taste Buds, one of Paul's favorite pre-dinner snacks.

Heleon started to leave Lothar's presence when he gripped her wrist.

"Paul didn't tell me about you."

"I'm new!"

She felt a strange vibration from him.

"I bet you are!"

He touched her face with his fingertip.

"Lord Lothar!"

Ona, the Afrikaniker, approached him.

She put her arms around his neck and seductively stuck her tongue down his throat.

Heleon watched the ritual they called "kissing."

Heleon had taken a course in Society and Tradition.

She scored high on her exam, but as she watched them actualize the kiss, she realized it wasn't like the visualization she had studied.

Paul entered the living room just as Velma Vinestreet was ordering Delti to flex his biceps.

The strongman holographic character stood on the third step pod as Velma stood on the first. She still wasn't as tall as he was.

"Paul!"

Zelman stood up from the couch where he was eating all the Taste Buds off the tray Pi had left on the vitafee table.

Yolanda Keefhotter was inhaling purple vita smoke as she walked up to Paul and kissed him on the cheek.

"I've heard so much about you!" she said.

She had Taste Bud crumbs on her chin.

Paul looked over his shoulder and noticed Heleon watching him.

He was unprepared for this little party. He'd thought they were going out.

"Music!" shouted Lothar.

Heleon immediately responded.

She didn't know why she selected the Mombo Symphony, but it seemed appropriate.

"Let's dance!"

Yolanda grabbed Paul and started to twirl him around the living room.

She was a computer choreographer at the Kennedy Center, and she knew how to move her feet!

Pi, Delti and Heleon stood on the third step pod and watched the actualization of this visualization they'd only studied at the Learning Garden.

Delti thought it was disgusting.

Pi was too busy refilling everybody's vitavino goblets to notice.

And Heleon wanted to dance with Paul.

Within an hour, three vitavino goblets had been crushed, one solar lamp was broken, the couch had been stained with Taste-Bud nourishment, and a rip appeared in Paul's tangerine atmospheric party suit.

But finally he was able to get Lothar, Zelman and the girls out of his house, but only after he promised to take them all to a restaurant.

"Sir certainly has interesting connections."

Pi was the first to break the silence after the party had danced off.

"Weak connections, if you ask me."

Delti lifted up the overturned solar lamp and straightened its shade.

His words jabbed the atmosphere around him.

"Well, nobody's asking you!" snapped Heleon, as her impulsive energy sapped the strongman's negativity.

Pi and Delti watched her carry the empty tray of Taste Buds back into the kitchen.

"H models have undisciplined pulsations," grumbled Delti.

Pi knew it was just the vibes of a female that made Heleon the way she was. It was really quite simple.

Pi decided not to respond to the strongman 's narrow perception of Heleon's impulses.

What good would it do? wondered Pi.

The three of them completed their respective maintenance with waning energy.

Delti dematerialized back into the H-wall where his energy felt most at home.

Pi and Heleon stayed up late communicating their observations of Paul's party. Both agreed it had been a visualization for sore eyes.

Heleon and Pi were becoming best of friends, each confiding in the other with increasing frequency.

Both agreed they felt negative energy from Delti. Neither understood why.

Both enjoyed maintaining Paul, for he made them feel part of a unit larger than themselves as he simultaneously emitted warm and welcoming vibrations, even if a little something went wrong with his maintenance.

All in all, the last few seconds, hours, days, weeks and months had turned out to be the positive visualization of the actualization they'd been trained for at the Learning Garden, and that was satisfying in itself.

"I'm turning in."

Pi yawned and rubbed his hands on Heleon's. Rubbing hands was a holographic's way of showing affection.

"I'll be along shortly."

She rubbed her cheek next to his. He felt her warmth, and his energy blushed a serene pink.

As he dematerialized back into the wall, he thought how wonderful H models were. Pi was so fond of her warmth!

Heleon waited for Paul to come home, but he did not return.

She moved through the all-computerized house touching different articles she knew he had touched.

Suddenly, she found herself in his bedroom. It was the most fascinating room in the house, she thought.

She wondered what it was like to hibernate on an air bed.

She turned around to make sure nobody was watching and then slowly crawled onto it.

She lay back and held a pillow against her. She could smell his scent on it.

Her eyes roamed the room.

She noticed the clothes closet, the secret cubicle Paul had instructed her to avoid.

The room was next to his closet.

She got up and walked over to it, looking over her shoulder to make sure Delti or Pi weren't observing her.

Her pulse raced.

She felt a strong impulse to open the door to the secret room.

Why didn't Paul want her to look inside?

She didn't understand "Paul," as she liked to call him in her private visualizations.

His reactions were so different from hers!

She decided to open the clothes closet even though she knew she was disobeying.

She rationalized to herself that the closet fell into her area of maintenance, and in order to understand her job better she should make an effort to expand her skills.

She pressed the closet button, and the door slid open noiselessly.

Inside she beheld Mary Quatro's clothes.

The variety was overwhelming.

Dresses in all lengths and colors and styles hung on elegant air hangers that gently "brushed" the clothes with a soft "current" that kept them wrinkle-free.

Heleon had only three variations of the H model form-fitting uniform!

She noticed a framed photo-image of Mary on the closet dresser cabinet. The heart-shaped neon gold-and-platinum locket was draped over the frame.

Heleon stood mesmerized by the visualization.

"So, this was Paul's wife, Mary!" she said out loud.

She touched the photo-image with her fingertip and felt Mary' s vibe.

A moment of sadness bolted through her. She responded to the impulse by immediately leaving the closet, pushing the "close" button and standing motionless for a moment.

"It was not meant to be!" she cried out.

She felt ashamed that she had intruded on Paul's privacy. She was sure he would send her back if he ever found out she had opened the forbidden closet.

Paul wobbled up the plastic pathway to his house.

He had had a very Up night.

He found it difficult to get Yolanda Keefhotter' s high-pitched voice out of his head.

She wouldn 't leave him alone that night!

She'd rubbed against him at the eatery, her ankle going up and down his leg, as Zelman entertained with his magic tricks.

He kept pulling colored eggs out of the girls' ears and then cracking them open.

Little yellow robotic chickletts roamed the table, bumping gently into everybody's vitavino goblets and sometimes knocking them over.

What a mess!

Paul's tangerine suite was stained with vitavino.

When Yolanda Keefhotter tried to dry it off with her cellophane napkin, Paul visualized that she was Heleon, towel-drying him in the bath.

When he excused himself to go to the cosmetic room, Lothar and Zelman followed.
As he dried his trousers with a porta blower, Lothar and Zelman teased him.

"She gives the best blow dry in the city!" Lothar shouted in his ear.

"You should have let her lick you clean!"

"Pass it around if you don't want it!"

Zelman pinched Paul's earlobe.

"Perverts!"

Paul laughed back.

It had been so long since they had triple-dated, and he'd forgotten how loud and raucous his two friends could be in public.

He watched them primp and pamper themselves at the cosmetic counter, splashing cologne on their faces, rubbing gelatin through their hair with the porta scalp massagers, and then dabbing opiated hankies to their noses as a finishing touch.

There! The intensity had really begun!

"Try it!"

Lothar pushed the hanky under Paul's nose. He got a good, strong whiff before he was able to push the Grand Potentate' s manicured hand away.

From that point on the evening began to swim in vibrant waves of color and distorted images.

Faces puffed out of proportion. Big eyes and tongues lolled out of gaping holes. Flagellant lips and lewd whispers told of unspeakable fantasies.

Paul thought the party was moving.

Everybody crammed into Lothar's antique Europa sports-copter and headed to the dance-a-torium.

They landed on the roof and took an elevator to the rotating dance floor where Yolanda Keefhotter turned into a shrieking flamingo.

Everybody turned to watch everybody else turn into an animal.

Lothar became a lion.

Zelman was a prancing hippo.

Ona, the Afrikaniker, was a black panther.

Velma Vinestreet swung across the dance-a-torium floor like a baboon in heat.

Paul found himself staring at an owl in the mirrored alcove of their booth.

189

As he pushed his face up to the reflection he realized the eyes of the owl were his eyes.

He started to laugh at his visualization.

Lothar and Zelman stuck their faces over his shoulder, and they all began to point their fingers at each other 's funny expressions.

Oh! It was a night for Paul Quatro to remember.

Zelman tickled Paul 's nose with another opiated hanky.

"It's time to get Up!" he croaked.

Paul agreed with the High Puba. It was time to get Up.

With a blink of an eye the party was arm in arm, strolling, laughing and dancing through the Pennsylvania Avenue videodrome, the finest videodrome in all twenty-five states in the union.

It had a three hundred foot high cyclorama vid screen, private balcony booths equipped with full-stocked food automats, and the best popcorn in town!

Usherbots escorted them towards the best booth on the balcony.

Paul could see the pedestrians in the lobby below staring up at them, whispering amongst themselves and pointing fingers at Lothar and Zelman, the media stars.

Neither could go out in peace!

"Lothar! Zelman!"

Paul didn't realize who had called their names until he saw a powerful man with clipped hair and massive muscles put his arms around Lothar and Zelman.

"It's Ronnie Chrome!" Yolanda Keefhotter whispered to Paul.

Sure enough, it was the big-ball jammer all star.

Paul didn't know his two friends knew Ronnie Chrome!

People began to close in on them, trying to hear what the famous duo were saying as introductions were made.

Ronnie Chrome presented his girlfriend, Pris Paisley, a professional cheerleader for the Washington Technicals.

Although it was a team rule not to date the cheerleaders, Ronnie was so important to the team that an exception had been made in his case.

Everybody loves a winner! Paul thought to himself as he entered the balcony booth in the videodrome.

The extravaganza was about to begin.

Paul noticed Zelman was passing out red, white and blue colored tablets. He called them Dreamsicles. Paul refused at first, but Lothar elbowed him in the ribs.

"Come on, Paul. It's the weekend!"

Paul opened his mouth to speak, but before he could make a sound Lothar dropped the tablet in his mouth and it tumbled down his throat like a flood of hot lava.

If the opiated hankies made everything a sea of colorful distortion, the Dreamsicles heightened its focus and made you feel you were starring in your own videotape!

The lights went out in the video-drome, and the party vibrations intensified.

Paul began to feel like a symphony conductor. He raised his hands and began to move them to the beat of each individual's vibration.

He visualized Zelman wearing a rainbow coat with a white halo over his head.

Lothar's ears, on the other hand, had begun to grow into a pointed elongation of their former selves. His eyes blazed with yellow light rays.

Ona' s fingers were long, hissing cobra snakes!

Ronnie Chrome bloated up into a big ball.

Paul thought of Millicent Chrome, Ronnie's former wife, whom he had met at the Bork's for dinner.

He laughed to himself.

What a couple!

Both were going for the big score, whatever that was. No wonder they'd had their marriage annulled.

He could see Pris Paisley, the professional cheerleader, metamorphosing into a small ball of pink mink that draped itself around Ronnie's neck.

Velma Vinestreet leaped to her feet with all the grace of a baboon still in heat.

She began ripping off her clothes as she babbled incoherently in the private screening room.

Her actions seemed to trigger the others into a similar impulse.

Everyone took off each other's atmospheric clothing.

Shoes, trousers, jocks, inchy skirts, penis-fitters, suspenders, blouses, stockings, jackets, snaps, zippers, bras, G-strings and buckles flew through the air like a closet-blizzard.

Through it all Paul stood in the center, motionless, except for his arms, which moved to conduct the vibrations.

As he conducted, he visualized Heleon, whose face appeared out of nowhere, then disappeared back into the crowd of naked, writhing flesh.

Suddenly, it was all too much.

He looked down and saw Yolanda Keefhotter clenching his zipper in her teeth and pulling it down.

Paul visualized one thing: the sexobot that had taken a bite out of Zelman's pink, fleshy penis at the Putney Inventor's Convention.

He became frightened.

He pushed her away.

She giggled and dove into the symphonic undulations of her fellow Upsters.

Tongues and legs intertwined. Nipples rubbed against lips as fingers searched out dark orifices. The sweet odor of sexuality carried everyone away.

It wasn't that Paul was a prude. He just didn't feel comfortable with the visualization as it was actualizing.

He backed towards the private screening room door.

The last visualization he remembered was Ronnie Chrome grunting like a big bear as he mounted Pris Paisley.

As he heaved into that cute little pink cheerleader, she sucked on Lothar's penis.

Lothar, in turn, was licking Ona's breast, and Ona was kissing Yolanda Keefhotter who, in turn, had her fingers inside Velma's vagina!

Zelman was wedging his pink tool between Velma's buttocks and oinking like a pig.

Suddenly, Paul tripped and fell to the floor as he headed for the door.

Stumbling back on his feet, he grabbed the doorknob.

It fell out of its hinge.

Panic-stricken, he didn't try to repair the damage but ran out of there without looking back.

It had been a night...a year to remember.

Beginning with Mary's death, the implementation of the new system, John Malone's sabotage attempts, the pressure to maintain his sanity and Elliot Richards' decision to run for the Presidency right on through to the arrival of the H-wall!

What an incredibly technological year!

And there was still some left!

As Paul entered the house he knew the evolution of robotics had reached its final end and that holographic characters would be the ones to work alongside the Together Generation in pursuit of their ultimate goal, Utopia.

The effects of the opiated hankies along with the hallucinations from the Dreamsicles were beginning to fade.

As he hung up his atmospheric overcoat in the hall computer closet he paused and stared at himself in the vibrational mirror.

He no longer resembled an owl.

His features had evolved into the features of a centaur. Half-man, half-horse!

He turned and entered the living room, only to be stopped by one of the most beautiful visualizations he'd ever actualized.

Heleon was asleep on the first step pod next to the H-wall.

He wasn't sure whether it was the vibrant glow of the wall or Zelman's synthetics that made her seem like a magical princess from a childhood fairytale.

She looked so sensual.

Paul wanted to touch her.

Heleon sensed his presence.

She opened her eyes and visualized him standing over her. She had waited for him, and now he had arrived.

An incredible energy sprang up between them.

"Heleon," he whispered as he kneeled close to her.

"Paul!"

She spoke his name for the first time. The word felt wonderful in her mouth.

She pressed her warm hands against his face in a spontaneous gesture of affection.

She hadn't stopped to think if he would understand the private ways of a hologram.

Her moist lips vibrated against Paul's. No one saw the sparks that ricocheted off their first kiss.

"I want you," Paul whispered into her hair.

She smelled of honey, beeswax, the back side of an angel's ear.

"I am for you."

She pushed her tongue between his lips and slid it across his tongue and down his throat. His mouth was on fire.

He lifted her up and carried her into the bedroom.

They lay naked on the air bed, their bodies wet with passion. Just before he entered her he knew the lady in his dream had been Heleon.

When he awoke the next morning he was clutching a pillow.

He was down. His cortex ached from a synthetics' hangover, his eyelids stung with exhaustion.

Never again would he allow himself such foolish pleasure!

He was a technocrat, not an inventor! He buried his head into the pillow and froze.

Heleon! He could smell her. He remembered last night, the warmth of it, the passion.

He shuddered. Surely it had been a dream. But the scent…the scent hypnotized him even as he lay there: her voice…her body…her warm, dusky scent…

"Good morning, sir."

Pi was standing next to the air bed with the customary tray of raid-morning nourishment.

"What time is it?"

Paul sat up in bed as Pi set the porto tray in front of him.

"Eleven-thirty p.m., sir."

Pi unfolded the napkin and tucked it into Paul's pajama top.

"What day is it?"

Paul sipped the vitajuice and felt his cortex fighting to regain sobriety.

"The eleventh of October, sir."

"The eleventh!"

Paul couldn't believe it.

"Yes, sir, the eleventh."

Pi poured a cup of hot vitafee and added the white aloa vera as he'd been instructed to do.

Paul tried to put the visualization into its proper perspective. Thursday was the ninth of October, the last day of the work week.

He remembered going to work, taking care of departmental business, sitting up in the balcony of the Pentagon media vid room, and then...?

Lothar and Zelman came to visit. Ona, the Afrikaniker computer cover girl, had been with them. A South Mexo native girl had been with Zelman. Paul couldn't remember her name. They'd all agreed to have dinner together that night.

Heleon! She flashed into his visualization. He fought to get her image out of the visualization and then he remembered Lothar and Zelman coming to his house with Velma Vinestreet, Ona and Yolanda Keefhotter.

Lothar and Zelman! The image of the both of them jumped into his visualization with greater and greater frequency.

The party! The eatery! The opiated hankies, the owls, flamingos, panthers, baboons, lips, eyes, winks, the dance-a-torium, music, oboes, harmonicas, electric flutes, violins, saxophones, drums, Ronnie Chrome -- the big-ball all-star jammer, the videodrome...

Paul couldn't remember his stained tangerine suit. He felt under the covers and felt his nakedness.

He didn't remember getting undressed.

Heleon! He remembered.

"Sir, I found this in the living room."

Pi was holding onto the videodrome's private screening room doorknob. He looked puzzled.

"You can dispose of that," shrugged Paul. He didn't want to explain it to Pi.

"Yes, sir."

The cherubic butler wanted to ask Paul where it came from, but he could sense that Paul didn't want him to.

Besides, it wasn't polite to ask one's controller too many questions. He'd learned this in the Learning Garden.

Paul, for the life of him, couldn't figure out what had happened to the tenth of October.

The image of Heleon flooded his visualization...her softness...her scent...the sex in her.

They were naked together. He knew it in his loins.

"Heleon."

Paul unconsciously spoke her name.

"She's in the computer library, sir."

Pi smiled at Paul.

"Thank you, Pi."

"Would you like me to request her presence?"

"No!" bellowed Paul. He checked himself, embarrassed.

"I mean, no," he said gently.

Pi nodded pleasantly.

"What about Delti?"

"Delti is working on the hydrophonic botanical garden outside."

Pi waited for Paul's response.

"Thank you, Pi."

"You're welcome, sir."

Pi wasn't sure whether Paul was complimenting him on the excellent breakfast or informing him of Delti's aggressiveness.

Paul spent the rest of the morning trying to piece together the tenth of October. The image of Heleon kept getting in his way.

He decided to give Lothar a transmission.

He pressed the digits on the vid phone next to the air bed and waited for his friend to appear on the small oval screen. He wasn't home.

Paul then pressed Zelman's digits and waited for him to appear. When he did, Paul wished he hadn't.

"Who goes forth to thy kingdom?"

Paul squinted at the screen. The face which spoke had sun, cloud, lightning and moon symbols painted all over it.

"I am Gorgo the Presto."

Zelman began speaking a language that obviously existed only in his imagination. He wore a crown of feathers, beads, bells, curlers, buttons and bows.

"Zelman, what happened to the tenth of October?"

Paul knew his question was unclear. He could still feel the effects of the synthetics he'd taken.

Zelman, the High Puba of the Together Generation, the greatest synthetist of his day, the inventor of the Root of Immortality, winner of three Gold Wrenches belched loudly and then screamed at the top of his breath, "Find it and you shall know the secret of life."

He lowered his head for a moment. Paul could see he'd begun to cry. His shoulders only shook like that when he cried.

"As for me," he continued, "there is no answer to my life..."

His tears destroyed the painted symbols on his pudgy face.

Paul's heart went out to his friend.

"Don't cry, Zelman," he called through the vid-phone speaker.

Zelman faced the vid-phone computer camera. His eyes were raving mad as he laughed hysterically.

"I'm not crying!"

The transmission went blank.

Paul pressed the digits again and again, but Zelman wouldn't answer the transmission.

What had happened to his friends? What had happened to him? What had happened to the tenth of October?

Paul held his face in his hands and pondered this question when he felt her presence.

He didn't want to confront her.

She was a hologram.

He was a technocrat.

He didn't know whether or not they'd committed a technological sin since holograms had not yet been introduced to the market in official status.

He knew he would have to make a decision, though, and he knew it would have to be now.

He would have to send her back. He just knew it.

But then something visualized in the center of his cortex: Heleon wasn't a robot! He wasn't sure what she was, but she was not a robot! There wasn't yet a law against their passion!

She stood next to the bed, afraid he might deny the impulses she felt surging through her essence.

She visualized that he had come home in the wee hours of October tenth. His energy had been very high.

She had waited up for him, and when he didn't come home, she lay down in front of the wall to rest.

Her next visualization was of Paul looking down at her with passion in his eyes.

They'd embraced. They had kissed. They had spent the entire day and night of October tenth in his air bed connecting their passions through sexual impulses.

He had been so gentle. She had been a virgin. At times she felt awkward, but he had guided her through the bumpy vibration until they reached a collective orgiastic energy explosion that was not taught at the Learning Garden. He called her H. His tone was textured with love. How many times had she wanted him to enter her? She'd stopped counting at thirty-three.

When he finally fell asleep, she touched his lips with one last kiss. Then she left him to dream.

Paul pulled his face out of his hands and stared into her eyes.

He could sense her fear. She was his virgin! Not even Mary had been a virgin.

"Hello, H."

He took her hand, and she sat down on the air bed next to him.

"Do you wish to send me back?"

Her words startled him. Could she visualize his cortex?

He could feel the energy ripples on her arms. She was shaking with fear.

"No, never."

He caught her energy tear on his thumb and kissed her. It felt magnetic.

"Oops!"

Pi had entered the bedroom and seen them cause sparks.

He was holding on to a tray full of nourishment which he had prepared for the controller's mid-afternoon brunch.

He dematerialized immediately. He hoped they hadn't seen him.

Paul hadn't. Heleon had.

She would have to speak with Pi about this. She knew he would understand. She and Pi were close friends.

Was she not trained in personal maintenance? Still…her vibes told her to be careful.

What if Delti found out? Her energies jumped. He mustn't!

She knew he would never understand. She knew, too, that any more negativity from Delti could upset the harmony within the household.

"Where's Heleon?"

Delti was riveting studs into the hydrophonic botanical garden's aluminum siding.

"Performing maintenance," answered Pi as he handed rivets to Delti.

He couldn't stop thinking about their kiss.

"What maintenance?"

Delti had a strong vibration for Heleon. He was frustrated that he hadn't been able to connect to her pulse.

"Computer library organization," mumbled Pi.

Delti scanned the P model's vibration. His pulsation seemed suspicious.

"She completed that maintenance this morning."

Delti stood next to Pi, towering over his portly frame. Pi noticed the rivet gun in the strongman's hand.

"Last-minute reorganization maintenance."

Pi was not equipped for lies, yet he knew that for the moment a lie would be the most positive vibration for the unit.

"I'll check her maintenance."

Delti dropped the rivet gun and got ready to dematerialize. Pi visualized fast.

"What will the controller say?"

He grabbed Delti's arm. His energy stopped Delti from the initial fade-out.

"Don't touch me. Don't ever touch me!" hissed Delti as he flicked his arm away.

"I am concerned about your position in the unit," he nervously blurted out. Pi was much more intelligent when it came to social etiquette than Delti would ever be.

"The controller did not give you permission to construct the hydrophonic botanical garden."

Pi could feel Delti's pulse. He knew Delti wasn't afraid of him.

That was the problem with D models.

They were absolutists. But their absolutism was also a greater part of their strength.

"He will understand that I visualized this situation correctly," Delti snapped.

"What if he does not understand?"

Pi's visualization caught Delti off guard.

"But he must understand."

Delti felt a loss of energy.

Pi immediately detected a weakness, and it gave him renewed purpose.

"Yes, let us hope so."

Pi left the strongman and returned to his kitchen. He had stopped Delti this time.

Delti stood next to the half-completed botanical garden and pondered Pi's visualization.

What would he do if the controller did not agree with his actualization?

The thought aggravated his pulse.

Pi continued to observe Delti through the kitchen window.

He had protected Heleon from Delti's prying eyes, but how long would it be before he found out about Heleon and the controller?

Pi had sensed from the very beginning that Delti had strong vibrations for Heleon. He could see it in Delti's eyes.

Every time she walked by, his pulse speeded up. Every time she stood next to the controller, his energy became hot.

"Thank you!"

Heleon rubbed her warm cheek against his.

Pi turned around.

"For what?"

He respected her privacy.

"For protecting our secret."

When she used the word "our," Pi, felt relieved that he'd been included in their love unit.

She had watched him from the bedroom window as he'd valiantly protected them from Delti. They sat in the breakfast vid nook and whispered about it.

"Does sir know that I know?"

Pi wanted to know everything.

"No," said Heleon, shaking her head.

"In time."

Pi understood everything when she actualized the story from her hand pulse into his.

Holograms had sixth, seventh, eighth and ninth senses by which they communicated, in addition to the standard Earth methods.

They even had their own pulse for love! When Pi felt the love pulse charge through her palm, he quickly responded.

"Be careful, Heleon."

He didn't want her to get hurt.

Before she could respond to his concern, Delti entered the kitchen, his face smudged with grease, his overalls stained from a hard day's maintenance.

As he passed the breakfast vid nook he felt his pulse charge up when he visualized Heleon. He wanted to communicate with her vibration, but he couldn't express his energy.

"Where have you been?"

His voice was deep and aggressive yet tender, too, in its pulsation.

"I do not have to answer to you, Delti."

She blocked his energy course.

Pi could feel the tension between them.

"Dinner will be at 6:30," chirped Pi, trying in vain to divert the bad vibes.

"I'll be in the wall," said Delti, as he left the kitchen.

Heleon had frustrated his energy again.

As Delti stood on the third step pod preparing to dematerialize, he couldn't understand what had actualized between them.

Here he was, a D model, capable of incredible feats of strength, an absolutist in maintenance, able to maintain better than all the other holographic models in the land and this…this…young vibe-o-gram was totally scrambling his vibes.

It was maddening.

He dematerialized in a glaring puff as he entered the tranquility of the wall.

Paul Quatro enjoyed his best weekend since the one before Mary died.

Heleon explained what had happened on October tenth.

The eleventh of October was spent in bed.

Heleon prepared an extra special bath full of high octane relaxo salts and vita bubbles. She switched the sauna steam on and pressed the dial over the Springtime in the Forest, a scent Paul particularly liked.

Paul soaked his aching muscles…remembering…

Her energy had been enthusiastic that night, unusually so for the first time, he mused.

Still, she'd been awkward at times, delightfully, childishly awkward.

When he guided her off into the right direction, though, she'd taken him on an incredible journey that had tested not only all six senses but also his stamina.

She was incredible!

The night of the eleventh Paul dined on a seven-course Inja meal fit for an emperor, complete with computerized chopsticks, synthetic ginger rolls, parsley puffs, squab-fried vita rice, mouth-watering duck strips and punji snips.

After dinner he sat in the computer library and sipped vita brandy from a snifter and listened to Heleon sing classical songs from the twentieth century.

She had a very pleasant voice and could imitate over five hundred of the most famous female singers of the century, from over sixty nations!

Paul invited Pi and Delti to sit in on the concert. Pi accepted the invitation and enjoyed himself immensely.

Delti asked to be excused after the dinner maintenance. He didn't like to partake in the fun of the unit.

After the concert, Pi excused himself and left Heleon and Paul alone in the computer library.

They stayed up until the early hours communicating.

Paul played over twenty cassettes that dealt with topics ranging from such diverse subjects as automobile racing to George Washington.

It was difficult for Heleon to totally visualize what the Indianapolis Five Hundred Speedway was, considering there hadn't been an automobile on Earth in over one hundred years.

Although she wanted to learn more about her inner sexual visualization, she didn't ask Paul to guide her that night. Nor did Paul attempt to guide her.

The entire visualization of their actualization was still a new and rather weird situation for Paul. He didn't want to totally abandon his logic.

As he kissed her good night her energy melted into his arms.

He had never felt any woman like Heleon before. He watched her dematerialize into the wall with an uncomfortable feeling.

What was he afraid of? She wasn't a robot...but what was she?

He decided to find out first thing Tuesday morning at the office.

Pi was confused. Why didn't the controller reprimand Delti for being so aggressive?

Delti thought the controller was a weak energy.

Sunday night Paul had dinner with Howard and Bernice at a quaint eatery in Computer Meadows where they served Europa dishes and had robot entertainment. Paul was deluged with thoughts of Heleon throughout the evening.

Howard ranted about the high sales figures for H-walls. Every household wanted one! Orders were backed up five months!

Paul noticed that Bernice seemed distant. Her once vibrant smile appeared frozen in sadness.

What Paul couldn't know was that Howard and Bernice had been arguing all weekend over whether or not to turn in Rob, their robot.

Howard wanted an H-wall.

"How do you think it looks? The Vice President in Charge of Purchasing doesn't even have his own H-wall?" Howard shouted into his wife 's grieving face.

She loved Rob.

"Why can't we have both?" she cried.

"Robots are obsolete!"

He was hoarse from screaming.

Paul was glad they hadn't tried to fix him up with one of their annulled friends.

When he returned home later that night, Heleon wasn't waiting for him at the wall.

He put on the computer glove and got ready to press her red index button but stopped himself before he completed the exercise. He didn't want to draw suspicion from Pi and Delti.

When he entered his bedroom, she was waiting for him on the air bed, curled up like a cat waiting to be petted. The Computer News was turned on. It felt wonderful to come home and find her there.

Heleon uncurled herself, stretched, and reached to undo his tie and shirt. Deftly, she reached for his two-piece sports jacket. Off came his four-piece recreation trousers!

He kicked off his atmospheric weather boots and lay down next to her.

They kissed. Her tongue slipped inside his mouth as he felt her warm fingers slipping inside his bikini jock. He slipped his hand inside her form-fitting panties and let his fingers spread her sex apart. Her vagina was shaped like Mary's but tighter and smoother. The patch around her sex was softer than mink.

She could feel his tongue trailing down her stomach. She didn't have an umbilical indentation like humans did. He loved her scent. It was fresh and clean, like some kind of wonderful, healthy animal. He licked her patch until his tongue searched her sex and found the small opening. It seemed to blossom around his face. His nostrils, his tongue, his penis, his entire being were inflamed with her hot vibrations!

Together they spun in their own private visualization. They sensed the danger of their illegal love, even as their passion exploded to stellar heights of bliss Paul had never known...not even with his poor, dear Mary.

October thirteenth. Monday. Paul went to church for the first time since Mary' s funeral, although he wasn't usually prone to such activity.

Most Together Generation members could leave religion just as easily as they could take it.

Most reasoned it hadn't done any good when trauma shock had come along. Most thought it was a waste of time to fiddle with something as non-profitable as religion.

Yet there were some, Paul concluded, who found a certain tranquility in religion that couldn't be found elsewhere.

It was wonderful to be able to sit in the cathedral and look up at the giant vid screen and listen to the priest read from the old cassette!

When he returned home after church, Heleon had a hundred questions to ask him about religion.

Paul took her into the computer library and set her down. He put a cassette in and she watched "The Greatest Story Ever Told," an old cinema movie from the twentieth century.

As she watched the movie, Paul went into the kitchen for lunch.

214

Pi had prepared synthetic hamburger and french fries complete with onions, pickles and relish...the works!

An authentic, twentieth century food, according to Pi.

Paul enjoyed Pi. With each meal he gave what Paul considered a fascinating account of the origins of the foods he had prepared.

By the time he got back into the computer library, Heleon was lying in the middle of the floor, weeping.

He had seen the old cinema film several times and never found it sad. Had she visualized something in it that he had missed? Monday night Paul felt it would be logical if he said good night to all three holographic characters and sent them back into the wall. He explained his logic to Heleon, and she understood.

He didn't want Pi and Delti to get jealous of her maintenance. She wanted to tell Paul that Pi already knew about their secret, but she felt the time was not right.

"Good night, Pi."

"Good night, sir."

Pi's cherubic energy dematerialized very gracefully into the wall.

"Good night, Delti."

"Good night, sir."

Paul felt Delti's uncomfortable energy weakening as he dematerialized.

"Good night, H."

Paul took Heleon in his arms and kissed her.

"Good night, Paul."

She tasted his mouth all through her body. He was delicious.

Paul pressed the red index finger button and watched her dematerialize into the wall. His heart ached as she left him for some peaceful world beyond his experience.

The weekend had been wonderful, yet deep down Paul felt that he was committing a technological sin. Yet he knew he was going to live with it.

Was it not part of the Together Generation's purpose to live life to its fullest? Wasn't pleasure one of the main principles?

And didn 't Heleon bring Paul total pleasure?

"Tuesday. October fourteenth...the first day of the work week. The new system is growing...The new system is multiplying...The new system's capabilities will do it all...The new system shall have peripherals...The new system has elements...each element shall connect to neighboring elements...a break in the primary hierarchical link will not cause the system to fail...The new system will not fail!"

Paul held the porta microphone next to his lips, lost in thought.

Miss James waited for him to continue.

She watched his mouth. It looked so young. His lips were puffy as if they had been kissed repeatedly. Of course, she thought to herself, that was not possible.

216

Her fingers rested on the rubber key pads of her transcriber. She and Paul worked well together.

Miss James knew that other transcribers in the Department of Technology had tendencies towards jealousy when she spoke of her relationship with the Undersecretary of Technology.

Most transcribers despised their bosses who, they felt, took unwarranted credit for work the transcribers did in their names.

It was an age-old problem, Miss James knew. This was why she respected Paul Quatro. He was a true technocrat visionary.

Someday he would be the Secretary of Technology, and she would be his transcriber. The thought at times almost took her breath away.

Holly James was a small Dome girl who had come to the Capital Dome when she was a teenager looking for employment.

A plain-looking little thing with a great pair of legs, she had a set of compact buttocks which she liked to say had been built for speed.

It was by accident that she had become a transcriber. The girl she roomed with was supposed to have gotten the job, but the day she was to report to work was the day she had come down with a bad case of neuro-contamination.

Holly remembered the girl whispering into her ear, "Take the job...I'm no good."

The girl then lapsed into a coma and died.

Being an opportunist and a member of the Opportunity Generation, Holly took the job without a moment's hesitation.

She also took the girl's identification application, as well as her name. Holly's real name was Freida Tewkzey. No one in the Department of Technology knew this about Holly's past.

Holly felt that in a world where full disclosure was the order of the system it was just fine to have at least one, good, fat secret. It gave her the feeling she was somehow ahead of the game...or at least her own game.

Two secrets? Holly felt that was a little "gamey," but one was fun, and good for the system!

"Integration...evaluation...involvement...identification... decisions...solutions...The new system will move society towards its ultimate goal...Utopia!"

Miss James's fingertips stopped before she transcribed the word ...the word...the word...Utopia. She scanned Paul's expression.

Never before had a technocrat expressed himself so honestly in transcription.

"P.Q., is that the right word? Utopia?"

It sounded strong...right.

Paul nodded with conviction.

"Yes," he said. The strength in his voice removed all doubt in her mind.

Paul knew he was expressing himself beyond the boundaries of his position as Undersecretary of Technology. As the Undersecretary, he did not express policy, he only actualized it.

Yet, if Elliot Richards was to become President, he knew he would be appointed Secretary of Technology.

If Elliot Richards was taking bold steps towards his own destiny, then Paul felt it was time for himself to leap over stated boundaries, too, and present his own, personal visualization!

It was time that Paul let it be known that he was a technocrat visionary!

He pressed the mobility button on his armrest, and the chair swiveled.

Paul scanned the Washington skyline. He was impressed with its harmony.

For a city that had almost been annihilated, it glistened under the weather dome brillance like an elegant symbol of decontamination...a reminder that democracy could, after all, withstand anything...even trauma shock!

"Will there be any more transcription, P.Q.?"

Holly waited to take her headphones off as her hands stopped in midair. She wore rubber fingertippers, too, to protect her from radiation.

Paul pressed the mobility button again, and the computer chair revolved back in her direction.

He wanted her to secure the H-wall cassette which would explain everything he needed to know about Heleon, but he was afraid to make his desires known, lest he be discovered.

What if Heleon was just an advanced robot? But of course she wasn't! She was a hologram! But what kind of hologram?

He didn't want to think of this wonderful girl (what was she, anyway?) as an appliance. The mere thought of that made him quiver with fear and outrage. But was she programmed like a robot only with a higher intelligence?

"P.Q.?"

Holly had been waiting for his answer for over two minutes.

Paul looked up and placed his porta microphone down, a signal that this transcription was over.

"No, that will be all."

He couldn't get Heleon's image out of his visualization.

He touched his nostrils with his fingertips. He couldn't get enough of her scent. He could feel his sex stirring at the merest thought of her. A bulge outlined itself against his trouser crotch.

He had to get back to work. He had to transfer the visualization.

The phone rang.

"Professor Sam Ludlum requests a moment of your time," said Holly, reverently.

Paul enjoyed that certain tone she affected for special dignitaries. The old man's bionic ear would enjoy it, too, he was sure.

"Put him through," he said, feeling important.

"Paul, my boy…I was in town on business, and I had a few spare ones."

Paul nodded into the vid phone.

"So I thought I'd drop by."

They sat down in the lounge section of Paul's spacious office. Holly brought them hot vitafee and chocolate pretzels, Professor Ludlum' s favorite snack.

"How is the new system corning along, Paul?"

"We're right on schedule," announced Paul.

"Good."

Sam Ludlum sipped his vitafee and savored his pretzel. He smacked his lips unselfconsciously.

"So what brings you to the Domed Capitol?" asked Paul, as he reached for a chocolate pretzel himself.

"Miss Vickers!"

The Professor had a twinkle in his eye.

"Miss Vickers?

"Ohhh…yes…Miss Vickers!"

Paul understood. He was glad the old man had found Togetherness.

"She's becoming quite famous, you know," said the old man. Paul nodded.

"Ever since she discovered the cure for Adolescent Decontamination Lung Cough she's risen to the top of the inventor's heap. She's been on the National Vid News. She's spoken at seminars. She's even been asked to appear in a videodrome extravaganza. She turned that last one down because the bank's credit wasn't big enough."

"What a girl!" exclaimed Paul.

Professor Ludlum placed his fingers next to his nostrils.

Paul noticed. He wondered whether the old man was smelling Miss Vickers' scent or if he was smelling the remains of his chocolate pretzel.

Paul's intercom clicked, and he turned to the Professor.

"Let me take this transmission," he said, as he switched the lounge panel couch button so that the inner-departmental vid screen could rotate its massive shape into viewing comfort.

"Technology before pleasure!" exclaimed the old man.

"Pleasure before technology" was a common phrase born of the Together Generation.

Paul resented John Malone's intrusion into his time, especially with Professor Ludlum in his office, one of his favorites, someone whom he didn't see enough anyway.

"What is it, Malone?"

He looked over at the Professor and thought he detected an ominous vibration.

"Mr. Undersecretary, the new system's hierarchical data link control panel does not fit into the network tube!"

Paul could hear the happiness in his voice.

"What? I scanned those diagrams myself!" said Paul, incredulous.

The minute he spoke he sensed a trap.

He glanced at Professor Ludlum. The old man looked stern.

"I've reported the omission to Secretary Richards," said John Malone.

He was wolf-like in his murderous stance, outside his boundaries and knowing it...liking it!

Would he be so bold without the Secretary's approval?

Paul wasn't sure. He felt like smashing his fist into the vid-screen image of John Malone.

"Mr. Malone, I want you in my office with a complete analysis of the actualization within the hour!"

Paul flipped the Off button, and the smug face of the young Assistant Undersecretary disappeared on the screen.

Professor Ludlum had observed Paul Quatro through biased eyes.

He'd watched this young man grow from the raw, idealistic student he had been at the Institute of Technology into one of the most brilliant technocrats the department had ever employed.

Now, with the entire strategy of the department at its greatest cross-circuit, he found himself wondering if whether the Undersecretary of Technology was the right technocrat to succeed Elliot Richards!

It did not occur to the old man that the Undersecretary of Technology would not be elected President of the United States.

He had placed his entire fortune at Elliot Richards' disposal, to be used for his campaign as he saw fit. Who would succeed Elliot Richards was his main concern.

If Elliot Richards won, Sam Ludlum would triple his fortune. If he lost, he'd be bankrupt.

He eyed the young Quatro suspiciously.

"Trouble, Paul?"

He scanned for weaknesses.

"Nothing that can't be repaired."

Paul tried to make light of the situation. Professor Ludlum had always admired that quality in Paul…that willingness to take it on the chin, no matter what the pain.

But, he also knew that Elliot Richards could not afford to miss the projected installation date for the new system. To miss that date would mean defeat!

"Good," answered the Professor.

"Then I shall leave you to your repairs."

The way the Professor stated the word "repairs" bothered Paul. He sounded tentative...as if he'd lost confidence.

"Professor, if you should speak with the Secretary, reassure him, please, that the new system will be operable on the projected date."

Paul escorted Sam Ludlum to the door.

"Good luck, Paul."

The old man squeezed Paul's hand as if to say, "Don't fail us. The consequences are too great."

Paul's heart was sinking fast as he watched his former Professor depart.

All the tension he'd forgotten over the weekend rushed back into his cortex. He needed to rebound from its effects before he met with Elliot Richards, for he knew the Secretary of Technology would probe the omission with an investigator's eye.

Before the hour was up, Paul had received an urgent transmission from Elliot's transcriber. She said the Secretary demanded to meet with his Undersecretary immediately.

Her voice quavered as she spoke.

Since Paul did not have the advantage of John Malone's data analysis of the omission, he would have to go into the Secretary's office cold and ad lib: a risky position.

He knew he had no choice.

Paul regretted he hadn't demanded John Malone's analysis immediately.

He had given the Assistant Undersecretary ample time to gather his data. Now he would have to suffer for his softness.

"Time is of the essence...How many more omissions can we afford? If the new system is not operable by the projected date, the entire security of the country shall be compromised...You promised harmony!"

Paul stood at attention in front of Elliot Richards' assault without speaking. John Malone was standing beside him, obviously feeling sublimely victorious.

As Elliot ranted, Paul wondered to himself how to convince the Secretary the data was correct.

He was certain John Malone, or one of his sub-section chiefs, had sabotaged the diagram.

How could Paul prove that without demanding a complete computer inquiry? An inquiry would take up too much time.

He glanced over at Malone. The Assistant Undersecretary had planned this strategy in advance. Paul knew it. He, too, knew Paul couldn't demand a computer inquiry.

"I have put the trust of the entire department in your hands. Are you up to the task? Time is running out, you know."

Elliot's nerves were under a tremendous strain due to the rigors of campaigning.

Paul had never seen him quite so out of harmony with himself. And then Paul made his move:

"Sir, the hierarchical data link control panel does fit into the network tube."

He spoke slowly, firmly and with emphasis.

He stood erect and stared directly into the eyes of John Malone. Obviously, the young Assistant Secretary of Technology was not prepared for Paul's bold stand.

It was clear he had been convinced Paul would sink into a whimpering sea of excuses.

"But Mr. Malone has stated it does not fit!"

Elliot turned and scanned John Malone.

Malone, too, was obviously quite mistaken about the Secretary.

Why, they had dined together at least once a week. Their private meetings were professionally intimate…ripe with promise.

Had not the Secretary hinted that he, Malone, had the qualifications needed for the position of Undersecretary of Technology?

No, he hadn't expected the Secretary to behave in this fashion.

He had been too busy campaigning! But then…

"I repeat, sir. The hierarchical data link control panel does fit into the network tube. I believe it is possible that Mr. Malone, in his eagerness to be totally efficient, accidentally analyzed test diagram 313 which did, in fact, show the panel would not fit. But we did not use 313 for that very reason."

Paul continued to stand at attention as Elliot Richards scanned the hierarchical data link control panel network tube diagrams.

He felt he'd done well.

As he rode up in the elevator to the Secretary's office, he couldn't imagine how he could possibly have made the mistake of which John Malone accused him.

The new system was a million miles of circuitry, one hundred tons of hardware, over five hundred million different programs!

John Malone was banking on the hope that Paul Quatro would be unable to find the smallest needle in the biggest haystack on Earth.

As soon as Paul saw Elliot's face light up, he knew he was safe.

The new system was still on schedule.

The Secretary took off his 5-D computer glasses.

Paul made gleeful note that John Malone had stepped away from the Secretary's high-backed chair. He'd lost his power!

"Paul, I appreciate you coming up here and clarifying young Malone's lack of insight."

Elliot's voice was restrained.

"There is no more important visualization than the actualization of the new system on the projected date."

Paul nodded his agreement.

Elliot continued.

"Mr. Malone, I'd like to thank you for being so diligent in your duties as Assistant Undersecretary."

Paul couldn't believe what he was hearing.

Diligent! The Assistant had been totally out of line! He had attempted to upset the chain of command in the department!

It took all of Paul's control to maintain composure as Elliot spoke.

Why was Elliot always protecting Malone?

What was the connection?

His chest tightened with tension as he rode the escalator down to his office.

It wasn't enough to be acquitted in front of the Secretary of Technology! He wanted to know why he was constantly being tested!

Was the Assistant Undersecretary being groomed for his position?

Was he being groomed for the top chair?

Was it possible that if the new system wasn't ready by the projected date, or, worse, if it didn't operate properly, could Elliot still win the Presidency?

Suddenly, the answer flashed on Paul. "Yes!" It was part of Elliot's strategy! A sacrifice must be made if the new system was a disappointment.

Surely a President could not promote the man responsible for the failure of the new system!

Someone had to be waiting in the wings in case it didn't work out. So obviously Elliot had selected John Malone to be that someone.

Paul was having trouble breathing.

He started to hyperventilate as his logic began to veer out of control. He visualized a white lamb on an altar, its throat being cut, blood squirting out its twitching jugular like a lubricant sprinkler.

By the time he entered his office his heart had slowed down, and the tension in his chest had subsided.

He was resolved: he would not be defeated. The new system would be finished on time.

Miss James handed him a transmission from Lord Lothar as Paul walked into his private office, his inner sanctum.

He placed the cassette in his transcriber and began to decipher the coded message. It was a code known only to Paul, Zelman and Lothar.

They had invented it when they were teenagers at the test tube orphanage. It had come in handy when they wanted to communicate in class; they used to pass the coded messages under their desks.

Even if a teacher found them, they would have been absolved of any guilt since no one could decipher the code.

Paul switched on the transcriber and decoded the urgent message from Lothar:

"Come quick! Have completed my great invention! Signed... Lothar."

Paul smiled inwardly as he turned to Miss James.

"I have to go," he said.

"Important business. Hold all my transmissions."

Lord Edwin Lothar lived and worked in what once had been the Smithsonian Institute, a large, gothic building that had housed ancient historical artifacts of unique importance to the twentieth century collectors.

The building was especially unique in that it had survived trauma shock: four walls had remained intact.

The roof, unfortunately, had been blown off.

Most of the contents within had been burned beyond recognition.

What was left was laced in cobwebs so thick it was nearly impossible to discern the shapes within.

In yet one more dramatic gesture, Lothar had bought the Smithsonian from the city for the tidy sum of one dollar.

Along the way he 'd sunk over one million dollars of bank credit into his little "investment" for restoration as his home.

It had become quite a showplace! Tourists piped to it every day, taking insta-photos of themselves standing on the steps.

231

Once Lothar confided to Paul that the former Institute had been used as a brothel during the 21st Century by the Undergrounders.

He said that during dome construction the roof had suddenly collapsed in on the Undergrounders, all of whom were left to die.

Apparently, a live Undergrounder had been discovered ten years ago, blind, healthy and estimated to be over one hundred years old.

Officials placed him in a custom designed miniature zoo which enabled tourists to view him at their leisure.

When last seen, Lothar said the Undergrounder was still alive and was often heard shouting obscenities as locals hurled synthetic food into his cage in hopes he would eat on display.

He never did.

In fact, he often went for months without moving, eating or smiling. His behavior baffled scientists.

Paul remembered visiting the zoo with Mary, remembered trying to communicate with the Undergrounder without success.

Once, though, as they walked away, Mary had turned and shouted back, "Are you the last Undergrounder?"

The Undergrounder had shaken his head suddenly and vigorously.

"No! There's plenty more where I come from!"

And then he'd thrown his head back and laughed.

Paul and Mary could hear his weird guffaws as they ambled towards the pipeline. Even now, sometimes, that laugh reverberated through Paul's mind.

Paul piped into Lothar's private pipeline.

He was immediately greeted by two nine-year-old blue-eyed, blonde-haired girls, each of whom had an I.Q. over 300.

Each was dressed very seductively in see-through transparent inchy skirts.

Each was bare-chested. Their little nipples had been painted red and blue, and their lips were camelia pink...soft...like flowers.

They took him by the hands and escorted him through the former Smithsonian Institute.

Lothar had restored it beautifully.

During the renovation he had discovered crates full of artifacts which had somehow withstood the abuse of trauma shock and two centuries of time.

One wall, though, had been left in its original state.

It was splattered with Undergrounder graffiti that seemed insane to Paul: "Suffocate the baby!...Can't stop crying!...Help!...Help!... Help!...Why?"

The nine-year-old nymphets pointed at the wall and giggled.

They reached for each other's hand and skipped along the echoing stone hall, their footsteps reverberating through

Paul 's ears like ancient chimes.

He felt a profound sadness that contrasted with the merry laughter of his little companions.

He walked slowly after the chattering girls.

As he reached a large, marble alcove, Paul noticed what he thought at first was a large bug.

On further inspection he saw it was an old airplane called the Spirit of St. Louis. He wondered if it had any importance, or if it was just a toy decoration for Lothar's amusement.

As he continued to follow the girls, he wondered what Lothar was doing with them.

Were they the children of friends? Was he tutoring them?

He imagined Lothar being suckled by the two little ones, then quickly jammed the visualization out of his cortex.

Heleon! What was she doing right now? Was she thinking of him? Was she sleeping in his bedroom?

"Paul! Thank goodness I've saved you from all this nastiness!"

Lothar hugged his friend.

He had been lurking in a dark hallway and intercepted him, separating him from the two girls who wandered ahead.

Paul was confused.

"Nastiness?" he queried.

Lothar's face had been made up.

Paul flashed onto Zelman's last transmission over the vid phone.

He prayed Lothar hadn't succumbed to Zelman's fate.

"What is this great invention?" he asked with excitement.

As he waited for Lothar to answer, he wondered where the two little girls had gone. Glancing back over Lothar's shoulder, he saw them holding onto Lothar's twenty-foot silk train, like bridesmaids in a procession.

"First we must eat!" roared Lothar, as he clapped his hands three times.

He looked like an Inja emperor as he led Paul into a large banquet hall.

Paul was glad to see Lothar was so happy.

He was glad to know he had finally broken through as an inventor, too, and was back at work. They sat down together.

The mood was festive as barebreasted women wandered through the banquet hall in scant clothing.

Suddenly, Paul jumped.

"Real red meat!"

He looked startled as a barebreasted butlerette set an elegantly arranged platter in front of him.

Her nipples brushed against his cheek as she bent over.

The delectable odor of the meat made him salivate.

"And real fowl!" Lothar shouted across the expansive table.

Paul looked up from his platter and watched Lothar pull the bird legs apart and bite off chunks of roasted flesh.

Then he shifted his gaze to the barebreasted woman, who had blonde hair and painted blue eyelids. Her lips were red, and her teeth were ivory white.

Her face resembled the nine-year-old nymphets, so much so, Paul thought that she must be their mother.

"Pheasant...quail...the heart of an eagle...turkey...pickled peacock tongues...food fit for an emperor!"

Lothar was gorging on his fowl, blood gravy dripping from his chin.

A second barebreasted blonde-haired woman with purple painted eyelids and purple lips walked up to Lothar and wiped his mouth with a large linen napkin.

It was then that Paul realized Lothar had been eating the fowl raw.

He looked down at the blood-raw porterhouse steak and felt like vomiting. He was afraid to ask Lothar where he'd found the meat.

"Eat and be merry for a new invention has been created by Lord Edwin Lothar!" belched the Grand Potentate of Up, "and I, the genius pinhead, am proud to be a friend of Paul the Pure...the truest technocrat visionary in the land!"

236

He roared, belched again and continued to stuff his mouth with the flesh of fowl.

Paul cut unevenly into his meat. He had never eaten real meat in his whole life. He had visualized cassettes in his computer library of flesh-meat, but seeing in the library versus seeing in real life were two totally different things! Even with scent-o-tron!

He stared across the incredibly long banquet table at the second blonde-haired, barebreasted woman.

He squinted his eyes to make sure his visualization was correct.

She seemed to be the twin of the woman who had served him his food! The two little blonde-haired, blue-eyed nymphets must have been their daughters!

He eyed Lothar.

Was it possible they were his children?

And if they were, why hadn't Lothar told him?

Lothar suddenly began to choke on a quail bone.

Chunks of flesh flew out of his mouth as the blonde with the purple-painted eyelids rushed to his side with a brass bowl Lothar later told Paul was a spitoon.

Spitoons, said Lothar, had been used during the nineteenth century.

Paul waited while Lothar regurgitated up the pickled peacock tongues, the heart of an eagle, the liver of a quail and the legs of a pheasant.

The blonde-haired woman named Shanta held onto the spitoon with great courage, Paul thought, given the unattractive nature of her job.

She looked at Paul.

"Would you like to puke, too?"

Paul nearly gagged.

"No, thank you," he whispered.

He learned later the other woman's name was Fauna, and that she, in fact, was the grandmother of the nine-year-old nymphets.

Shanta was her daughter.

The two of them served Lothar out of some bizarre feeling of loyalty. In turn, Lothar gave them shelter, food and sex.

As direct descendants of the last curator of the Smithsonian, they felt it was their duty to see that things were kept in order.

The taste of red meat would stick to Paul Quatro's tongue for a week, and he would never forget its pungent odor. He was glad, though, he had finally actualized the visualization of red meat.

Still, he knew the people of habitable Earth would never want to eat flesh the way their ancestors had during the twentieth century.

The Great Trauma Shock had taken care of that.

Livestock couldn't survive that ghostly transition.

Most had died. The rest had been contaminated, thereby put to death.

A steer, in Paul's mind, was much the same as a dinosaur.

After the feast of flesh, as Lothar referred to it, the two little girls performed a tap dancing opera complete with four costume changes.

Their high-pitched voices carried across the banquet room like spastic harps from a bygone era.

When they'd finished, Lothar walked over to them, lifting both in his arms like a giant gorilla.

He wanted to kiss them. They cooperated by straddling his waist with their legs and squealing as he slobbered into their dainty necks.

When Lothar finally put them down, Shanta and Fauna brought Paul and Lothar a box that had something called "cigars" inside.

Paul had never seen a cigar, although he'd visualized cassettes, again at the library.

"I found them in the treasure room!" bellowed Lothar.

"You're supposed to smoke them!"

He lit his with the flame of a candle.

He motioned for Paul to pick one, then lit it for him.

Paul inhaled deeply.

He coughed.

239

His head felt fuzzy.

It was delicious!

"Don't inhale the damn thing," said Lothar.

"It's not a vita smoke! These things used to kill people, you know."

Paul didn't hear him. He was too busy feeling the smoke circulate through his nasal passages.

He turned to Lothar.

"So where's the invention?"

Lothar recited his favorite poem:

"Patience...patience is the jewel of the general's crown...alone ... alone we must fight the odds...We must fight on! And on! Until the dawn of enlightenment bathes our wounds in victory!"

Lothar hoisted a goblet filled with wine that had been preserved from the twentieth century. It dribbled out of the sides of his mouth as he arched his head back and let it drain down his throat.

His voice, no matter what he did, was always elegant.

Paul remembered the poem.

He and Lothar had found it back when they were in the test tube orphanage together. It was scrawled on a computer toilet seat.

Lightning cracked outside.

He glanced at his computer watch and read the date: October fourteenth. His mini-weathervane registered "Lightning storm - rain - begins at 7:00 p.m. to continue 'til midnight. Three inches of rain."

"And now...the invention! Shall we go?"

Lothar gestured to Paul.

Automatically, it seemed, the lights shut down, as if they were sensitized to Lothar's commands.

Shanta and Fauna screamed, hugging each other as they crouched next to the large fireplace that blazed continuously with a crackling, synthetic fire.

Lothar held a candalabra that had eight candles. It was a Menorah! A Middle Judean icon!

Paul followed Lothar down the narrow winding staircase, the blazing Menorah lighting their way.

The explosions of lightning were frightening in their intensity.

The dome computerphonics caused an echo that was ten times the audio vibrations that had occurred during natural storms before trauma shock.

The two men reached the third underground level.

The light from the Menorah produced magnificent monsters made out of shadows. The monsters danced across the high-ceilinged walls.

"Where are we going?" whispered Paul.

Lothar turned around, the flames distorting his handsome features.

For a moment Paul had an anxiety rush he thought might have been induced by some horrible potion he'd unknowingly consumed during the banquet.

"Ahhhhhhhhhh!" Lothar let out a shrill yodel.

Paul jumped back, not sure of Lothar's state of mind.

A clawlike hand landed on his shoulder.

Paul jerked around.

A stuffed gorilla glared down at him.

"Noooooo!" he shrieked.

He leaped away, crashing into Lothar and knocking the Menorah out of his hand.

"Paul, don't run away!" called Lothar.

It was too late.

Paul was running through the darkness towards anything but that gorilla.

His head pounded as he ran.

He couldn't hear Lothar laughing, nor could he visualize his friend as he picked up the massive candelabra and blew out the flames.

He didn't know Lothar had a computerized flashlight in his pocket, nor did he know that, as he stumbled into the blackness, Lothar was lumbering down a secret hallway to intercept him before he tripped over the banister and fell those twenty stories into the pit...that endless labyrinth of vaults that contained all those priceless, twentieth century treasures.

Lothar knew the treasures he'd uncovered would make any historian' s mouth water.

The problem was, historians had been abolished into extinction!

The new society, disappointed with their lack of accuracy in predicting the future based on the past, had declared them an illegal species.

It was all so sad, anyway death...war...torture...the Plague... prejudice...avarice...destruction...slavery...anti-semitism...anti-isms of all cultures...all religions.

Oh! The Earth's s history was repulsive! So many people inflicting so much pain.

"Stop! In the name of technology!"

Lothar's huge hands held Paul at bay, just as he was about to trip over the banister. As he did so, a bolt of lightning exploded outside, the flash so bright it seemed to burn through the heavy stone walls.

"Are you mad?"

Paul was half-crazed with fear as he looked into Lothar's smiling eyes.

"Calm your nerves, my friend, for I am no more mad than you are."

"I have never been in such a place, Lothar."

Paul's logic began to assert itself.

"Behold the wonders of the past!"

Lothar turned on a light.

They were standing in the middle of a hallway underneath the centrix of four arches.

Paul stared over the banister and shuddered.

The pit was slick and filthy below.

"Get up!"

Lothar's words ricocheted off the high-ceilinged walls of the arched hallway.

"I'm Up!"

Paul tried to reassure his wild-eyed friend.

"Then follow me, and you shall actualize the greatest invention since the pipeline!"

Lothar pulled out a metal key that reminded Paul of a computerized hacksaw.

He slipped it into a keyhole, and it made a creaking sound.

They waited.

The door squeaked as Lothar pushed it inward.

They entered the treasure vault.

Paul hesitated for a moment until Lothar whispered, "In here!"

"Gurglers, jagglers, hooplas, dipster dippeys, lancers and walkabouts...notice the kneeler and the taunter with three eyes and six ears...And over there...see the quitter of quilted pens!"

Lothar used an ancient Watusi warrior's battle spear as a lecturer's tool.

Paul found the Undergrounder murals fascinating.

Lothar explained to him that the muralists had preserved a short-lived but important evolution of American culture.

As Paul listened to Lothar's dissertations on the twenty-first and twenty-second centuries, he began to wonder if Lothar wasn't really mad after all.

"After trauma shock, the people fled to the underground dwellings that had been constructed not for such a ghastly event as that but, ironically, for a variety of cultural events which identify each sub-civilization: basements, rec rooms, storage bins and, in the case of the Smithsonian Institute, treasure vaults ...rooms in which the history of the world happens to have been stored."

Paul wasn't sure what Lothar meant.

"What is a gurgler?"

"Gurglers were people who had screamed so loud during trauma shock that they lost their vocal chords. All they could do thereafter was gurgle."

"What's a quitter of quilted pens?"

Paul suspected that Lothar's logic was consistently illogical.

If Lothar thought the discovery of a weird-looking mural was a great invention then he'd become as loony as a deranged service robot.

"Quitters of quilted pens were people who had tried to write down the events which led up to the day of trauma shock. They were castigated for being the bearers of bad memories. They used quilted pens to write down their memories, and people used to walk past them and tell them to quit. So that's how they became quitters of quilted pens!"

Paul glanced at his computer watch and saw it was 11:00 p.m.

"Look up at the shooter!" commanded Lothar.

"See what he has in his hand!"

Lothar pressed the Watusi warrior's spear tip next to an ominous-looking painting of a man.

"What's a shooter?" asked Paul.

He had never heard of a "shooter." He couldn't make out what the gruesome-faced man was holding in his hands.

"Paul, I thought you had one of the most comprehensive libraries in all of Washington, D.C.!"

"But nowhere, Lothar, nowhere have I seen a gurgler, a jaggler, a hoopla, a dipster dippey, much less a shooter. And I have absolutely no visualization as to what that man is holding in his hands!"

Paul was beginning to feel irritable, a trait never before associated with the Undersecretary of Technology.

Lothar sensed his discomfort.

"Yes, I am afraid you are like all the others in the world who have forsaken the knowledge of history!"

Lothar lowered his pointer.

"What's a shooter!" screamed Paul in frustration.

"I'm glad you asked that, Paul."

Lothar grinned and continued on his historical travelogue.

"Trama shock produced such huge mounds of human suffering that it was impossible to placate the suffering bodies, not to mention the suffering souls. Doctors, nurses, and first-aid helpers were all dead, dying or maimed beyond repair. The few that escaped with their lives fought for their own individual existence but were unable, due to the extreme nature of that time, to help others."

"As in most such tragic events, Paul," Lothar glared at Paul the way a parent might glare at a squirming child, "leaders surface. They take charge, heal the sick, orient the disoriented, provide meaning for those who have lost their way. In so doing they insured their own survival. But for many their arrival meant death. The leaders chose only certain men and women to survive. They had to choose. There was no way the handful of leaders could save so many millions of trauma-shock victims."

Lothar paused as if to take a breath.

"The chosen few were allowed to live. The group included men, women and children. All were given guns by the leaders."

"Guns?" Lothar's words stunned Paul.

He'd had a cassette which had been given to him by Professor Ludlum entitled, "The Good, The Bad and the Ugly," a cinema movie that visualized life in the old American West. In it, a man with a big gun went around shooting everybody.

"Shooting!" Paul whispered the word to himself several times.

Lothar could see Paul was visualizing his story well.

"Yes, that's what shooters did with guns. They shot and killed the mounds of humans who at that time were writhing in excruciating pain. And when the last shooter had shot the last human he turned the gun on himself and used the last bullet."

"Lothar, what does this have to do with your new invention?"

His throat was hoarse from screaming and shouting, and from smoking that fat cigar and eating that fresh, red meat.

"This!"

Lothar pulled an object wrapped in gold-threaded cloth out of his shimmering Inja robe. He laid it down on a crate in the middle of the chilly room and unwrapped it.

"Lo and behold, my friend, for I have invented the raygun!"

He gripped the chrome and black ivory-handled object in his right hand and cocked it. He pointed the gun at the chandelier lights above and quickly fired off two bolts of blueish bullets.

The energy burst from the evil-looking nozzle with red-hot flashes. All the light bulbs in the room exploded.

Paul covered his head with his hands, hoping to avoid the shards of razor-sharp glass.

"It works, Paul! It works!"

Lothar jumped up and down like a little kid with a brand new toy.

"But what does it do besides blowing up light bulbs?"

Paul was amazed at the extent of his friend's illogic.

"Do?"

Lothar seemed to have lost the conversation. Then he regained his visualization and began to giggle.

"Catch it!"

He threw the raygun to Paul, who caught it with both hands.

It felt hot and dangerous, and Paul wanted nothing to do with this technological aberration.

"Lothar, I do not want it."

But Lothar wasn't listening. He'd already produced another gold-threaded cloth from within his Inja robe that had another raygun in it.

"I have my own."

"Lothar, what does it do?"

"It's yours," he cackled.

"Try it and find out! Press the power dial and then cock it and fire!"

Lothar twirled his raygun around his head like a baton and cocked it in midair.

He began to fire at a row of aluminum bottles he had set up on a shelf at the far end of the treasure vault. He blasted them into a million pieces.

Obviously, he had been practicing.

"Try it, Paul...please...I need your approval if I am going to ask the Department of Technology to support my invention."

Paul could feel Lothar's need for approval through his frenzied madness.

So! This was the invention the public had been waiting for all these years!

He leveled his gaze at an ancient statue of a potbellied man sitting in the lotus position. Ming Dynasty!

Without hesitating, he 'd pulled the trigger again. The Buddha's stomach was annihilated.

"Doesn't it make you feel good when you pull the trigger?"

Lothar waited breathlessly for Paul 's response.

"Yes," he said. "I like it."

He held the raygun in his hand.

It felt almost as good as the computer glove to the H-wall! Yet Paul couldn't imagine that the raygun would give him as much pleasure as Heleon did.

"I knew you'd understand," croaked Lothar, hoarse with excitement.

He glanced at the ceiling.

"But what does it do besides blow up ugly statues and aluminum bottles and colorful light bulbs from a hanging chandelier?"

"Do?"

Lothar seemed to be unsure of himself.

Every time he explained his research, every time he tried to explain the origins of his invention, Paul asked him what the invention did!

He would have to help Paul understand. He gestured to Paul to sit down.

"It could be a toy…" he began.

"I can sell it to construction companies who are blasting their way through mountains..."

251

Paul listened.

"...It's a new game of pleasure...a sport...a luxury item...a piece of performing art."

He looked at Paul for signs of comprehension.

"The world has no need for an army if there is no war...Soldiers, armies, wars, all are obsolete."

"No, my friend."

Paul put his hand on Lothar's huge shoulder.

"It has no positive purpose."

"It does, Paul...I know it does. It has to, or why would I have invented it?...Do?...What does my invention do?..."

Paul convinced Lothar to take a sedative and get some rest.

He had been living life at the fullest pace imaginable, and it was obvious he was tired. His logic was damaged.

Still, in spite of Lothar's rantings and out of loyalty to his brilliance, Paul promised to take the raygun home with him to try and visualize a way to use it in society.

Lothar was ecstatic with this agreement, so ecstatic, in fact, that he kissed Paul on the lips.

They really were the best of friends! Paul the pure...Paul the dream...Paul the technocrat visionary!

Lothar knew he'd discover the true meaning of the raygun.

At half past midnight Paul piped back to Computer Meadows and took the late-night conveyor belt sidewalk home.

He was exhausted when he entered his computer home and walked through the living room with dragging feet.

He stopped for a minute and stared at the wall.

He was too tired to tell Heleon what had happened today.

The invitation arrived in the transmission box.

Because it fell under her maintenance duties, Heleon sorted through Paul's personal transmissions and placed them on his computer library desk.

He was in the habit of going over his transmissions before he returned home to hibernate through the night.

At first the invitation didn't stick to her consciousness.

Most of Paul's incoming transmissions were either communications from other technocrats or personal transmissions such as the ones that came in from Mary's mother.

And, of course, there was always the stray garbage transmission: some idiot selling more technology.

Heleon lifted up the cassette and held it in her hands. She scanned the return address:

> Howard and Bernice Bork
> 600000 Utility Drive
> Computer Meadows, 08808

She wanted to know what was in the invitation.

She knew it was an invitation because "invitation" was printed on the cassette container.

She couldn't understand why Paul's next door neighbors went to so much difficulty to send a personal transmission when they could walk across the synthetic lawn and speak with Paul personally! Or they could press his digits and vid-phone him up!

Sometimes things were so confusing outside the wall!

"You are cordially invited to attend Howard and Bernice Bork's eleventh wedding anniversary. Please bring an escort. Atmospheric tuxedo requested. November 21st. At the Bork's all-computerized home."

The announcer was a professional inviter!

Heleon stared at the transmission.

Who would be Paul's escort to the celebration?

She felt a strong vibration rattle through her system.

When she asked Pi about the transmission and its effect on her pulse, he could only say it might have something to do with her vibe towards the controller.

"Why do I resent the vision of Paul going to the Bork's without me?" she said out loud, as she and Pi chatted softly in the kitchen.

Pi was busily stirring a vat of red batter.

"I get a weird sensation when the controller does not allow me to complete my maintenance," he said, as he twirled the batter at the end of a long computer spoon.

"Do you feel hostile sensations?"

She wondered if Pi had discovered the secret of her rattled vibrations.

Pi stopped stirring the batter and stood, motionless, for a moment.

"Hostile is too important of a pulse to insert," he declared gently.

But I can say this.

"Whenever the controller dines away from the house and I know he is nourishing on another's menu I feel my maintenance is not being fully appreciated!"

He turned to Heleon.

"Does that clear things up?"

"Yes!" she blurted.

She turned her back on Pi with embarrassment.

Heleon was surprised by her own reactions.

As she sorted through her vibrations she gazed out the window in a kind of daze.

Rob, the homebot, was standing in front of the Bork's house, his small metal briefcase in hand. What was he doing there?

Delti's coarse voice broke through the vibrations of the moment.

Both Pi and Heleon jumped.

"Visualize hard. Robots are history."

His arrogance annoyed Heleon and Pi, both of whom found themselves defending the heritage of the robot.

"At least robots have the freedom to travel wherever they choose!"

Heleon pointed out the good side of everything, most of the time.

"I wonder where Rob will travel to!"

Pi's comment sounded innocent as the sad little homebot boarded the conveyor sidewalk. His metal shape glistened proudly as he glided away.

"The nearest junkpile," snickered Delti.

Heleon shivered inside.

Delti revolted her. Her disgust brushed his rippling, well-defined body.

He winced.

Sometimes Heleon gave him the distinct vibration that he technically disgusted her as she exited the kitchen in a cloud of sweet air.

"She has a sensitive pulse."

Pi tried to ease the strongman's rising energy before he exploded and destroyed the entire neighborhood.

Delti rotated his gaze away from Heleon, who was standing in the living room, to Pi, who continued to stir his batter.

"What are you maintaining?" asked Delti.

"Synthetic meat," explained Pi.

"Sir has requested a porterhouse steak for his evening nourishment."

The visualization revolted Delti.

He put his head down to shield his vibrations from the visualization when suddenly Heleon screamed.

Delti bolted from the kitchen to her rescue as Pi dropped his bowl of synthetic meat.

The runny liquid splattered all over the floor.

As he ran after Delti he left tiny red footprints on the floor. He wanted to rescue Heleon, too!

"Who are you?"

The visitor had startled Heleon, and she asked for clarification.

Delti materialized beside Heleon.

He put his arm around her protectively as he raised his head to face her visualization.

"Never fear, Pi is here."

The cherubic butler waddled into the living room tripping over his own little red feet and very nearly sliding headfirst into Delti's leg.

With an embarrassed frown he raised himself to his knees as Delti scooped him deftly to his feet.

All three holographic characters stood silently before the visitor, who stood on the first step pod of their very own H-wall.

He was as strong and powerful as Delti.

"I am Beta."

His voice was firm as he scanned each of them with interrogating eyes.

"Where do you originate from?"

Delti stood his ground, ready to confront this imposter hologram at a moment's notice.

All three of them sensed Beta's superior strength.

"My origins are of yours!" boomed the stranger.

His scan caught Heleon. She felt helpless under his visual grip.

"You...you...graduated from the Learning Garden?" asked Pi.

His voice was even higher than usual.

"I am a courier...Come! I will show you the dimension that is being built throughout the city! In households throughout the land...all of which possess an H-wall!"

Beta extended his mammoth hand to the three frightened holograms.

"No!" barked Heleon.

She took a step back from Beta.

Pi stepped back, too.

"There is no danger. You have a right to do as you wish!" said Beta, as he stepped onto the third step pod.

He scanned Delti's inquisitive eyes.

"I will follow you," declared Delti, as he reached for Beta's hand.

The two strongmen clasped each other's hands until a small flame jetted out from their grip.

"Delti! You do not have the controller's permission!" said Heleon, reminding Delti of his place.

For a split second, Delti hesitated.

"What the controller does not know will not hurt him," commented Beta.

Heleon and Pi knew this was not so as Delti willingly dematerialized back into the H-wall with Beta.

Six hours passed.

Heleon and Pi stood at the end of the dining room table and watched Paul cut into his synthetic steak without Delti.

Even though the strongman had negative vibrations he had been bred into their unit, and the experience of separation was a painful one for a hologram bred for a unit.

They had been taught at the Learning Garden that they must work amongst other holograms to form cohesive units in order to properly maintain a controller.

They both sensed Paul's exhaustion at night and both felt it was up to them to relieve him of negativity acquired during the working day.

"Excellent, Pi!"

Paul finished the last piece of synthetic steak.

"Thank you, sir."

Pi's confidence pulsed strongly when the controller was complimentary.

Paul continued to chew the last of his nourishment. He'd had a craving for meat all day.

He kept visualizing Lothar...the raygun...the night at his residence in the Smithsonian Institute...red meat!

Where did Lothar find real red meat?!

Paul looked down at his empty plate and studied the red blood gravy.

He found synthetic steak milder on the palate…less gamey…with a sweeter, less overwhelming aroma.

He glanced at Heleon and Pi, both of whom looked worried.

"Where is…?"

Paul stopped his question in mid- sentence.

Heleon and Pi were sure he was going to ask about Delti and they would be forced into making a decision as to whether or not tell the truth. Their respective pulses were vibrating at an incredible frequency.

"Dessert, please!" said Paul, as he rubbed his stomach.

Pi served the synthetic chocolate chip cheesecake a la Europa which he'd carefully stored under the plastic star-shaped serving container as a surprise for the controller.

Paul was delighted as cheesecake was his favorite dessert.

After dinner he adjourned to the computer library to go over his incoming transmissions. Heleon followed him into the room.

Pi completed his kitchen maintenance, satisfied with the evening.

Delti had yet to return home.

Heleon observed Paul as he scanned the Bork's invitation. With a sigh he tossed the cassette into the refuse basket and continued through the stack of transmissions.

Heleon was impatient to know what he was thinking. She wanted to know who he was going to take to the party!

"Who will you go with?"

She felt it was her right to know the answer to this puzzlesome question.

Paul was absorbed in his own visualizations: Would the new system be ready on time? Would Elliot Richards win the election and become President? Would he, Paul Quatro, become Secretary of Technology? Where did Lothar obtain real flesh? What purpose did a raygun have in a world with no soldiers? No armies? No wars?

"Who are you going with?"

Heleon's voice was more insistent this time. Her pretty face pushed towards him like a synthetic rose.

Paul's eyes drifted open as Heleon continued to massage his feet.

He had been soaking in the hot sauna for over thirty minutes as Heleon massaged his muscles with vitamin-packed oils and gels.

They were both naked.

Before he could answer her, she had her hand on his penis.

Her touch was electrically charged as he felt himself harden under her spell.

"Why do you want to know?" he asked.

"I want to go with you!"

Her words rolled off her tongue like candy.

Paul sat bolt upright, suddenly awake. He was shocked at the idea.

The two of them sat, facing each other in the hot, steamy sauna for another thirty minutes.

No words were exchanged as Heleon's sixth, seventh, eighth and ninth senses penetrated his mind.

They lay on their sides, their tongues drawing images across the well-formed ripples in their stomachs...small bites...lips grasping muscles as their faces touched...his tongue slipped into her hot, moist, throbbing essence.

Whew!

She rolled him over, her back arched as he faced down into her sex...her hands spread his buttocks apart as his nostrils inhaled the scent of her...and then he rolled her on top like a circus performer, and together they went higher...higher...and he remembered the raygun...electric bolts of energy exploding through that barrel and she tasted his excitement... moaning and moaning and moaning they rolled over each other... penetrating...connecting...desiring...they'd never get enough...

But the question wouldn't go away.

"Who are you taking to the party?" asked Heleon.

They lay together, exhausted. She was afraid, and she didn't know why.

"Why do you ask?"

Paul, too, was afraid.

"I want to go with you."

Her answer so honest…so caring…so loving…it broke Paul's heart.

They spent the rest of the evening connecting, disconnecting, reconnecting, but never reaching a comfortable place together.

The visualization of taking Heleon to a social gathering outside his own computerized house haunted Paul into the night.

He knew he had to make a decision.

The new system was to be tested on the twenty-second of November, the day after Howard and Bernice' s eleventh wedding anniversary.

The days leading up to the test were unbearable for everyone involved.

Tension ran high.

Paul was receiving negative energy from two sides: Elliot, who interrogated Paul constantly; and John Malone, who seemed ever biting at his heels, always hoping for a fall.

Through it all Paul found strength from the H-wall that Howard had experimentally placed in his home, and from his three unusual helpers who worked so hard to rid his body of the tensions and ills that go with high stakes and fast times.

Lately, though, Paul noticed Delti's maintenance was declining.

Recently, he'd left the Roto-Rooter in the hallway, and Paul had tripped over it as he stumbled to the cosmetic room late one night without turning the lights on.

He'd cut his knee, badly, on the blade. Luckily, Heleon had been innovative with her tongue and in licking it had healed it immediately.

But the memory of Delti' s oversight remained.

And Heleon! She seemed down when he came home.

She seemed almost to nag at him...always wanting to know where he was and when he got there...and who he'd been with!

Her recent lack of enthusiasm was confusing.

And Pi! Pi, who was always there with those fantastic, fattening dishes.

Paul had put on ten pounds since Pi entered the household!

He was a wonderful butler but with Delti's strange, almost hostile behavior, and Heleon's confusing vibrations, poor Pi was just half of his regular, jovial self.

Howard. That Howard.

He kept asking who Paul's escort would be. The questions drove Paul to distraction.

Furthermore, he kept mentioning potential escorts for Paul as if Paul couldn't take care of himself!

Howard was incredibly happy these days.

H-walls had become the rage of the technological world, and orders came in from as far away as Middle Judea, South Mexo, Inja, Austral and Europa!

Techno stores shipped them out as fast as they could, but it was hard to deliver H-walls to all the stores in twenty-five states in the union, let alone the world.

But, as Howard often said these days, grinning from ear to ear, "I'm so Up I'm Upping out of my head with joy!"

And why shouldn't he be Up!

Talk had been circulating at the store recently that Howard was due for a big promotion after all these sales.

Howard deserved a raise! Hadn't he been Vice President of Purchasing when the decision was made to order H-walls in the first place?

Now just who had been behind that little babe?

Howard snapped his fingers and whistled a little tune.

"Me!"

The wonderful answer popped out of his mouth like a sweet dream...except he was awake!

"Me! Me! Me! Ha! Ha!"

He rubbed his hands together. Had he not been the one to put his career on the line and...in the style befitting a genuine member of the Together Generation...won?

"Ha! Ha! Me!" cackled Howard.

Oh! Life was Up for Howard Bork! Things were A-O-K.

He loved his new H-wall! He loved his new holograms, Beta and Omicron!

Howard stopped and thought for a minute about Paul. He felt there was something mysterious happening between Paul and Heleon, but he couldn't for the life of him imagine what it was.

He'd tried to draw him out on the subject, but Paul was evasive so Howard had decided to let things be.

He and Paul were the best of friends, and, Howard figured, if Paul had something to tell him he'd do so at the right time.

Paul worked late on November 21st, the day before the new system was due for testing.

All the pieces had gone to the testing grounds located in the old Lincoln Memorial building. The test grounds boasted the most advanced technology in the world and were operated by the most gifted, logical, dedicated technocrats available through mankind.

As each piece was assembled by hand, Paul maintained constant communication updates with his staff.

Everyone held the unspoken question within: Would the new system work?

The answer lay in tomorrow, November 22nd.

Paul stayed in his office a full two hours after the department doors had officially closed. He had his own key.

When Miss James left for the evening, she gave Paul a kiss on the hand and reassured him that the new system would work.

Her voice wasn't convincing.

After she left, Paul organized his desk, arranging final visualizations for the next day's test at the Lincoln Memorial test grounds.

He analyzed every component more than one hundred times.

He scanned thousands of primary circuits and attempted to connect fifty-five thousand diagrams into one complete new system.

Then he picked up his computer pen and began to write down his alternative visualization if the new system didn't work.

How many days would be left before the official unveiling?

How many seconds, hours, days would he have to correct any mistakes he might have made?

He knew his deadline was just nineteen working days from now...New Year's Day.

The new system was allowed only one test before official presentation on that projected date.

If tomorrow was a fiasco, he had one more chance.

The eyes of the world, Paul knew, were upon him.

Every cell in Paul's body was being squeezed to the breaking point, yet he still experienced pleasure in this dangerous pursuit.

"You can't win if you don't play" was a popular slogan for the Together Generation, and Paul embraced that philosophy wholeheartedly.

Building a new system was as exciting to Paul as a big-ball game.

Technocrats were every bit as tough as big-ball players, weren't they?

And more intelligent, too! thought Paul to himself as he walked up the plastic pathway to his all-computerized house. He noticed the sprinkler system was working, and this made him feel good.

Paul did not like confronting Delti. A power struggle existed between them that Paul found disarming.

He never felt that kind of tension with Pi, or -- God forbid with Heleon…nor with any other service robots he'd been in contact with in his lifetime.

He thought once the new system was a success he'd have Miss James transmit the H-wall cassette into his transcriber so he could discover the essence of Heleon.

As soon as he entered his house, he could feel the Up music stroking his mind.

Pi was waiting to take his atmospheric trenchcoat.

"Good pleasure, sir."

The beaming butler took Paul's fedora hood, too.

"Thank you, Pi."

Paul had such warm feelings for Pi!

"I hope you like your vitatini dry, sir."

Heleon was holding the long-stemmed vitatini glass. It had been weeks since Heleon had greeted Paul with a vitatini!

"Thank you."

He took the drink and raised it to his lips.

The smile on Heleon's face relaxed him. He was glad to see her energy was back up, especially the night before the new system was tested.

Even Delti seemed in a positive energy.

As Paul passed the H-wall, he noticed Delti was exercising on the first step pod.

"Good pleasure, sir."

Delti's voice still had arrogant darts in its texture, but it sounded less negative than usual.

"Thank you, Delti."

Paul walked towards his bedroom followed by Heleon.

She stared at Delti as she followed Paul.

Although he smiled at her, Heleon wasn't fooled.

Ever since Beta had introduced himself, Delti disappeared regularly.

And although his negative energy had softened in tone, it remained focused in the same direction.

And even though he seemed less aggressive towards Heleon, she continued to distrust and dislike him.

Delti scanned Paul and Heleon as they disappeared from the living room and headed towards the bedroom.

He no longer felt unsure about his position in the unit, thanks to his trip with Beta to the meeting wall in the Techno department store's basement auditorium.

He was glad Heleon and Pi hadn't been with him. Anyway, they wouldn't be able to help.

The connection would always be most complete, he knew, between the A through E hologram models.

To Delti's mind, they were the most finished and, of course, the most intelligent.

So he'd prefer to connect with the models of his own atmosphere.

Delti was glad, too, that the controller was going to the Bork's this evening.

It would allow him to attend another meeting. Tonight he was honored to be representing Beta, who would be working at the Bork's anniversary party.

Delti stood quietly for a moment.

Someday Heleon would be his, and the controller would understand. He began to laugh...the first time he had experienced such an impulse.

"Why are you laughing, Delti?"

Pi looked up at the strongman.

He'd never seen Delti like this. Something wasn't right.

"Because I am happy!" howled Delti, as he dematerialized into the wall.

Pi remained behind, pondering Delti's vibration.

Heleon was busy laying out Paul's atmospheric tuxedo which was complete with top hat and computer cane.

She had prepared his sauna tub complete with favorite vitamins and relaxo bubbles with special salts.

Paul found her energies to be enchanting tonight. She was so attentive to his maintenance!

Not once did she ask him who he was taking to the anniversary party.

In the sauna tub she became a seductive mermaid.

All his aqua-erotica-sexo-fantasies were aroused as she played an imaginary flute.

Accidentally, they pressed the computer panel for the mechanical arms.

Soft sponge hands began to unfold out of the air. They gently pressed their arms and legs, lifting them both to their feet, positioning them in outrageous postures which were simultaneously sexy and funny.

Inside out…upside down…angled and spread…by the time they crawled out of the sauna tub they were not only clean and steamed but their bodies had been sexually perfumed.

Paul closed his eyes and allowed Heleon to towel-dry him all over. Her hands pressed against his body amidst the softness of the towel, absorbing the wetness with tenderness and compassion.

"We'd better get dressed or we'll be late for the party."

He opened his eyelids and smiled.

She didn't know what to say at first, and then she whispered, "But I don't have anything to wear."

Paul draped the towel over her body and dried it. He kissed her neck, behind the ears and between her shoulder blades.

"I've taken care of that."

He held her hand as he pressed the button to Mary's clothes closet. The doors slid apart slowly. He hadn't opened them since Mary' s funeral.

"I'm sure you can find something in here that's appropriate."

Energy droplets trailed down Heleon's face. She was ecstatic. It had worked!

273

All day she'd been trapped in a foul energy source. It got so bad she was ready to shut herself down for a while, but Pi had suggested she take a walk to the controller's computer library and sit in his chair for a special visualization of a certain cassette.

Together they'd watched an old twentieth century movie called "Gone With The Wind."

In the movie, Heleon saw two women: Scarlet, who she couldn't understand, and Melanie, who she identified with completely.

But her lesson was learned from Scarlet. Heleon saw that she got whatever she wanted with the right kind of flirting.

Pi, on the other hand, fell in love with Rhett Butler.

Loving Rhett, he swore to himself that very night, would be his secret. He would never tell any energy…not even Heleon!

But he couldn't hide his feelings, and by the end of the movie they were both crying and hugging each other and huddled together like babies.

Both so wanted to be in love with a good man!

Heleon chose a majestic, full-length synthetic mink gown with a hood. It draped over her curvacious body like a thin layer of oil on water.

Although she was not accustomed to spiked, atmospheric heels, she was determined to wear them.

As Paul turned to look at her from the multi-tiered mirror in his dressing room, he thought she was the most gorgeous woman he had ever visualized.

He took her in his arms and slid his tongue between her lips and down her throat.

"You're beautiful, H," he said softly.

She pressed her body against him, holding his hard penis through the atmospheric material of his suit.

"Let's go," he said.

He gave her a last kiss on the lips and straightened his trousers. He did not want to walk into the party with what appeared to be a computer rod in his pocket.

Before leaving, Paul scanned the H-wall computer pamphlet to discern the limit, if there was a limit, on the distance Heleon could travel from the wall.

He wanted to be sure she would be safe, not to mention energized, at the Bork's, which was the farthest Heleon had ever been from her "home."

He also wondered if Heleon would be able to draw power from Howard's H-wall. But the pamphlet didn't say.

They left holding hands. Pi watched them walk down the plastic pathway to the conveyor belt sidewalk in front of the house.

They looked happy, he thought. He leaned his neck out as far as he could so as to enjoy the last possible visualization.

Within seconds they'd glided to the Bork's and disappeared inside.

Pi felt an ominous vibration jitter through his system.

He turned and went back to the breakfast vid nook where he switched on his favorite show, "Up Up and Away," the most popular game show on prime-time vid that the Together Generation had ever actualized.

As Paul and Heleon approached the Bork's door, they felt nervous. Paul turned to look at Heleon as he reached to press the door chimes.

He could read her mind! It was a fantastic way of communicating.

"Paul! So glad you could make it!"

At first Howard didn't see Heleon. He shook Paul's hand and escorted him in to the hallway of his computer house. The party was at an all-time high.

"Good evening, Mr. Bork," piped Heleon.

Paul didn't like the subservient tone in her voice.

Howard's head swiveled on his neck as his eyes popped.

"Well, I'll be Up!"

Howard scratched his head and scanned her body.

"Happy anniversary!"

She reached to rub his hands in an endearing effort to show affection. Howard understood and offered his hands.

He led Paul and Heleon into the living room where the upward members of the Together Generation gyrated to the latest dance craze, The Spin.

"Hey! Everybody! Look who's here!" shouted Howard.

His voice sounded mischievous as he stepped aside, inviting everyone to gaze at Paul and Heleon as they stood together in the living room entranceway.

It was impossible not to hear the snide whispers that floated around the party.

Bernice broke the tension.

"Paul, I'm so happy you could enjoy our pleasure.

And who is this ravishing child?"

Her voice was full of sympathy.

"Heleon," gulped Paul.

Howard slapped him on the back catching Paul by surprise. He coughed.

"Paul couldn't get a human escort, so he ordered a hologram!"

The room buzzed with rustles and titters. But then, that didn't surprise Paul.

The Together Generation had lost much in the way of sensitivity and open-mindedness up the upward mobile ladder of success.

Often he thought their hearts were at large the way one's petbot might run wild if left too long without supervision.

"He's a perverted technocrat who's gone and stuck his connector into the wrong socket," hissed an overweight matron covered with feathers.

"A blue-nosed digbot without a hole!" agreed a middle-level executive in a top hat.

"No hole. No hole, whatsoever."

All of the couples were married.

Most had ordered H-walls, some of which had already been installed.

None had ordered the three-unit wall, though, not even Howard and Bernice.

Paul had been Howard's experiment with the three unit, the luxury wall!

Obviously, mused Howard as he observed his friend, the three-unit wall had been good for Paul.

As the music resumed, several men approached Heleon and asked her to dance. At first she felt obligated to be Paul 's partner, but he encouraged her to partake in the festivities without him.

Each man she danced with took liberties with her, bumping and grinding their bodies against her,. touching and squeezing and poking their fingers into her luscious curves.

Suddenly, it happened.

Abner Truaxton, President of Techno department stores, jerked Heleon away from Miles Look, an account executive for Solarium Enterprises, the largest manufacturers of solar technology.

He'd been sniffing opiated hankies all night, and his lust for Heleon grew with every whiff.

Her dancing drove him wild! Other men, too, were mesmerized by her undulating twirls.

The women held back, frowning. This creature was a threat!

A threat for everyone but Bernice, who found Heleon's movements a refreshing break from societal restraint.

Paul was chatting with Evelyn Grunewald at the time, unaware of the adventure taking place.

Abner Truaxton grabbed Heleon's breast and pinched her nipples.

Even though she had been mauled all night, Heleon felt it would be wrong to object to his actions.

She was afraid that if Paul looked her way and she was expressing negativity to one of his friends he would be offended. She didn't want to offend her controller!

But when Abner Truaxton unzipped his atmospheric tuxedo trousers and yanked out his pale, angular penis, Heleon said no.

Abner was incensed.

"Take it, whore technology!" he bellowed.

He grabbed her hand and placed it on his unappealing knob.

"No!" she cried out.

He clutched the back of her neck and pushed her face towards his.

His long, slippery tongue coiled out of his mouth like a serpent's.

She thought she'd gag if he came any closer as the room around her began to swirl and pulsate.

Her pulse was weakening.

Paul Quatro had never struck another human being in his whole life.

It wasn't done in the Together Generation's society.

Abner Truaxton, too, was unused to physicalities of this nature.

As the blow struck he reeled backwards and fell into the buffet table. The weight of his body collapsed the legs of the table, and food tumbled down over his head.

Paul held Heleon in his arms. She was losing her pulse!

"Why did you bring her here?" shrieked Mrs. Truaxton venomously.

"It was an experiment," said Paul evenly.

He caught Heleon before she fell and heroically lifted her into his arms.

She fainted immediately.

As Paul pushed his way through the crowd to the front door, he saw Beta standing on the first step pod next to the Bork's H-wall.

Beta had seen the whole thing.

He had observed the effect Heleon had on men; he knew how wild they became at the mere sight of her; he had witnessed their loss of control…the demise of their logic.

He folded his arms and smiled.

"Beta, put some music on," shouted Howard.

"Yes, sir!"

Beta took two steps down and ordered Omicron, their skinny, fidgety and overly-proper holographic butler to put some music on.

He sounded like a general when he spoke.

"Yes, sir," said Omicron.

He always obeyed Beta, for fear of being destroyed if he didn't.

The Bork's H-wall wasn't as happy as Paul's was.

Howard ran outside and called to Paul, his voice making angry echoes through the night.

"Damn you, Paul, for spoiling my eleventh wedding anniversary party!"

But Paul wasn't concerned about Howard or Howard's party.

He was worried about Heleon.

Pi opened the door as soon as he heard the chimes.

"Sir, what's happened?"

Paul carried Heleon over to the H-wall and lay her down on the first step pod.

"She's lost her pulse!"

He held her tightly against his chest.

"Sir, let me help."

Pi took Heleon from Paul and rubbed her hands with his.

In a matter of seconds, she woke up. She looked refreshed.

"Paul!"

She kissed Pi on the lips. He thought he was going to have an energy attack on the spot.

"No, Heleon, it's me. Pi."

He moved aside and allowed Paul to hold her again.

"H, will you ever forgive me for jeopardizing your energy?"

Pi stood by, tears welling in his eyes.

Heleon didn't answer, because she didn't have to.

Paul could read her mind.

As Pi dematerialized into the wall they headed for the bedroom. They lay together on the air bed, talking.

"Is that all it was for you? An experiment?"

Heleon's voice was thick with hurt as her pulse beat sadly against Paul. Droplets of energy trickled down her face.

"Is that all I am? An experiment?"

She repeated the words again and again as if saying them would make the thought go away.

Paul dabbed at her moist little energies with a soft hanky. He kissed the hanky in-between dabs.

"No," he whispered in her ear.

They held each other all night long, absorbing each other's pain.

When the first light of dawn sprinkled through the bedroom blinds, kaleidoscopic colors bled softly across the floor and walls.

Paul was still awake as the colors stirred into his awareness. He was thinking about Heleon…and what was happening to them …and he was wondering whether the new system would Work…knowing that both Heleon and the new system were integral to his future.

CASSETTE NUMBER THREE

THE NEW SYSTEM

Howard Bork avoided Paul Quatro's attempt to apologize as they glided across Computer Meadows towards the pipeline on the conveyor boulevard sidewalk.

Paul thought it was an ominous way to begin one of the most important days of his life.

"Howard, it was an experiment."

Paul felt worthless compromising his apology.

"Leave your experiments in the lab," barked Howard.

There was bitterness in his voice.

They reached the pipeline without further communication.

Paul wished he hadn't apologized.

Heleon had done nothing to provoke this vulgar actualization from both Howard and his Together Generation friends.

As the neon door to the pipeline began to close, Paul stared at his friend, and they knew they could never be close again. \

Howard was more like the idiots at his anniversary party than Paul had realized.

Paul despised those fools! They took the top off the profits technology offered but were unable to accept and love its essence.

As he stepped out of the pipeline, Paul had a nagging headache.

He yearned for Heleon's healing touch.

Paul headed for his favorite vid-news stall.

"Good morning, Art."

Paul clapped his hand to his mouth. Art had been replaced!

"My name is Zeta, and you are Mr. Quatro," said the holographic newsboy.

He handed Paul his mid-morning news without mentioning the big-ball game's score.

Paul scanned the news with weird sorrow in his heart. He'd grown attached to the newsbotboy, Artie. He was going to miss him.

"President Ricarda promises a more humanitarian Administration...Elliot Richards promises greater prosperity with a brighter technological world for all people...Washington Technicals 489 -- Georgia Cylinders 513..."

He tossed the vid screen into a disposable bin as he headed up.

Anxiety gnawed at him like static. Besides, whenever the Washington Technicals lost a big-ball match he never failed to have a horrible day.

As he took the elevator to his office he wondered how the Washington Technicals could lose to the Georgia Cylinders...the worst team in the league!

He visualized little Artie the robot. He wondered where he was.

He remembered the robot pieces twitching by the hanging cliffs in his dream.

He had to get ahold of his logic! He had to flush away the negative images in his head and concentrate on the best visualization possible.

The new system must work today, and today that was all that mattered.

He remembered Heleon lying in his arms, her warm energy calming him.

The image of her gave him strength, for Heleon was good and she had made him very happy. He would not allow anyone to abuse her ever, ever again.

"Good morning, P.Q.!"

Holly was as nervous as he was!

As Paul proceeded past her into his office she commented to herself on how magnificent a technocrat he was.

Paul, on the other hand, focused on her hairdo. He thought it was lovely, just lovely!

How, he asked himself, can I think about my transcriber's hairdo on a day like this?

But he had, and it made her happy.

Holly James had lit nineteen candles in the vid cathedral before she came to work.

286

As she prayed she'd looked out at the giant weather dome that arched magnificently over Washington, D.C. and prayed, "Let the new system work!" She prayed "He" was listening.

Paul walked immediately over to his computerized wall safe and pressed the combination digitals. The iron door swung open, and Paul took out an oval container made of high-grade nickel alloy.

Inside was the key to the new system.

He pressed the computer combination on the oval container and watched as the digital combination spun around.

The oval container made a clicking sound, and the lid snapped open.

Inside was a silver-encrusted magnesium computer key.

Paul held the key between his fingertips.

He could feel the rapid pulse throbbing inside the key as the spark needed to start the new system built to its maximum force.

He replaced the key and snapped the oval lid shut. The time drew nearer.

He placed the container inside his computer briefcase and prepared to pipe to the Lincoln Memorial test grounds.

If one could invent a vacuum that could suck the energy of tension into a combustible mechanism then a new power source would be available!

Paul walked quickly along the gleaming hallway at the Department of Technology.

People scanned his essence as he passed, knowing he was carrying the computerized oval container that contained the key to the new system.

"But will it work?"

Their invisible thoughts echoed from the mind of every technocrat Paul saw.

Their careers! Their lifestyles! Their entire actualizations were dependent on the success of the new system!

As Paul walked up the steps to the Lincoln Memorial he stared up at the headless statue of Abraham Lincoln, a prominent figure in pre-trauma shock civilization.

He had been the sixteenth President of the United States! Imagine that! Sixteenth!

The thought was difficult for Paul to grasp. He entered the test grounds building.

"Good pleasure, Mr. Undersecretary."

The young technocrat engineers greeted him with respect.

"Good day, Mr. Quatro."

They all knew if the new system worked Paul would be Elliot Richards' eventual heir, even if Richards lost the election, for such a feat would surely undermine the Secretary himself and lead to his downfall.

Paul had spent many a work day in the Lincoln Memorial test grounds. It was on the grounds that he was able to actualize his most profound understanding of technology.

For Paul the test grounds were the promised land...heaven or hell...depending upon whether your invention withstood the rigors of the test!

Paul visualized Lothar's raygun and knew he'd never be able to bring it in for testing.

It wasn't meaningful enough. It lacked purpose. No, he couldn't bring it in.

A migraine headache squeezed in on his logic, and time began to take on a different dimension.

He couldn't breathe. He fought to maintain his strength and his logic.

Logic! Logic works! Logic! Logic! Logic! Logic works!

The hall doors slid apart as he entered each section of the test area.

When he reached the grand test ground auditorium, he stood at the top of the circular sunken room as hundreds of technocrats from every sub-section in the Department of Technology were seated. The more successful the technocrat, the closer they sat to the front of the stage.

Tension hissed in the air like poison gas.

The new system had been put together by a thousand hands...piece by piece...checked, re-checked...double checked, triple-checked and then the next piece connected.

Now, as it was about to be turned on for the first time, Paul rested his eyes on the greatest technological source of energy in the inhabitable world...for the new system had been designed as the source of all power to serve all of the technological world.

The walls moved in as Paul grabbed the railing that led to the front row of seats on the rotating platform. His heart was beating like a computer drum.

His cortex screamed.

His mind raced ahead, poring over the future, licking at his past.

It wouldn't stop. Why? asked Paul.

Why must the new system work?

The visualization struck him by surprise as he scanned the new system. It was like an elegant techno-god, so opulent in its vulgar power.

Paul felt faint.

Why? he asked.

Because it doesn't matter! Paul answered himself.

If the new system doesn't work, the world will function just like it did the year before...The old system works, too...it's just not as efficient.

Paul struggled with his logic as he continued down the steps towards the new system.

Even though the new system had a new design…had a new way of transferring power…was able to deliver multiple sources through one circuit…had multi-colored wiring…a brighter and clearer screen…and four more digital keys…its purpose was still the same!

The same! The same!

As Paul walked down the steps towards the new system his head throbbed with these realizations.

He was finding it difficult to balance his logic. Had he worked all these seconds, minutes, hours, days, weeks, months and years to find out it didn't matter?

Beads of perspiration percolated on his forehead as his heart slammed against his chest.

He could feel the exhausted screams of every technocrat protesting his awareness.

He wanted to shout at them all, "It doesn't matter!"

He locked into Elliot Richards' eyes.

The Secretary waited for him at the bottom of the steps next to the new system.

Paul walked towards him.

But it does matter! he thought to himself.

How could it not? It has to matter! It has to!

Yes, it did! He worked too hard for it not to matter!

Paul braced himself as he teetered on the balance beam of logic.

"Good day, Mr. Quatro."

Elliot Richards was technically precise.

There was no room for kindness in his voice, no place for friendship. The only feeling in Elliot Richards' voice was, "Does it work?"

"Good day, Mr. Secretary."

Paul, too, sounded technical. He wanted to emulate the Secretary perfectly this morning.

"Are you prepared for the test?"

Elliot's voice was strained with anticipation, and Paul knew it.

They all knew it. Everybody in the department was at a high point of energy stress.

Everyone had a migraine headache, everyone was having difficulty breathing, everyone felt faint. Everyone teetered on the balance beam of logic.

"Yes," whispered Paul to the Secretary of Technology.

Everyone in the auditorium craned their heads trying to discern the conversation between the two most powerful men in the department, without success.

He noticed that John Malone stood just behind Elliot.

He had dark, sallow rings under his sunken eyes, and he appeared to have lost a lot of weight. The atmospheric collar around his neck was drenched with perspiration.

And then Paul smiled.

He didn't know why he did it, nor was he sure he actually smiled.

Later on he would visualize the effect of that smile, but by everyone's interpretation, Paul smiled directly at John Malone.

Maybe it was a facial twitch! Nonetheless, he smiled.

Everyone knew Paul and John were enemies, but the fact that Paul smiled was seen and understood by all as a calming force.

"Lights out!" Elliot Richards barked in a loud, cracking voice.

The lights at the Lincoln Memorial testing grounds grand auditorium blinked out.

As Paul opened his computer briefcase and took out the computerized oval container which held the computerized key to the new system, a strange shadow crossed his face.

His hands were wet as he took two deep breaths.

He felt a vacuum in his lungs.

For a moment he panicked as a bolt of pain ran up his right arm and traveled across his chest.

A bubble of blood rose on his fingertip from a cut he 'd gotten from the zipper on his atmospheric suit pocket.

As he observed the blood spurting gently across the top of the oval container, his legs began to go to rubber.

His equilibrium was malfunctional as he spun the computerized combination on the oval box.

He waited for the container to open. It didn't.

He'd dialed the wrong combination.

Every cell in his body fought panic as he summoned his last morsel of strength to try again.

He pressed the combination again and watched it spin around.

Black swirls danced before his eyes. He turned and caught Elliot Richards' face.

He looked like Rodan's The Devil.

Paul felt like falling…falling…falling through space.

The container made a neat little click as it snapped open.

A ray of light from the computerized key shot into the cornea of his left eye causing his head to straighten up. He felt as if he'd been given an injection of extra-high maximum potency vitamins.

His equilibrium stabilized, his breathing back to its regular rhythm, Paul felt awake and healthy, ready for anything.

He held the key to the new system over his head the way a big baller who had won the game for his team might hold the victory ball aloft for all to see.

He stepped onto the rotating oval platform and put his right hand on top of the new system. It felt cold.

It seemed massive, a frightening complexity of technology.

Paul knew…just one short-circuit…just one omission…one faulty part...one miscalculation...one mistake, and the new system wouldn't start.

He jammed the computer key into the computer keyhole.

The force of its entry generated a sexual vibration through Paul's loins.

He knew in an instant. He had turned on the new system.

He looked down and realized he had ejaculated all over his conservative suit pants.

The new system worked!

It purred in his ear…Paul could hear the audience applause but he was afraid to turn around...afraid everyone would see he had lost control at the very last second.

They were carrying Elliot Richards on their shoulders up the aisle steps.

He was being touched by all the technocrats. Many were on their knees crying.

Several had fainted and were being carried off by nursebots.

It didn't matter! The new system worked, and that was all that mattered!

Paul noticed John Malone was one of the young technocrats who was carrying Elliot Richards out of the auditorium.

He turned and stared at the new system.

He hated what it had done to him as he felt the stickiness of the ejaculation seep through his atmospheric bikini jock and spread a wide circle on his conservative atmospheric pants.

As he left the auditorium he removed his coat and held it in front of his trousers in an effort to obscure his stain.

As he descended the Lincoln Memorial stone steps he paused to look at the sixteenth President of the United States.

"Thank you, Mr. President," said Paul.

He knew he had been tested to the maximum of his being and he'd been able to withstand the pressure because of his logic!

Wasn't that something Abraham Lincoln would have understood?

He decided not to return to the office immediately. He needed time to sort through the activities of the morning.

He walked up Pennsylvania Avenue and stood across the street from the White House. How beautiful this replica of the original seemed to him!

It was complete with synthetic shrubs, golden brown oak leaves that had fallen realistically around the house, and a synthetic national Christmas tree which service robots were busily erecting.

Paul knew this would probably be the last year he'd see service robots at work. Holograms had moved in!

Much as Paul liked his household holograms, he had a wistful attachment to robots. They were old-fashioned, quaint and romantic.

He felt a little sad imagining life without robots.

He stopped in front of a bronze plaque which reminded everyone who saw it that at one time the Washington Monument had stood in its place.

The air was clean and crisp, forty-six degrees with a stiff breeze.

Paul felt a slight chill, but he was too embarrassed to put on his coat.

Somehow he wandered into the ruins of the old Supreme Court building.

A family of Injas asked if he would take their insta-photo, and for a brief moment he forgot about his trouser stain.

As he focused through the viewfinder he noticed they laughed and pointed at his trousers. Paul deliberately distorted the viewfinder to give them round eyes in retaliation.
The Department of Technology was suffering from mass hysteria.

The new system had worked in the test. Would it work on the projected date?

As soon as Paul entered the waiting room to his office Holly James's arms were around his neck, and she was kissing him.

He was so startled he opened his mouth and gave her the encouragement she needed to complete the move.

Her breath had a musky scent to it. Her tongue was thick. As soon as her hand brushed against the crotch of his trousers, he knew she could feel his ejaculation.

"Congratulations," she smiled.

She was happy he had had a successful climax.

Paul was not in the mood to play sex-o-tag with Holly that day, so he requested his afternoon transmissions.

Immediately, she straightened herself.

His cassettes were brought in as soon as she could get them.

She watched him disappear into his inner sanctum. She knew they would never mingle together, but the visualization was delicious.

He scanned each congratulatory transmission.

Every Assistant Undersecretary except John Malone had sent one. Every section chief and sub-section manager had sent one.

But the two transmissions which made him happiest he discovered last:

"With my deepest gratitude I want to send my congratulations. Please accept my apologies if I have caused you unfair criticism. Sincerely, Elliot."

By the tone of his transmission, Paul knew the Secretary had regained full confidence in him.

"The future is yours! Congratulations! I have always had the utmost confidence in you! Sincerely, Sam."

The old man's transmission had many hidden messages in it, and Paul knew it.

The Professor had never ended a transmission to him with a simple signature by first name.

Paul saw this signature as the Professor's indication he had at last accepted Paul as an equal, if not in wisdom, then at least as a colleague.

His worries began to disappear as he began to accept the new system as a viable solution to the trauma shock energy problems.

"The future is yours!" Professor Ludlum's statement made Paul feel as though he'd just been anointed with holy water.

He pressed the intercom button on his inner-office vid screen, and Miss James's proud smile came into bright focus.

"Yes, P.Q.?"

"Miss James, I want the complete transcription on holographic H-walls from A to Z transferred into my transcriber when you have time."

"You'll have it within five minutes." She flashed him those teeth.

299

He switched off the vid screen and leaned back into his chair. He was exhausted as Christmas music breezed through the open windows in his office.

Test day always signified the first day of the holiday season.

The refreshing rhythm of the music lifted Paul from his foul spirits in a much-needed respite.

He thought of the four-day weekend ahead.

As he made his way through the crowded hallway of the Department of Technology, the spirit of the season filled his heart.

Technocratic men and women, who just hours before had been on the verge of emotional collapse, were suddenly able to dance, sing, kiss and go shopping with renewed vigor and purpose.

Paul shuddered to think what it would have been like if the new system had failed.

As he stepped out of the pipeline and boarded the conveyor belt sidewalk, he felt a raindrop hit the tip of his nose. He raised his atmospheric trenchcoat collar and pulled down his fedora hood.

The drops came faster until they fell with lightning speed...faster than the conveyor belt moved!

He checked his computer watch and scanned the weathervane meter: 100 percent chance of rain, November twenty-second, twenty-third, twenty-fourth, twenty-fifth and twenty-sixth.

Of all weekends to get a rainstorm!

As he scurried up his plastic pathway he noticed the sprinkler system was dousing the emerald-green lawn with blue lubricant.

Paul dreaded the thought of confronting Delti with this mistake, but he knew he had to.

By the time Paul opened the door to his all-computerized house he was running a temperature of one hundred and three degrees.

"You're going to bed!"

Heleon's concern was so reassuring!

"I'm just tired, H," said Paul, knowing he was deathly ill.

He sneezed and had a coughing convulsion.

Heleon pressed her lips to his mouth and began to suck out the congestion that was causing Paul 's convulsion.

He immediately stopped coughing as she helped him across the living room towards bed.

"Where's Delti?" asked Paul.

He remembered the sprinkler system as he passed the H-wall.

For some reason the wall reminded him of the difficult strongman.

Quickly, Heleon decided to lie to Paul. She had never lied before, and she dreaded it, but she felt she had to in order to preserve the sanctity of the unit.

"He's in the attic organizing the illumination sockets."

301

There! Only half a lie, really.

Delti had been in the attic, and he had been organizing the tiny sockets, but she hadn't seen him for over an hour. Not since he dematerialized into the H-wall and said he was going to a meeting.

"I want to speak with him," Paul whispered weakly.

"First you get well, Paul," said Heleon.

She slipped her right arm around his waist as her left hand held his hand. He stood helplessly in the cosmetic room as Heleon carefully stripped off his rain-soaked clothes.

His body shook as his temperature took off on a roller coaster ride of feverish highs and bone-chilling sweats.

"The new system works," he coughed.

Heleon nodded as she held a spoon of steaming synthetic chicken soup to his lips.

"I know," she whispered back.

Delti had told her that afternoon. He'd told Pi, too.

Delti had found out from Beta. Both Heleon and Pi had been happy about the news but worried that Delti had been the one to tell them.

She watched Paul as he lay his head back on the air pillow and took a breath.

She could vibe the pillow cushioning the storm that raged inside him.

She knew there was no medicine to cure him, no vitamin that could impart better health.

He was exhausted and needed to rest. Nothing else would help him but sleep.

That night Paul had a fever dream. As he thrashed beside her, Heleon pressed her body against him to assuage the chaos; absorbed his sweats; stood watch over him as he writhed and cried.

She could see him dream through her ninth sense, but she couldn't save him from the demons that plagued him… Judgment Day is on its way…the echo slammed against Paul's eardrums, causing them to bleed…he climbed a jagged mountain full of thorns…broken glass and razor blades…all alive… scratching, slicing, cutting his hands and knees and ankles and feet as he climbed up a mountain of pain he could see the top… a warm, red glow…a peaceful vibration…and then a ghost… skeletons with swords…aberrations huge and small, powerful and deformed, warts…oozing boils…sores full of pus…He saw the ladder…the savior…the only one…and grabbed the rails… They were greased with blood…he stepped…the bottom rung…it broke…he pulled himself up, and up, and up with his hands…each rung breaking after he stepped to the next rung… the faster he climbed, the farther away from the top of the mountain…the rails of the ladder were scaly snakes with poisonous fangs snapping at his eyes…he slid…down the ladder…holding tightly, tightly, tightly to the rails…his hands were bleeding…the snakes at his fingers…his knuckles…his wrist…his elbows…he tumbled backwards, his back was stabbed…the thorns went through him…razor blades…broken glass…the top of the mountain…a warm, red glow, the peaceful vibration was becoming as small as the top of a computerized pin.

He had no hands...a flying monster had taken them...he had no
arms...they'd been swallowed...he had no feet...no legs...a torso
was left...and the monster gouged a thick piece of meat from
between his groin...his testicles exploded...his penis twisted and
screamed in horror as the flying monster shredded it in his
beak...his kidneys...his liver....his spleen...his heart were
flipped in the air, and the monster caught each on the tip of its
hairy tongue...let each roll down into the volcanic foulness of its
guts...falling faster...his bleeding eyes scanned a gold coffin
below...no hands...no feet...no heart...no penis...why my
penis? Paul cried out...Judgment Day...the voice...and he
passed the image...one hundred feet away from the gold coffin
...one hundred feet from the explosion of his head...he was
floating, and the monster's head was just a butterfly with day glo
rainbow veins...and he landed in a garden as the butterfly lit on
his vision to clear it from him...a magnificent waterfall lay
before him...horses, lambs, men and women frolicking naked in
a magical pond...no technology...no devices...no circuits...no
new systems...no pressure...just humanity...and he waited for
Heleon to step out of the waterfall, her hair wet, her lips moist...

"I love you." She gently pressed her lips against his.

"I love you, H."

He kissed from the dark and lightness of his soul and opened his
eyes. Heleon. Her lips caressed his as her naked body pressed
against him.

The dream was over. He was well.

"How long was I asleep?"

He sat up in the air bed and began to consume the fantastic array
of nourishment which Pi had prepared in his honor: fresh

strawberries flown in from the synthetic domed farm-op, blueberry bran waffles, a Denver omelette, muffins with juicy raisins, vitafee, orange juice, and a nine-pound raw porterhouse syntho steak.

For dessert Pi had prepared Paul's favorite: chocolate-chocolate-chocolate cheese cake with chocolate-chocolate-chocolate ice. Pi hadn't wanted to overdo it on the ice since the cake had been so dense. He knew Paul would understand.

"Twenty-one hours."

Heleon dabbed the bloody juice from Paul's chin with a cellophane napkin.

"Thanks!" he said.

"For what?" she asked.

"For being by my side."

He leaned forward and kissed her forehead affectionately.

She hoped he'd stay in bed all day, but Paul felt restless. He wanted to scan the H-wall transcription.

He could hear the rain beating down on the roof as Pi and Heleon helped him to the computer library.

I'm so weak! he thought as he placed the transferred cassette into the transcriber.

He turned to them.

"I'd like to be alone right now, if you don't mind."

The holograms nodded and left immediately, closing the library door.

Paul pressed the button on the transcriber and leaned back in his cushioned chair. What he was about to see would change his entire life.

"H-walls!..." The interrogator was the well-known bi-educator, Dr. Z. X. Quid from the Learning Garden, the also well-known home laboratory known for the construction and manufacture of H-walls.

"From the beginning was the invention!"

Dr. Unatin was the creator.

Dr. Gilbert Unatin's cassette album of images twirled in front of Paul's face.

Sam and Cille Unatin holding three-month-old Gilbert Unatin ...Five-year-old Gilbert Unatin rocking back and forth on a robotic rocking horse...Eleven-year-old Gilbert Unatin wearing an honorarium robe from the Institute of Technology...The youngest graduate in the history of the Institute... valedictorian ...maxim cum laude...Gilbert Unatin and the former Jean Kent, a nine-year-old Middle Judean Princess on their wedding day... years of public service...honors...awards...fame and fortune...A vid-news article about the brilliant young geneticist ...Dr. Unatin transfers genes from a wolf into a human embryo ...A mysterious child is born...an animalistic child with an I.Q. topping 500...with the strength of a carnivorous beast...Dr. Unatin is arrested for unethical practices in science against Mankind...A public trial...The death penalty...reprieved... pardoned...banishment...

And the cassette ended on the life and times of Dr. Gilbert Unatin.

The cassette disturbed Paul. How could a man of Dr. Unatin's notoriety be allowed employment at the Learning Garden, a publicly-funded, scientifically-computerized corporation?

Paul scanned the cassettes for more information on this man.

Outside the library door Heleon paced. She wanted to know what he was doing that she had been asked not to witness.

Pi had urged her to leave the controller alone, but she wouldn't listen. She felt he was rejecting her maintenance. She waited.

"Hologynic: inherited solely in the female line through transmission as a recessive factor in the nonhomologous portion of the X chromosome...Holographic metabolism...holographic myarian: having the muscle layer continuous or else divided into two longitudinal zones without true muscle cells...Hologamous: having gametes of essentially the same size and structural features as vegetative cells...Holocrine: producing a secretion containing disintegrated secretory cells...Holoblastic: having cleavage planes that divide the whole egg into distinct and separate blastomeres...Holmium: a metallic element of the rare earth group that occurs with yttrium and forms highly magnetic compounds..." The interrogator's voice was above reproach.

Paul's mind was racing as fast as the cassette scanner dealt images through the transcriber.

"Technology: the totality of the means employed to provide objects necessary for human sustenance and comfort...Tectum: the dorsal part of the mid-brain...Technetium: a metallic element obtained by bombarding molybdenum with deuterons or neutrons and in the fission of uranium...Computer: a

307

programmable electronic device that can store, retrieve and process data...Gene: an ???? as a computer that performs one or more functions for control or computation."

Then Paul saw the final epilogue of information which confirmed his visualization:

"Humaputer Genes: the crossover of computer hierarchical genes and human genes that creates a hereditary structure which is able to incubate into a technological specie capable of reproducing itself."

Paul stopped the cassette transcription. This was the most beautiful technological transcription he'd ever visualized.

Heleon had the genetic make-up of a human and a hologram …simultaneously.

She was the ultimate technological advancement! A new creation!

Yes…Paul was beginning to understand…As man evolved from an amoeba in the ocean, so did technology evolve from the primate tools employed by a cave man to its own species!

A species that could procreate with itself! Heleon!

Paul studied the remaining portions of the cassettes.

He realized that most of the H-walls were being sold in the stores without the ultimate holographic character capabilities.

Obviously, the creator wanted to train holograms to the ways of humans before allowing them to run rampant into society.

Paul knew that certain experimental models were being transplanted into the mainstream and that they were being monitored carefully.

They did not need the wall!

Paul wondered whether Heleon could leave the wall. Was she capable of procreation with him?

He scanned the H-wall cassettes but couldn't find an answer.

When he requested the list of models that were capable of this humanistic miracle-feat, he found access blocked by inter-status-symbols: "Top Secret Classification - Stay Back."

He wanted to transcribe the list anyway.

"Request Rejected."

He made a note to inquire about the information with understandable feelings of frustration brewing beneath his calm demeanor. Why wasn't his top-level technological status enough to get him through this computer red tape?

He subconsciously knew the answer: certain information was available only to the Secretary of Technology himself.

Paul yawned and stretched. He felt stiff!

He glanced at his watch and gasped. He'd been sitting for fifteen hours.

He walked to the library door.

"Heleon," he called, knowing she'd be there.

She was sitting on the floor, waiting. She jumped to her feet and flew into his arms.

"Everything is going to be perfect," he called softly into her sweet-smelling hair.

They danced around the hallway in childish joy. They were so glad to see each other after all these hours.

"Not right." Delti's voice was firm and cruel.

They looked up as the last blue smoke cleared. He had dematerialized before they could see him.

"Come back, Delti."

Paul was angry.

"Paul, D models have no visualization of love," said Heleon, her eyes wide and sad. She tried to calm Paul, but he was agitated.

"I must communicate with him," said Paul, as he headed up the hallway. Heleon followed.

"It won't do any good!" she cried, but Paul didn't listen.

Logic no longer applied to what had happened behind the walls of Paul's computer house in Computer Meadows.

He felt a connection to these holographic characters.

He knew, too, that they were the future of mankind, that man and the hologram together could attain Utopia and allow evolution its rightful conclusion on this battered planet, Earth.

Pi observed Paul as he put on the computer glove and pressed Delti's blue fingertip button.

The cherubic hologram was frightened for he knew, instinctively, that Delti was dangerous.

"Delti, I order you out of the wall!' commanded Paul.

His patience, Pi knew, was stretched thin.

Delti appeared on the first step pod, then descended to the second and finally settled in full color and dimension on the third.

"Sir, I obey your command."

Delti's stare was forceful, full of hate and arrogance. Paul gathered his strength and spoke.

"Delti, I want you to know you are welcome in this house."

"I obey your commands."

Delti's face bulged with taught muscles. Rage skittered crazily in his eyes.

"Yes, of course, you obey commands…We all have our place in this house…But, I do not want you to resent your position in the unit."

"I obey!"

He held his stand, folding his arms across his chest, taunting Paul with his superior strength...

"Then you may return to the wall!"

Paul was weakening under Delti's massive stare.

He pressed the blue button to dematerialize Delti, but Delti maintained his position on the third step pod.

Paul pressed the button several more times, but Delti would not go back into the wall.

The strongman began to laugh, a long, lugubrious laugh, as Paul continued to push the blue button in vain.

His terrifying bulk began to fade as he laughed on and on and on until slowly he'd gone from view.

Pi turned away from the frightening visualization. Chaos was imminent.

Without a word he returned to his kitchen and continued his maintenance, his heart heavy in his chest.

Heleon didn't know whether to tell Paul about Delti's disappearances and his meetings or not.

She was afraid any further awareness of the hologram evolution would threaten his life.

"D models are so boring." She tried to make light of the actualization.

"I can understand his frustration," said Paul, as she rubbed his hands. He appreciated her display of affection.

He felt he understood Delti's frustration. Here was a brand new species trying to find his proper place in the unit. An unsettling position for man -- and hologram to be in.

Paul could understand that!

It didn't occur to him that something far more dangerous was troubling Delti.

Although it rained all that weekend, Paul decided to take Heleon out. He wanted to further his experimentations with her away from the H-wall.

They decided to go shopping for a synthetic Christmas tree at the Computer Meadows shopping arcade.

Heleon was both nervous and excited as she pulled Mary Quatro's raincoat and rain boots out of the once forbidden closet.

Pi was concerned about their outing and told them so. He didn't want a repeat of what happened at the Bork's wedding anniversary party.

But Paul felt strongly that everything would be fine.

Heleon had never felt rain before. As soon as it splashed against her bare hand it sizzled and evaporated!

Paul showed her how to wear the gloves Mary had left in the coat pockets. Heleon was amazed at what a difference gloves made.

She wondered if they made gloves for faces, too, as stray raindrops dashed and sizzled against her cheeks.

Pedestrians stared at them along the way, and snide whispers followed them everywhere.

One obviously spoiled tweenage girl stuck an accusing finger in Heleon's face and screeched, "Look, Mommy! A hollygrammy!"

Paul pushed the girl's finger away from Heleon's face and led her away.

Both the girl and her mother shouted obscenities after them as they disappeared into the crowd.

Somehow, and in spite of the commotion over and prejudice against "mixed couples," Paul and Heleon managed to enjoy themselves.

Only once, when an old-world shopkeeper refused to sell them Christmas decorations, did Heleon cry.

She couldn't understand the anger against hologram/human attachment.

She wanted to know everything about Christmas, what it meant, how long it had been celebrated, and why people bought trees and exchanged presents.

When Paul introduced her to the mall's Santa Claus she sat in his lap and gleefully told him what she wanted this year: "Paul!" she announced happily.

The old Santa pinched her bottom, and she leaped out of his lap, squealing.

Paul felt like kicking the ancient geezer in the shin but let it go for the sake of Christmas.

"What do you want for Christmas?" she asked Paul, as together they set about decorating Paul's Christmas tree.

"I haven't thought about it," said Paul, stringing synthetic cranberries across the synthetic tree.

He glanced at Heleon. Her face was drawn in sadness.

"What's wrong, H?"

"You don't want me for Christmas?"

Paul lay the last string of cranberries on the tree and took a deep breath.

"Yes, I want you, H, for Christmas."

He took her in his arms and kissed her eyelids, both sides of her face, under her chin, the side of her neck and then nibbled on her earlobe, guiding his tongue around her smoothly curved ears.

Then he kissed her eyelids a second time, gave her a quick kiss on the tip of her nose and finally pressed his mouth against her warm, full lips.

Her figure melted into the strength of his body.

He began to be aroused.

He wanted to lift her inchy skirt up and pull down her synthetic mink panties that once belonged to Mary. He wanted to drop to his knees and press his face inside her luscious sex, insert his tongue into her warm, sweet vagina. He could smell her being this close.

His penis hardened as she pressed her hips against his and began a soft, rhythmic movement against his hips. He placed his hands inside her panties and felt her firm, well-rounded buttocks. His fingers pulled her sex apart, probing and pressing,

315

inserting, searching, always searching for that climax that brought them home, together…relief.

Whether he was pipeing to work, riding the conveyor walk at the department, in a conference, speaking on the vid phone or giving Miss James an important transcription, he couldn't get Heleon out of his visualizations.

He couldn't stop these intense urges towards her.

Sometimes the itch between his legs was unbearable.

"Sir, your big ball game is on!"

Pi entered the living room and couldn't tell what they were doing on the other side of the Christmas tree.

Paul had asked Pi to remind him when the game was about to begin.

Heleon giggled.

"What bad timing!" said Paul.

His response confused Pi. What could the controller possibly be up to now?

"Sir, I have the popcorn ready," Pi continued.

He took several more steps towards the Christmas tree, and then all at once he understood: Heleon was pulling up her mink panties!

"Greene's got the ball…Major Elias takes the crash and elbows a piledriver…Hancock…the all-star sticker throws his spear…it's a miss…out of bounds…Chicago! Evelyn takes the inbound

316

kick...Benny heaves his spike...The Chicago kicker's feet are blown apart. No point.

Washington's ball. Ronnie Chrome takes the slam. He punches his way through the circle...Bukowski, the behemoth grinder for Chicago, leaps in front of the all-star jammer... Chrome is down! No!...he's back up...Bukowski is hurt... Yes! He's hurt! Chrome is going to score...He's at the two hundred line...Two-fifty! Three hundred! He's going to score!"

Paul leaped to his feet and shouted encouragement to Ronnie Chrome.

"Go, Ronnie! Go! Score! Score! Score! Score!"

And then Heleon and Pi jumped to their feet screaming and shouting their encouragement.

"Go, Ronnie! Go!"

Pi was enamored of Ronnie Chrome's physique.

"Score! Score! Score!"

Heleon jumped up and down, knocking the popcorn out of Paul's bowl.

"Ronnie Chrome has scored," came the announcer's silken voice. He was obviously excited, too.

Paul, Heleon and Pi hugged each other in spontaneous ecstasy.

"We've scored!" Paul shouted.

"We've scored!" echoed Heleon as she kissed him.

317

"Ronnie scored! We've scored!"

Pi was so overwhelmed he had to sit down.

But there was only one problem: no matter how many times Heleon and Pi watched the game with Paul they couldn't understand how it was played!

With thirty-three players on each team it could get pretty confusing, thought Heleon to herself.

Each player holding onto his own computerized technological device with its own purpose...that was difficult enough to comprehend when you didn't even understand the function of the player!

Each time a big ball match came on the tube, Paul would try to explain it.

"There are thirty-three players on each side. Each team is organized into four, eight-number squads. The Major directs all four squads which include the Score Squad, the Defense Squad, the Hit Squad and the Killer Squad."

Pi and Heleon understood the breakdown and organization of the four, eight-member squads. They understood that the Major directs the coordination of the squad.

But when it came to sluggers, strikers, punchers, slatters, blasters and thumbers they got confused.

"For instance," Paul paused and collected himself.

How could he explain it to them? In the end he realized he couldn't, but it didn't matter at all.

Pi and Heleon shouted down the referees when a bad judgment call was made; they booed an opposing player when he made a great play against their favorite team, the Washington Technicals; and they wept for joy when the Technicals won, because they knew when the Technicals won, Paul was happy.

"The Ballbearings have the big ball on the Technicals' two hundred yard line...It's a fake...No, it's a reverse...Overy has the ball...She hikes it to Winston...He slams it over Hoskin's head...Harsalis is speared in the neck...Rosemary just took a crowbar in the hose...Winston is breaking through the Defense Squad's curtain...He climbs over the piledriver...He batters, one, two, three punchers...Winston is going all the way...Oh no! Ronnie Chrome has taken his computer saw and cut off Winston's head! Time out! Washington's ball!"

"What's it like inside the wall?"

Paul rolled over on his side and whispered into Heleon's ear.

They had spent the afternoon watching the big ball game and eating popcorn.

Pi had prepared a magnificent dinner of synthetic swordfish, corn on the cob, coleslaw and sourdough biscuits.

For dessert he had baked a synthetic brandy custard cake with whipped cream frosting.

Heleon felt his stomach against her back. His penis was wedged comfortably between the crevice of her buttocks as his hand gently stroked her right nipple. They had finished making love for the thirteenth time.

Heleon found it hard to communicate in human words the visualization of her actualization inside the wall.

319

They lay there, gazing at each other, for over an hour, the warm breeze from the air bed sighing gently over their bodies.

Paul could imagine the feeling of dematerialization from his experiences on the pipeline each morning as he went to work, but· the sensation he sensed from Heleon and the wall was different.

Dematerializing through the pipeline felt numb. From the moment you entered the pipeline until the moment you materialized at your destination you had no visualization at all.

The sensation Heleon transmitted expressed consciousness: supreme visualization to a heightened level which Paul had never imagined could exist.

He wondered if she was hiding something from him. He suspected she was.

He probed her seventh, eighth and ninth senses. He didn't probe her tenth.

She wouldn't give it over.

If he could have had access, he would have discovered the truth about Delti's disappearances...about the meetings he attended at the Techo department store...about the dimension Beta had transmitted into their visualization.

Paul drifted into a deep sleep. He was satisfied, satiated and serene.

Even Mary couldn't send me off to dreamland quite so well, he thought, as he closed his eyes for the night.

Heleon kissed them shut and lay her face close to his heart. She loved to hear it beat.

What Paul and Heleon didn't know was that Delti had been observing them all night.

He had hidden inside the circuitry of the vid screen over the air bed and watched them as they had sex thirteen times. He had never visualized such a thing.

At first the sight was horrifying to him, but he soon became jealous of the freedom they experienced together.

Pleasure was a vibration Delti could not understand.

"I shall have you, Heleon," muttered the strongman through clenched teeth.

The next morning Paul asked Heleon if she'd like to go to church with him.

Heleon wondered what "church" was. She asked Pi to explain.

"I think it's a place where the controller goes to shop!" he whispered.

"Shop for what?" Heleon was puzzled.

Pi just smiled and shrugged. He didn't know.

The church was the weirdest actualization of Heleon's young life.

Paul said it was called a vid cathedral, and it was awesome in its solitude.

Not even the H-wall could compare to such a vibration.

When the vid priest appeared on the giant screen behind the altar and delivered his sermon, Heleon was moved to energy tears that softly splashed on the little computer Bible she held on her lap.

"The words of a whisperer are like delicious morsels."

The vid priest's words seeped into her visualization.

"They go down into the inner parts of the body."

Heleon flashed on Paul's flesh.

"Like the glaze covering an earthen vessel...are smooth lips with an evil heart...he who hates dissembles with his lips...and harbors deceit in his heart...when he speaks graciously, believe him not...for there are seven abominations in his heart though his hatred be covered up with guile...his wickedness will be exposed in the assembly...and he who discards a pit will fall into one...a stone will come back upon he who casts it forth..."

Paul could feel the hatred in the parishioners' glances as they squirmed in their pews to get a better look at Heleon. Happily, she was unaware of their negative vibes.

"How abnormal," they whispered.

As they walked out of the cathedral Heleon noticed that Paul dropped a credit card into the computer offering. She wondered what the vid priest meant by saying, "He who hates dissembles with his lips."

She was overwhelmed with questions. Paul attempted to interpret the sermon, and at times he succeeded.

In the end, though, Heleon did not totally understand the meaning of any of the vid priest's words.

Still, and in spite of that disturbing aspect, she liked church. Her vibes basked in its essence as, almost in mockery of the priest, she reveled in her love for mankind.

Even if the vid priest hadn't said such awful things she would have felt the true vibrations of the church, for she had no awareness of hate in her pulse...she didn't know about wickedness...or guile and, because she didn't have a heart, she couldn't even understand the concept of "seven abominations!"

Heleon didn't have a heart, she had a pulse!

As Paul and Heleon walked the twenty blocks back home they held hands quietly without speaking.

It was often this way for them, and they could spend long periods without words. They didn't need them much, anyway. Their sixth sense prevailed.

Delti could see Heleon kissing Paul goodbye as he left for the department on the morning of Tuesday, November twenty-sixth. His energy tensed as he caught their warm vibrations.

"Maintenance to the controller!"

His contemptuous voice jolted Heleon out of her serene pulse. She turned around and faced Delti, feeling a need to defend herself and her poor, dear maintenance.

"Sir is a good technocrat!" she hissed.

She turned to walk away from him, but his bad vibes blocked her passage.

"Humans are an inferior species," he breathed down at her. He desired to take her passion.

"Delti, you shouldn't visualize such negative energy."

How she despised his arrogance!

He wanted to take her in his arms and express his true vibrations, but he was unprepared for such a bold actualization.

"Why? Because I am a hologram and have no rights?"

He let her brush him aside as she entered the living room to escape his disturbing vibrations. He followed her until she spun around, frightened.

"We were created to maintain mankind!"

He grabbed her and forced his lips against her.

She slapped him hard, causing red-hot sparks to ricochet off his face. He let her go.

He was more surprised than hurt, more embarrassed than frightened.

"Someday mankind shall serve us!"

He looked at her for what seemed to Heleon to be eons. He had the strangest expression on his face as he dematerialized back into the wall.

The vibrations he left behind were confused and searching.

Pi reached to put his arm around Heleon as she struggled to maintain composure.

"I fear Delti is flawed in his purpose," he said protectively.

Heleon pressed her face against his chest as tears of energy droplets streamed down her face.

"On behalf of the Techno department stores, I present to you, Mrs. President, our one millionth H-wall!"

Paul observed Howard Bork as he made his presentation to President Ricarda from his office computer desk vid screen.

The presentation was being televised over the multi-national channels.

Paul couldn't help but be a little impressed.

His former friend had been promoted to senior vice president in charge of all Techno department stores! He was Up!

"Thank you, Mr. Bork. Although…it saddens me to visualize the actualization that service robots are no longer needed. I want to thank each and every one of you who helped contribute to the rebuilding of not only our nation but all nations of the World Unity Council. Evolution, when directed in a positive path, can only be perceived and experienced as a celebration. I accept this H-wall on behalf of positive evolution. I know how much the holographic characters mean to all of you out there, and I know, too, they will take their rightful place on the evolutionary ladder of success," said President Ricarda.

Paul flicked the transmission off and pressed the mobility button on the armrest of his computerized chair. It turned and positioned him toward Miss Holly James, who had just entered the office.

"Your request for the H-wall priority cassette has been denied."

She was as surprised as he was.

"Denied!"

Paul leaned forward in his computerized chair.

"Only the Secretary of Technology has a clearance code," said Miss James, as she placed the denied trans- mission cassette on Paul's desk.

"Do you wish for me to put a transmission in to the Secretary?"

She waited for his response.

"No!"

He decided not to press the interrogation.

He pressed the mobility button as Miss James turned to leave, rotating the chair ninety degrees.

He flicked on his personal vid screen.

He knew that when he became Secretary of Technology he would have full access to all top-secret cassettes.

He scanned the morning transmissions as he pondered the virtues of logic.

One cassette caught his eye.

"Your presence at the annual test tube orphanage awards dinner as an honored guest is hereby transmitted to Paul Quatro, Undersecretary of Technology, December twenty-fourth."

The announcer was S.M. Beckett, the Principal of the orphanage. Always proper, always firm, always with a sense of play, Mr. S.M. Beckett had not changed over the years.

Oh, his eyebrows were thicker, the wrinkles under his eyes were more wrinkled. But his voice still resonated with kindness.

Paul took his computer pen and wrote down the date in his computerized notebook.

He thought of Lothar and Zelman. He wondered whether they'd be at the awards dinner.

"Miss James, please contact Lord Edwin Lothar and Monty Zelman on my multiple private vid screen."

He wanted to check in with his buddies!

"I'm afraid Monsieur Zelman is unavailable for transmission."

The holographic character who spoke to him was an L model with a French accent.

L models were trained in the laboratory sciences.

They were very intelligent, proper in etiquette and yet they seemed cold.

"Tell him Paul Quatro is transmitting."

"I'm sorry. Monsieur has given strict instructions."

Paul remembered how he had tricked service robots into countermanding their original instructions.

He let out an exasperated sigh.

No such luck with holograms!

"Yes, well, tell him I transmitted."

Paul couldn't hide the frustration in his voice.

But why shouldn't Zelman have an H-wall? Everyone else had one! Including Paul!

"Paul! So good of you to transmit! How are you?"

Lothar's voice was full of opiates.

He was seated on an ancient elephant-tusk throne from a long-annihilated tribe of Afrikaniker warriors.

They stood in a high-tech salon which Lothar had constructed on the third floor of the former Smithsonian.

Seated in the lotus blossom position were the two blue-eyed, blonde-haired nine-year-old genius nymphets.
They were barechested and wore colorful Inja skirts. Their tiny nipples were painted pink and powder blue as were their lips and eyelids.

"Lothar, Did you receive Principal Beckett's invitation to the test tube orphanage's awards ceremonies?"

Paul observed the richly-brocaded black-and-gold silk pajamas from Middle Judea which Lothar wore.

There was certainly nothing conservative about Lothar!

"But, of course! I wouldn't miss Zelman getting his award for anything...for worthwhile contributions to society..." mused Lothar.

The five-time Golden Wrench award winner sniffed.

"I was only 'Inventor of the Year'..." he said, reaching for a day glo lavender-and-yellow opiated hanky.

His head nodded back, and his eyelids drooped.

"I didn't know Zelman was getting an award!"

Paul waited for over two minutes for Lothar to respond to his exclamation.

"You know how he always shined Beckett's slippers," growled Lothar.

He sounded contemptuous. Paul wondered if Lothar really felt contemptuous or if the opiates had exaggerated his tendency to jealousy.

"We all shined Beckett's slippers," said Paul, trying to make light of their strained communication.

"None brighter than that pudgy little syntheticist!" snorted Lothar.

He took a lime-green hanky from the little nymphet on his left and handed the day glo lavender-and- yellow hanky to the little nymphet on the right.

The one on the right disposed of the used hanky in a round, marble urn between her lotus-blossom feet. Paul noticed it was full of used hankies.

"Where is Zelman?"

Paul had never heard Lothar so unhappy...so bitter. He felt bad for his friend.

"Edwin, where is Zelman?" mimicked the Grand Potentate.

It was obvious to Paul that Lothar was very, very down.

His chin was resting on his chest, and mucus dripped from his nostrils. His eyelids closed over the most bloodshot, watery eyes Paul had ever imagined.

"Lothar! Lothar! Wake up!"

But the genius pinhead couldn't hear Paul's sincere shouts.

"Lothar!"

And then the little nymphet on the right picked up the marble urn with the disposable hankies and flung it at the vid screen, cracking the pyrex. Many of the hankies stuck to the screen. Then the transmission went blank.

Paul panicked and asked Miss James to put through a second transmission, then a third transmission.

But Lothar wouldn' t accept the communication.

"P.Q., he doesn't seem to be answering."

"Then that will be all for today, Miss James. You may go to noon brunch."

He pressed the mobility button with his elbow, and the computer chair rotated another forty-five degrees.

Paul was able to scan one hundred and eighty degrees of the Washington, D.C. skyline. It was a beautiful, crisp, clear day!

Pedestrians glided along the conveyor walks carrying armloads of Christmas presents.

The new system had tested successfully, and an atmosphere of celebration still rang out through the land, almost three weeks since the happy day!

The only tension that remained was the tension of anticipation: the Inaugural submission had to be made on January first.

Paul breathed a secret sigh of relief remembering Lothar's raygun. He was glad Lothar hadn't asked him about it. He hadn't figured out a use for it yet.

December was the most energetic month of the year, according to Paul.

Once the new system had been successfully tested, all visualization was then immediately directed toward the departmental parties held annually by each section and sub-section.

The Secretary of Technology's ball, which came last, was held at his estate in Middleburg, Virginia, where, it was said, horses once roamed those magnificent hills.

This year the season promised to be especially potent with the added ingredient of the election looming seductively seven days hence. January seventh…just one week after Elliot' s bash!

Everybody voted on Election Day! It was a law!

And just in case you didn't make it in the physical sense, a "death law" required each citizen to cast a "death ballot" so that, in the event of their passing, a vote could be cast in their memory.

Post trauma-shock citizens of the world were convinced that if the citizens of the twentieth century had voted there would never have even been The Great Trauma Shock to begin with.

The mystery of its occurrence had yet to be solved as decade after decade political scientists conducted new interrogations in what appeared to be eternally futile efforts to understand the origins of that horrifying event.

December was also one of the most boring times at the department.

On several occasions Paul piped over to the Lincoln Memorial test grounds and looked in on the new system. Once he even held the key.

And on another occasion he felt the strong urge to re-test the new system, but he knew re-testing was against regulations.

He evaporated that visualization almost as soon as he'd conceived it.

Still, later on he found himself wondering why the new system was tested only once.

Such an important contribution to society, thought Paul, should be tested again and again and again in order to ensure its safety.

But he knew, in spite of the thoughts, that part of the challenge in being a technocrat was the ultimate trust which the citizens had bestowed upon the government.

The logic, the meticulous absolutism was constantly under the glaring gaze of a test interrogation.

In the end the technocrats always came through for the citizens. And why shouldn't they? The Department of Technology was the most successful department in the whole government!

Paul made a mental note for himself: when he became Secretary of Technology he would make certain changes in the department.

As a member of the Together Generation he felt it was his responsibility to help the world evolve into a Utopian state.

Yes!

Paul felt good as his thoughts moved quickly through his brain.

He had read that morning in the Computer News that Elliot Richards was six percentage points ahead of President Ricarda.

Somehow, the computer journalist had gotten certain information which stated that the new system worked.

Just what the Secretary needed to become President of the United States...

With so much extra time on his hands, Paul was able to take an hour off from work to go shopping since most of the technocrats in the department were working only half days during the December lull.

"Would Madame like an atmospheric five-piece leisure suit?"

The holographic salesman wrung his hands with anticipation of a sale as the holographic fashion model materialized, twirling magnificently, on the first step pod of the fashion H-wall.

She looked a little like Heleon except she was skinnier…more made up.

She strutted towards Paul, stopping to strike dramatic poses at perfectly-timed intervals.

Paul found himself wondering if Heleon would walk like that if she put on the leisure suit.

"No. It's not her," said Paul with conviction.

He had to smile to himself. If only they knew he was buying clothes for a hologram!

"I see!" said the hologram.

His grin indicated he'd penetrated Paul's thoughts.

Paul glared back at the salesman who continued to rub his hands together in a most unattractive way.

"Thank you for your help," he said, barely moving his lips.

He turned and left the showroom.

"Do not run away!" called the hologram salesman.

"We have many designs for the abnormal..."

Paul could hear him cackling as he continued down the boulevard.

Everywhere Paul shopped he was waited on by a holographic salesperson.

He hated salespeople!

They were always trying to sell some new and completely useless technological device to the department...always pushing something ridiculous on an otherwise perfectly functional person ...always there with that sales smile.

He was amazed at how quickly the holograms had taken over the functions of the service robots. It seemed they'd appeared literally overnight.

How did that happen? It was obvious that holograms were most efficient...that they even had charm!

Although sometimes they seemed a little cold...But perhaps that was just due to their high level of intelligence.

In fact, thought Paul to himself, holograms are their own species!

But it never occurred to Paul that they might want their own rights.

Besides, he thought, as he rounded a curve in the sidewalk, technology was an evolution designed to serve mankind.

Even if technology designed a species which would procreate, the species would remain a technological species. And as long as they remained so, their duties would remain in service to mankind.

Yet…he sensed a certain uneasiness lately…as if they might be up to something.

He knew the citizens trusted their holograms the way they'd trusted their robots for over two hundred and fifty years.

Even before trauma shock there had been robots!

Of course, robots hadn't made any terribly important contributions, mind you, but in a way -- in a very quiet, unspoken way -- it was the robots who somehow helped men evolve through trauma shock.

Paul shook for a minute as a lightning bolt of sadness streaked through him.

He knew robots wouldn't be coming along with mankind towards Utopia -- a Utopia that they, too, had hoped for in the name of their programmers.

He could visualize Utopia -- a certain portion of it set aside for the beloved robots -- even if they weren't needed when the Final Generation entered the pearly gates of the Holy Zone.

Robots deserved recognition! As Secretary of Technology he would be sure to lobby on their behalf.

"That will be one thousand bank credits."

The holographic saleswoman handed Paul the computer pen and a salespad. She needed his signature. He signed with a proud flourish.

He had bought Heleon a magnificent three- piece erotic nightgown complete with spiked heels and lace gloves. The nightgown was see-through with a beautiful butterfly-wing design that reflected all the colors of a rainbow.

Paul had become extremely aroused when the holographic fashion models stepped out of the H-wall and strutted their wares around him.

Each model was more seductive than the next.

Each wore a more daring, more erotic nightgown than the next.

In the end Paul had been so excited it had taken him over ten minutes to find his wallet!

The saleslady was used to such antics as most men reacted the way Paul did. But none were quite so excitable as this man.

Most felt embarrassed that a holographic woman could turn them on so explicitly. But not this one! She couldn't help but smile to herself.

"Thank you for your help," said Paul, obviously embarrassed.

He did everything he could to shut his visualization down from the holographic saleslady's eighth sense, but without success. "I hope you enjoy her as much as she enjoys you!" beamed the saleslady as she handed Paul the gift-wrapped box.

"I'm sure we will," said Paul proudly, as doubts and fears about Heleon began to further recede.

His honesty obviously shocked the saleslady.

337

Human kindness, not to mention love or pride, had not been consciously created as part of the hologram's system.

They had been created for total maintenance. In this regard, they could be very immature when it came to human emotion.

Paul discovered this with Heleon, and he also observed Pi's nervousness when trying to express his true vibrations.

Certainly, Delti took the computer cake overall!

Paul thought he was the most immature hologram he had ever visualized. He was so strong physically but so weak when it came to communication!

The holograph saleslady was taking notes as Paul left her shop.

She wrote down his name and address so it could be added to the "list" that was being assembled at the meetings.

"Have you discovered the purpose?" Lothar grumbled.

He sipped a rather inexpensive goblet of vitavino.

"No," Paul whispered back.

The annual Test Tube Awards ceremony was underway.

December twenty-fourth, the date of the ceremonies, was a date that was remembered as the anniversary of trauma shock.

December twenty-fourth, therefore, had been officially pronounced as Trauma Shock Day.

It was a world holiday.

All credit banks, computer schools, governmental departments and pleasure resorts were officially closed.

Every citizen wore a black-and-blue and blood-red armband.

Trauma Shock Day was a day of great sobriety.

It was a time when citizens were encouraged to visualize the pain mankind had actualized on itself.

It was a day set aside for award-giving...for honoring those who had made the most important contributions to their society.

"He is a man who was incubated in this very school, from a seed in a test tube to a responsive adolescent. Courtesy was his attitude. He was always polite to his teachers."

The speaker at the computer podium was R. Bennet Crawford, Assistant Vice Tutor at the test tube orphanage.

Paul and Lothar had driven him up a computer circuit more than once during their escapades at the "Big O," as they liked to refer to their origins.

Both Paul and Lothar sat at the "most-honored" table which faced the auditorium guests.

They had come to bear witness to the greatness of Monty Zelman, inventor of the Root of Immortality...the High Puba of Up...the finest syntheticist in the world.

"I remember young Zelman as if it were only yesterday. He was just a pudgy-faced boy who always had his nose inside a computer bank!" said a blubbery-looking woman who sat nearby.

339

"If only she knew where pudgy old Zelman's nose has been lately!" said Lothar, out of the side of his mouth. He elbowed Paul in the ribs.

"Shhhhh!"

Paul didn't find Lothar's loose tongue particularly appropriate on this somber occasion. Trauma Shock Day had always meant a great deal to Paul.

"It gives me honored pleasure to introduce you to the most revered tutor of tutors, principal of all principals, the founder and keeper of the test tube orphanage, S.M. Beckett!"

Everyone jumped to their feet, applauding wildly.

As they waited for Zelman to make what Paul knew would be a flamboyant entrance, he noticed Lothar dabbing both nostrils with a pink hanky.

As he dabbed, his eyes grew watery, and he began to laugh. Paul quickly grabbed Lothar and pulled him to his feet.

"Bravo! Bravo!" shouted Lothar.

It was obvious he was opiated to the gills as he shouted more loudly than everyone else.

Suddenly, he stopped cheering and began rubbing his face as if consumed with some weird, animalistic anxiety.

"Control yourself! " barked Paul.

Lothar looked at him with the ruined eyes of a spoiled child.

"Find a purpose for my raygun, or I'm ruined," he moaned.

He slipped out of Paul's grasp and thumped to the cushioned chair.

Paul could feel Principal Beckett's disapproving glare as his beloved Professor strolled to the computer podium and adjusted his eleven-D computer bifocals.

Paul shook Lothar, but nothing worked.

The once-brilliant inventor and five-time winner of the Golden Wrench Award was sucking his thumb and rolling his eyes in a circle like a circus robot clown!

As R. Bennet Crawford took his seat next to Paul, Lothar stuck his foot out and kicked him in the seat of his pants. All the students laughed at Lothar's Up gesture.

Principal Beckett hushed the audience and began his speech.

"I stand before this procession of past and present students with great sobriety in my visualization. Let us never forget Trauma Shock Day. Although there are some who believe trauma shock could have been avoided, I am of the opinion that its occurrence was inevitable. Evolution occurs only through trauma and sacrifice. I believe it is through this sacrifice that great advances are made in the name of humanity. With these advances comes a creation and a contribution towards a better future for ourselves, our children and our children's children.

A society cannot evolve without a contribution from each individual. While some contribute more than others, it is important to note that even the smallest contribution to our world matters. It matters. Montgomery Zelman has not only contributed to our society in a generous and profitable way, but he has given us the actualization of the test tube baby. I would

341

expect. nothing less from all of my students both past and present than to follow Mr. Zelman's example of sacrifice and good citizenship. It is an honor to honor this year's recipient of the Trauma Shock Award, Mr. M. Zelman!"

Principal Beckett folded his eleven-D computer bifocals and lifted the five-pound synthetic eyeball trophy so that the entire auditorium could see it, the symbol of trauma shock!

The auditorium fell deathly silent. Everyone waited for Zelman, the High Puba of Up, to emerge on the stage and receive his award.

Suddenly, Lothar stood up and leaped across the table, knocking R. Bennet Crawford off his chair and onto the floor.

"Lothar!" yelled Paul.

But he couldn't stop his friend.

Then someone spotted Zelman squirming across the floor like putrified computer squish…stark naked except for a pink bow that had been gaily tied around his penis. An opiated hanky dangled from his nose.

"I deserve the award! " declared Lothar, as he yanked the five-pound synthetic eyeball award from Professor Beckett's hand.

"Lothar, take your seat immediately," roared Beckett.

"I'm a centipede! I'm a centipede!" squeaked Zelman, as he wiggled toward the podium on the shiny floor.

Paul watched both Lothar and Zelman with heartbroken disgust.

342

His two best friends were making fools of themselves in front of an audience of people who admired, revered, very nearly worshiped them!

It took seven students to subdue Lord Lothar when they finally caught him.

He fainted as they gently tugged the trophy from his sticky, quivering hands.

As he felt the trophy slipping through his fingers, Lothar saw himself naked, prostrate on a wheel, his hands and feet bleeding from the nails that had been driven through.

As he suffered, he imagined a thorny computer circuit had been wrapped around his head. It pulsed and stabbed his mind with very sharp sticks of knowledge.

"What is the purpose? What is the purpose?" Lothar's mind was an echo of questions as he suffered.

"Will he be all right, Doctor?"

Paul stood over Lothar as his friend rested in the orphanage infirmary.

Zelman slept in the bed next to Lothar. Both had been given strong sedatives.

"Only a cortex probe can determine that!" said the doctor as he closed his computer bag.

Paul knew the doctor detested him because of his close association with Lothar and Zelman.

He watched the vid screen as it monitored all their bodily functions. Then he looked at Lothar and Zelman.

Zelman wore a smile of contentment as he murmured, "Go west! Go west!"

Paul wondered what he meant.

To go west of Washington was to go toward the uninhabitable regions of Earth. Nobody did that. To go west of Washington just wasn't done.

"Go west!"

Zelman licked his lips and laughed.

But Paul knew it was against the law.

He turned and looked at Lothar, the once handsome pipeline inventor.

His face twitched and contorted as he breathed in what appeared to be some pain. He looked a million years old as he entered no more than the twilight of his youth.

"Such a waste!"

Paul was startled by Principal Beckett's comment.

He turned around and faced the man who had brought him up, the man who had instilled in him the desire to contribute.

"They've been under incredible pressure!" said Paul, trying to protect his friends. But he knew the tutor of tutors was right.

Lothar and Zelman were wasting away into opiated ruin.

"To live life without pressure is to live without contributing," said Beckett. Obviously, he felt there was no excuse.

"But they have contributed!"

Paul attempted to build a case.

"It's not what you contributed yesterday but that what you contribute is a true contribution. Still, I can understand your feelings of loyalty. In spite of those feelings, Paul, you must never let friendship blind your purpose."

Principal Beckett took a peaceful breath as he placed his hands on Zelman and Lothar's foreheads.

He closed his eyes and leaned back as Paul watched the old man perform his strange ritual.

He knew Principal Beckett was a man of many mysteries. He had witnessed his fantastic visualizations as a youngster while he'd been in the orphanage.

The Principal's wisdom had flourished especially well in the classroom, like an oasis in the desert of youth.

Paul didn't know very much about S.M. Beckett, where he came from or what his life had been before he became Principal of the test tube orphanage.

There were rumors he'd once been a computer trader, an ambassador to South Mexo and the inventor of the multi-national vid channel, but nothing was ever verified.

In fact, nobody really cared because the Principal was S.M. Beckett, Principal, loved and respected by all.

But the language he spoke as he pressed his hands against Zelman and Lothar's foreheads was strange.

As he pressed against them, they began to sweat, and bloody mucous started to drain from their eyes, ears and noses. Their bodies shook and convulsed.

Zelman's smile seemed to be laughing at the pain that was coursing its way through his cells.

Lothar gasped for air, choking and gurgling on his own saliva.

It seemed as if both of them would have flopped off their air beds and landed hard on the floor had they not been strapped down.

When they awoke, both were like little boys who had been mischievous. Neither one had been sober for over a year.

Principal Beckett admonished them for wasting their lives and being a detriment to society.

"I'm sorry, Principal Beckett," said Zelman, as he kissed the old man's hand.

"It won't happen again, sir," said Lothar who, though not the humblest of men, had genuine tears of regret in his eyes.

He kissed the Principal's other hand. He turned to Zelman.

"You never should have invented the opiated hanky," he shrilled, slapping Zelman across the face.

Zelman was surprised, but not hurt.

"Not all hankies are opiated," he said, turning to Principal Beckett to pursue the matter.

The Principal wasn't interested.

"You don't deserve the Trauma Shock Day award," he declared with conviction.

"I am not deserving." Zelman mumbled meekly.

"You two have disappointed all of us at the orphanage. You've compromised our integrity."

"But, Principal Beckett! We have contributed!" said Lothar.

"Oh, you have, have you?" said the Principal as he approached Lothar with his fist clenched.

Before Lothar could say "Jack the robot" the Principal had flicked hard on the Grand Potentate of Up's Roman nose.

"Ouuuuchhhhhhh!" bellowed Lothar, cupping his nose in his hand.

"Paul! Tell Principal Beckett about me...my...my..." and then he stopped himself.

He knew it was useless to try to explain to the old man about his invention -- the invention that had no purpose. Explaining it could only dig him further into the circuitry of glitches.

"...About my good deeds, right?"

Paul was relieved Lothar had caught himself in time.

There was something ominous about the raygun, and Paul felt certain that the less people knew about it the better.

"I've been very stupid," said Lothar, kissing the Principal's hand.

Zelman nodded vigorously over his shoulder. The two Upsters were obviously drained of energy.

It seemed to Paul almost as if they'd been sleepwalking as they stood before the auditorium procession.

The Principal stood between them. When he raised his voice and demanded that they kneel, they knelt.

Paul watched the ceremony without surprise. He had suffered such admonishments and then been forced to submit when he'd been a boy growing up in the orphanage.

Still, he was impressed that Lothar and Zelman permitted the Principal to chastise them like ordinary citizens.

And he knew, too, it was good for the both of them to remember their humble beginnings.

He hoped the actualization with their beloved Principal could perhaps elevate them back into the right visualization, a visualization which would revitalize their abilities to contribute.

Suddenly, what appeared to be a miracle occurred.

By allowing themselves to submit to their Principal on what was their humblest common denominator, both Zelman and Lothar actualized themselves on their highest possible level, right there in front of the audience!

Paul could see the event as it affected the eyes of the people in the audience.

"No one citizen is greater than all of the citizens!"

The old man's voice was a holy grail.

"Let those who contribute the most, reap the harvest for all citizens!"

Beckett's voice sounded like music as he spoke.

Paul's heart filled with it as he began to understand.

He moved his gaze towards the Professor.

To his amazement, he was in the process of disappearing.

A hushed murmur rippled through the auditorium.

Paul had to rub his eyes to make sure he wasn't mistaken.

Principal Beckett had disappeared!

"Hail to Zelman!" said Lothar as he stood up.

"Hail to Zelman!" Everybody shouted and smiled as Zelman stood up.

"Hail to Lord Edwin Lothar!" said Zelman as he stood.

"Hail to Lord Edwin Lothar!" shouted the audience as he stood up.

Everybody shouted and everybody stood up except Paul.

When the students seated in the front row marched up and lifted Lothar and Zelman from the stage, it seemed as if a holy miracle had just been witnessed by all.

Men, boys, women, young girls, even tutors reached to touch the two men they could now adore in real life.

Their actions reminded Paul of the day the technocrats had carried Elliot Richards out of the Lincoln Memorial test ground auditorium when the new system had been declared successful.

Lothar wanted to give Paul a ride in his "new" medivacopter, an ancient copter which had been restored to perfection. It was his most recent addition to what had become a nationally acclaimed collection.

Paul waited for over an hour as he stood by the medivacopter, which Lothar had parked next to the big ball field at the orphanage.

The big ball field, his beloved Principal used to say, was a perfect miniature of the pro fields.

Paul tapped his foot with frustration and checked his computer wristwatch.

The big hand was on the ten, and the little hand was on the twelve.

He decided to take the pipeline home.

As he walked quickly across the big ball field he noticed Mr. Beckett standing next to the ironbox goal flags.

For a split second, Paul thought he was glowing, but then he was just Mr. Beckett again, dressed in his usual bright, six-piece atmospheric suit. Paul breathed a sigh of relief.

"Leaving so soon?" asked the old man as he approached Paul with his hand extended. He was smiling.

"Thank you for inviting me, sir!"

Paul took Mr. Beckett' s hand and felt the warmth and strength of him in his grip.

"I'm so glad the new system tested out all right."

Mr. Beckett held onto Paul's hand almost as if he wanted to shackle him as a prisoner.

"Yes, it tested out well, didn't it?"

Paul had to restrain himself from asking Mr. Beckett how he was able to disappear. He knew such a question would alienate the old man for good.

"Remember, Paul, the visualization you visualize may not be the actualization you actualize."

Mr. Beckett sounded as if he was trying to impart something very important to Paul, but then Paul mentally chastised himself for trying to read into everything.

As Mr. Beckett' s gaze left Paul's, Paul nodded good night.

His former Principal glided into the darkness of the night, leaving Paul with many questions whirling in his brain.

He felt instinctively that Beckett was trying to tell him something without coming right out with it...that this time his instincts were right.

Paul pondered the equation. What was Beckett trying to say?

"Tis the season to be jolly..." said Heleon. Her voice sounded like the video cathedral choir.

Paul opened his eyes and feasted on her beautiful face. She finished her carol, and then he lifted up on one elbow and put his left hand around her neck so he could kiss her.

"Merry Christmas," he said.

This was their first Christmas together.

"Merry Christmas, Paul."

Heleon still felt a little funny calling Paul by his first name. A bit of formality had been bred into the hologram essence to ensure what scientists had hoped would be a proper working distance. Then Pi arrived with a tray laden with delicacies.

"Merry Christmas, sir."

Pi held back his awkward vibrations of embarrassment. He was never sure whether it was right or wrong for the controller to be kissing Heleon.

Secretly, Pi hoped Paul would kiss him instead, but he was too well-trained to let down his guard just because his pulse felt weird.

"Yes, Merry Christmas, Pi."

Paul let go of Heleon who detected his discomfort.

"Let's open the presents."

Neither Heleon nor Pi had ever opened Christmas presents before. The synthetic tree that blinked on and off was, to them, an exotic treasure. The fantastic neon ornaments stimulated all their vibrations.

Unfortunately, Delti found the whole affair rather fraudulent.

Pi's present came first.

"Thank you, sir. I shall maintain the integrity of the cassette, you can be sure of that!"

Pi tried very hard to hold back his enthusiasm as he held onto the Encyclopedia of Cooking cassette which Paul had given him.

"I'm sure you will, Pi," said Paul, as he handed Delti his present.

"Merry Christmas, Delti."

Delti's hand grabbed the red, white and blue container with belligerence.

"Sir!" said Delti with obvious surprise.

Paul was delighted by his reaction as red, white and blue paper floated down around the strongman's feet like feathers.

Delti had never been given a gift, and, for all his pomposity, he couldn't help but be touched.

"Try it on," piped Heleon.

"Lift up your arms!"

Pi grabbed control of the situation.

"I shouldn't accept this."

Delti was having a hard time interpreting his vibrations.

"Delti, don't be an old short-circuit.."

Heleon's statement jolted Delti into submission.

Paul sat back on the sofa and watched Pi and Heleon assemble the seven-piece atmospheric all-purpose suit over Delti's surface.

The suits were the latest in maintenance fashion and had been air-bopped in for the season from Europa! Zippers, snaps, suspenders, latches, buttons, clasps, locks and clips were connected with the greatest of ease.

"You look smart, Delti," said Paul.

He enjoyed the fact that his D model was uncomfortable. Not that he wished Delti ill.

It's just that Delti had intimidated him all these months with his arrogant attitude.

"You'll be the most fashionably-dressed D model in Computer Meadows!"

Heleon's comment made Delti blush. He so wanted her to like him!

Heleon turned her back on Delti's vibration as Delti watched her kneel in front of Paul as he sat on the sofa.

She opened her hands and held out a small red gift-wrapped container.

"Open up your present, Paul!" she said, nearly breathless with excitement.

It was hard for her not to openly declare her love at that very moment.

Delti seemed to know.

Within moments he had stepped up to the H-wall and began dematerializing into the warmth of it.

Heleon glanced in that direction, but his abrupt departure seemed unimportant to her.

"I made it especially for you."

Heleon didn't care whether or not Delti grasped her true feelings toward the controller. She only knew she wanted Paul...every pulsation in him!

Pi felt uneasy about Delti's departure, but he preferred being alone with Paul and Heleon.

It was so much more relaxing. And, of course, he felt accepted as part of a unit.

"H, it's…"

Paul 's voice was tentative and choked as he held the neon crucifix star in his hand.

The exquisite cross surrounded by a Judea star dangled from

an elegant string of day glo beads which Heleon had strung together herself.

"Do you like it?"

Heleon was not sure if she should have given Paul such a present at Christmas. She wished they'd taught her how to maintain during a holiday such as this at the Learning Garden!

Paul put the beautiful treasure around his neck.

The warmth of his chest ignited the crucifix star to blink every seven seconds. He felt gently infused with a golden hue of energy.

"I've never had a crucifix star before," he said softly. And he hadn't.

"Does that mean you don't like it'?"

Her voice was near panic.

"I thank you very much."

Paul stood as Heleon looked up at him, still on her knees.

She pressed her face next to his trouser zipper.He could feel her heat penetrate his loins.

He looked over at Pi, who didn't know what to say.

He, too, was flushed with excitement as Paul reached deep into the atmospheric pocket of his favorite smoking robe and retrieved a narrow silver cylinder which had been festively tied with a big red bow.

"Merry Christmas, Heleon," he said as he lowered his hand.

As she looked up at him with her electric doe eyes he thought she looked mysteriously sad, as if some awareness from far away was so acute it almost hurt her.

"It's for you, H. Here...take it."

He placed the silver cylinder in her trembling hand.

"For me?"

She whispered the question with pure surprise.

"Open it, Heleon, before I explode!" burst Pi from across the room, simultaneously nodding his instinctive embarrassment to Paul.

His outburst seemed to help Heleon into the present-getting mode as she quickly opened the mysterious package and gasped.

"What are they?" she asked everyone.

She held aloft a magnificent pair of earwings.

"Pi, come and help me put these on her!"

Paul took one of the long diamond earwings and placed it on Heleon's left ear. Pi affixed the other earwing to the right ear.

When Heleon emerged from their shadows into the light, both Paul and Pi stood back and exclaimed their pleasure.

The earwings had shaped her face into a magnificent female-icon. Hologram and human were speechless over her beauty.

"Amazing," said Pi.

He'd accidentally let his tongue slip. He'd been taught at the Learning Garden to always let the controller speak first. But Pi's slip notwithstanding, everyone had a Merry Christmas.

Everyone, that is, except Delti, who had chosen to attend a meeting instead of the Christmas celebrations which included a special feast made by Pi in honor of the day.

Paul wanted to spend at least part of the day outside in the special Christmas computer snow.

Like most Washingtonians who lived in Computer Meadows, Christmas computer snow was an annual event.

The beautiful white flakes began falling every year just past midnight on December twenty-fourth and stopped at precisely six o'clock the following morning, just in time for the little ones to get in their first snow-romp before breakfast!

Neither Heleon nor Pi had ever seen computer snow, nor made a snowball, nor constructed a snowman.

Paul busied himself as teacher, and the three friends forgot themselves as they rolled balls across the lawn, stacked them neatly, and then decorated their snowperson into life.

Heleon wanted a snowgirl.

Pi was too embarrassed to admit that he'd much prefer a snowboy.

Paul wanted Heleon to be happy, so snowgirl it was!

The three of them laughed and joked like a real family as they gave their snowgirl "hair" and "breasts," even a shapely "derriere!"

Howard Bork observed his next door neighbor with his holograms through hazy eyes as he dabbed his nostrils with an opiated hanky.

His new success had afforded him the indulgence of some very expensive addictions. He experienced his feelings as the drug lumbered through his cortex.

He resented Paul Quatro, disliked the relationship Quatro had with his holograms.

Howard's relationship with his holograms didn't exist, and that's the way he wanted it.

Howard didn't quite trust holograms.

At the bottom of his soul he was frightened of them.

He wished he could have Rob the robot back.

Robots obeyed every whim, and that's the way Howard wanted holograms to be. But, unfortunately, they weren't.

Holograms were self-determined.

Oh, they were more efficient, Howard knew, than robots.

They were so efficient they made Howard feel inferior!

Especially Beta, his newly materialized B model.

Bernice, too, was having trouble.

She'd still not forgiven him for sending Rob away, even though she seemed to find holograms perfectly acceptable as performers.

But she wasn't engaged with her holograms the way she'd been engaged with Rob.

He dabbed his nostrils once again with a fresh orange and yellow opiated hanky as his heart thrilled to the sight of Heleon ice skating around Paul Quatro's frozen pool.

It was sad, he mused.

Once he and Paul had been friends. But then Paul made the fateful decision to bring that...that...hologram to his eleventh anniversary party.

Howard gurgled audibly.

It was a disgusting thing to do. And not only was it disgusting, it was immoral! A human and a hologram together!

Yet, watching them play together...they looked like two swans gliding in synchronized harmony around the frozen pool as they skated.

Howard slammed the kitchen reflectors shut and turned his back on the happy scene.

It's too much, he grumbled to himself as he headed for the vid nook. He was going to try to catch some news...

Pi applauded as Paul and Heleon made their third turn around the frozen pool.

"Come join us!"

Paul extended his hand to the apple-cheeked Pi.

"But...sir! I have never performed such maintenance!"

Paul grabbed his hands as Heleon led him from behind onto the ice.

"This is not maintenance, Pi. This is pleasure," said Paul as he held Pi up.

Pi's ankles collapsed inward as he struggled to maintain his balance. Paul noted with amusement that Pi was definitely not an athlete.

"Pleasure?" Pi turned to Paul, confused.

"Yes. Pleasure." Heleon spoke as if she were an authority on this new phenomenon.

Paul had to turn away.

He was afraid Heleon would ask him why he was laughing!

The rest of the day was magic as the three friends skated around together holding hands in a chain, then breaking off to skate for a while in single file.

Pi became proficient after only a short time. Heleon, of course, was acrobatic.

Sometime during the afternoon a second batch of elegant white computer Christmas snow began falling. It covered their hoods, their arms, and the surrounding roofs, making everything seem pure and good.

Oh, what a fantastic Christmas this has been! Paul thought to himself.

And what a hard year, too. Mary's death. Completing the new system. The battles with John Malone. The paranoia and doubts about Elliot Richards. And then, of course, the H-wall! Heleon.

Yes, it has been a profitable year, Paul thought to himself.

Christmas dinner was a revelry.

They all sat at the circular computer backyard table with its solar umbrella and ate their Christmas feast, synthetic cranapple sauce, raisin-pear stuffing, a large, moist, butterball turkey block, orange yams, cornbread and gravy.

"Take a bite!" said Paul, as he held a luscious chunk of turkey block on a computer fork to Heleon's mouth.

"But I've never had nourishment," said Heleon, as she averted her face. She didn't want to disobey his order, but her impulse shied away.

Holograms were a self-nourishing species and could draw energy from everything from the sun, the moon and heat to ice, rain -- even another species!

But she loved Paul, a human.

She took the piece of turkey block into her mouth and chewed, the way Paul chewed when he consumed the nourishment so carefully prepared by Pi.

Her mouth felt unusual!

Not electric, the way it felt when she nurtured Paul's penis but nonetheless interesting.

It brushed against her tongue and tonsils, making them itch.

She'd certainly not be counting on this "nourishment" for energy. She got more of that from one ray of sunlight!

"Technically interesting!" Pi swallowed a scoop of synthetic raisin-pear stuffing.

Paul could feel Heleon's leg against his thigh as they enjoyed their holiday meal.

No one, not even the holograms' ninth sense, could sense the danger that lay before them.

At first Paul thought a perma-frost cloud had lost its buoyancy and was floating with benign recklessness towards the house.

Once, several years ago, the same thing had happened during the first Christmas he and Mary spent in Computer Meadows. He just called the local weatherbot who calmly ejected the cloud back into a far corner of the weather dome.

But this horrifying, pre-historic un-technical, audio-sensory echo startled the little Christmas party.

But not until Heleon's inner-ear-shattering whistle scream did Paul actually see the flying monster he'd battled in his own dreams.

With a wing span of over thirty feet and fangs as sharp as a laser beam, the creature seemed to promise an evil that didn't belong on Earth.

363

Its fangs dripped venom more powerful than the synthetic cyanide sleeping pills used to put trauma-shock victims out of their misery.

Its claws, eighteen inches long, were encrusted with dessicated flesh, eyes ripped from sockets, and bits and pieces of human hearts and brains. The stench caused Paul to vomit on the spot.

The tail, encrusted with feces and hair, was as strong as a whipping arm.

The thing went for Paul.

He had just enough time to leap out of its grasp. The solar umbrella went instead.

Heleon and Pi were knocked off their chairs.

She picked up a snowball and threw it at the monster.

The monster attacked Heleon as Paul dove to knock her down before it impaled her in its killer beak.

"Help! Help! Help!" called Paul to Howard and Bernice.

But Howard was in a deep sleep due to his hanky addiction, and Bernice was underneath her computerized hair massager getting a hair-zap.

The monster grabbed Heleon by the ankle with its talons, cawing through its beak like a carrion crow.

Its tongue was bloody.

The stench of death was everywhere.

Paul grabbed Heleon's wrist as the monster started to flap its filthy wings in a satanic effort to pull her away.

Pi, who had recovered from a dead faint, grabbed onto Paul's legs, but the monster was pulling all of them off the ground.

It snapped its tail and flicked Paul and Pi off as if they were ticks who had unsuccessfully tried to burrow into the fur of a dog.

The two of them landed on a snow mound close to the pool.

"You've got to save Heleon, sir!"

Pi was beginning to get close to the energy burn-out he'd been taught to avoid at the Learning Garden.

If he burnt out, Pi knew he'd blow up and, in so doing, he would detonate everything and everyone in Computer Meadows, a most undesirable thing to do.

"Sir, don't run away!"

Paul was running towards the computer house without looking back.

Pi's squeals for help seemed to barely prick the silence of that winter afternoon.

He felt desolate and shocked and disgusted, most of all, by Paul's behavior.

His own controller! A coward!

Just then he noticed the flying monster hovering above the computer house. Suddenly, it landed on the giant antenna which was stationed at the far end corner of the roof.

Heleon was caught, pale and silent, in its putrid talons.

Pi picked up a snowball, but he was so hot it melted into water within seconds.

Heleon made a stunned effort to escape from its grip, but she was so hyperkinetic she wasn't in full control of her powers.

She couldn't dematerialize!

The monster lifted her up to its prehistoric eyes, obviously enamored of her beauty and strangeness.

It had never seen anything like her.

Its long, slithery tongue licked her legs. It sniffed her buttocks.

Heleon banged its head with her tiny fists, but the monster didn't feel it.

Paul charged outside and pointed Lothar's raygun at the monster. He quickly fired off two bolts of energy.

The monster screeched in pain and lifted off the roof, flapping its wings as snow whirled around it from the wind force of its strength.

Paul blasted off another bolt, hitting the monster in the tail, blowing half of it off.

Destabilized, the monster was forced to make one final assault on its enemy.

Paul froze with fear as the venomous thing flapped its jagged, stinking wings and came towards him.

He pulled the trigger on the raygun again, but the contraption didn't fire.

The monster's ugly head threatened total destruction as it came towards him, Heleon screaming and undulating in its talons.

It was then Paul noticed the computer gauge on the side of the raygun. He switched it to max high and re-aimed with only split seconds to go.

The blast from the raygun was so powerful it knocked Paul backwards into the circular computer backyard table and across the frozen pool.

The yellow-red energy light briefly blinded him, and a strong, pungent odor of burnt flesh and smoke wafted through the backyard. It was an odor he'd never forget.

"Sir, are you functioning?" Pi kneeled next to Paul and helped him to his feet.

"Yes, I believe I'm in one piece!"

Paul checked his arms and legs and squinted to recapture his focus. Then he visualized Heleon.

"H!"

A bolt of panic jabbed through his chest as they both jumped up to look for her.

Pi slipped on the frozen ice as he ran towards the carnage.

Paul scooped him to his feet.

The destruction they'd wrought was beyond imagination.

A large mass of bloody flesh, bone, cartilage, pus, venom, mucous, feathers, cracked ivory teeth, busted veins, broken wings, bent neck, torn liver, ruptured heart and burst eyeballs oozed down from the northwest side of the computer house roof and seeped into the synthetic astral turf which had been drenched with blood and excrement.

"Heleon!"

Paul clawed his way through the bloody slush like a wild big ball player making his ninth-hour point.

Pi followed close behind, knee-deep in ooze. Suddenly, he felt the monster's gnarled claw grip his ankle.

"Sir! Help!" screamed Pi.

Paul turned and kicked the reflexed claw off Pi's ankle. Then he saw Heleon's hand push up through the eye socket of the monster.

"H!"

He grabbed her wrist and pulled her body through the eyeball slime and held her in his arms. She was wet with bloody mush, yellow phlegm and black bile.

"H, you're alive, you're alive," he said, as he kissed her face again and again.

"You saved my life."

Heleon's voice was weak, and she was shivering from shock.

Paul carried her into the house and placed her in the sunken sauna tub.

He set the computer dial on extra relaxation. The tub fluids showered the slime off her body and warmed her depleted energy.

That night a holographic clean-up crew employed by Computer Meadows maintenance vacuumed the monster off the roof and out of the astral-turf.

Naturally, computer journalists rushed to the scene of the actualization. No one had ever witnessed such a monstrosity!

A holographic security investigator spent over an hour interviewing Paul.

"What were you doing in the backyard?"

"Celebrating Christmas."

Paul didn't like this sterile-voiced holographic character.

He was an S model, security maintenance. His tone annoyed Paul.

"What were your holograms doing outside with you?"

"Celebrating Christmas with me!"

Paul knew he was walking a fragile tightrope when he admitted to such an actualization.

"Holograms do not celebrate. They maintain."

The holographic security guard sounded slightly imperious.

"I meant they were maintaining my celebration."

Paul watched the holographic guard record his answers in a porta-transcriber.

"How did you destroy the danger?"

The guard hadn't been trained in prehistoric monsters, but he knew how to handle danger, general danger.

"It hit the antennae and triggered an electrical malfunction that penetrated a deadly current into its system."

Paul was not about to tell this idiot about dear Lothar's raygun.

"I would like to interview the holograms."

The hologram guard penetrated Paul's sixth sense for the truth. Paul closed his mind so the hologram couldn't see in.

He was so angry he didn't know whether he could contain himself.

"What I want to know is how that monster broke through the weather dome security system, that's what I want to know!"

He jumped to his feet in outrage.

The hologram guard was distracted for a moment.

This thing "human anger" -- always ricocheted his eighth sense probe. He couldn't remember what he'd been talking about with this...Mr. Paul Quatro.

The hologram cleared his throat.

"We're investigating the actualization."

His confidence faltered as it always did when he couldn't give a totally maintained answer to a question.

"I want answers, not excuses!" barked Paul, as he glared at the guard with total disgust.

The guard stepped back, uncomfortable. He fumbled with his porta-transcriber.

"You!   Are!   Diiismissed!" hissed Paul.

The hologram bowed his head.

"Yes, Mr. Quatro."

Paul watched as the hologram left his house.

The following day Paul sent a full report on the monster to the authorities by Computer Express Mail.

The monster was classified as an ancient species, since all history in all the sciences had been abolished except for the computer sciences.

Since Paul had successfully deflected the holographic security guard's intent to interrogate Pi and Heleon with his "human anger," no further requests had been ordered by the probing guard.

As the official report came back to Paul over Computer Express Mail, Paul read it with interest and some amazement:

The ancient species, destination unknown, purpose unknown, was able to fly, due to its non-metallic substance, through the sensory beams. Damage assessed at thirty thousand bank credits to Mr. Paul Quatro. The carcass of the monster was disposed of at the Computer Meadows garbage disposal.

And that was it!

No further investigation, no further interviews. No further study of what Paul knew for a fact was an incredible actualization.

And although the computer journalists had swarmed all over him and his house taking insta-photos of the monster and asking a million questions, nothing was reported on the Vid News.

"Why?"

Paul unconsciously spoke the word aloud as he sat in the breakfast vid nook and took sips of his vitafee.

Heleon and Pi did not know the answer to that question, nor were they sure what he meant.

"Why what?" asked Heleon.

"Why didn't the computer journalists report on this occurrence on the Vid News?"

Paul switched off the vid screens and faced Heleon and Pi.

Both wore puzzled expressions as they tried to find answers to the controller's question.

Delti arrived with an armful of computer sockets and plugs.

He had been informed by Beta of the monster occurrence. Beta had strong connections to the holographic security force, and he made sure important holograms, such as Delti, were kept informed.

"Delti! What are you doing?"

Paul was suspicious of Delti's actualizations of late. He could sense the tension that poisoned the effectiveness of the unit.

"Maintaining the repair of the damaged roof, sir."

Delti's inflection was sarcastic.

"That's efficient!"

Paul made an effort to smile at Delti. He had an enormous amount of last-minute work to do on the new system, and the last thing he needed was a confrontation with Delti.

"I want to thank you for the very thoughtful Christmas gift, P.Q.!"

Miss Holly James greeted Paul as soon as he entered the office. Her smile was genuinely cheerful and welcoming.

"I hope they fit!"

Paul returned her enthusiasm with his own as he briskly proceeded into his own inner sanctum.

"Oh! I've always wanted a pair of solar earmuffs!" she cried.

She loved the fact that he'd thought about her ears at all!

"Incidentally, P.Q., I've bought myself an H-wall. A two-unit version."

Paul half-listened as she jabbered happily.

What caught his real interest was a top-secret transmission from Elliot Richards.

He closed the door of his office and immediately slipped the cassette into its priority transcriber. The image of Elliot appeared on the screen.

"Meet me at the Lincoln Memorial test grounds!" he commanded.

"Tell no one!"

Elliot's voice hoarded the threat of danger.

With only three days left to the unveiling of the new system, Paul knew danger was a very real possibility.

Once again the old tension squeezed his chest and stomach.

He quickly wrapped himself in the atmospheric scarf Miss James had given him for Christmas and entered the pipeline.

Upon entering the test ground auditorium, Paul immediately spotted Elliot Richards standing with Professor Sam Ludlum.

The two of them just happened to be conversing by the most important technological device in all the world.

Paul shivered. The auditorium was cold.

He noticed Elliot had his overcoat unbuttoned, while Professor Ludlum was bundled up in an atmospheric down vest and mittens!

In spite of all that clothing, the old man was shivering. Now why, Paul wondered, was Elliot Richards so comfortable when Sam Ludlum was so cold?

He pulled himself together.

"Mr. Secretary. Professor Ludlum."

Paul didn't want to make any unnecessary mistakes this late in the year when it came to making or not making introductions. It was better to overreach than not to reach at all.

Paul had learned his lesson once before, and he did not need to learn it again.

"Paul, Professor Ludlum and I wanted to have this private conference with you because we didn't want the department to interfere."

Elliot's eyes were beady and cold. His voice was both attentive and professional, deliberate and plotting.

The Professor extended ·his hand.

"Young man, I want to thank you for such a personal Christmas gift!"

He smiled at Paul but, in Paul's mind, he wasn't above suspicion.

He'd sent over a box of South Mexo smokettes, the Professor's favorite brand.

He thought it was nice of the Professor to thank him personally.

He also thought it rude of the Secretary not to thank him for the computerized pen and pencil set he'd given him for Christmas. But never mind, he said to himself, turning to the both of them.

"In three days we shall unveil the new system to all the world!" said the Secretary of Technology.

His voice boomed out across the ice-cold auditorium.

He knew he was on the brink of greatness, and Paul sensed how much his success meant to him.

"I have no doubt the new system will be everything we want it to be, sir," said Paul in a reassuring tone.

Professor Ludlum took a seat in the front row of the auditorium.

Paul followed behind him and was soon sandwiched in on the other side by Elliot, who seemed to press in unnecessarily.

In spite of the close quarters, Paul was honored to be included in their plans. They were two of the most important men in the history of technology!

"Paul," said Professor Ludlum, "we must be assured there will be no mistakes on January first, New Year's Day!"

The old man was obviously leading Paul into the plan as Elliot put a dry hand on Paul's shoulder.

"My election to the Presidency depends on the new system," he proclaimed with a quiet tone.

His words ticked like a metronome. They were without rhythm or warmth.

Paul sensed the threat.

"But, sirs…the test was successful."

Paul didn't understand what they wanted.

Ever a technocrat visionary, he was unaware of the politics behind this meeting.

"As Undersecretary of Technology, you are first in line to succeed Elliot as Secretary. That is…upon his election as President of the United States."

Sam Ludlum was a master of understatement. He'd made his career as a technocratic strategist, as the man who knew more about the Department of Technology than any man in the history of the department.

"Paul, we must be positive the new system will work." Elliot squeezed Paul's shoulder to emphasize his point.

"What are you asking?"

Paul would have preferred not being with these two men right at the moment.

He could sense a desire…or something larger than life. And that frightened him.

"The night before the new system is to be unveiled we want you to switch it on and give it a second test."

Professor Ludlum's statement was like a bolt of lightning entering Paul's chest.

He reflexively clutched at his heart in an automatic gesture of self-protection.

"A second test, sir? But that's against the rules."

There was a long pause. Elliot and the Professor exchanged glances as they waited for Paul to come to his senses.

Everyone knew Paul's ascendancy on that upward, mobile ladder to success was due, in large part, to their making.

Whether or not he chose to receive the balance owed was up to him.

Paul 's voice was weak with submission.

"If that is what you would like."

"Son, it's the only way. We must be assured of its total success if we are to be victorious and lead the world into Utopia."

Sam Ludlum took Paul's hand.

His words sounded reassuring, thought Paul. His eyes were fatherly, and his hand held Paul's with great strength.

"Son."

The Professor had called him "son." The endearment eroded his morality as he faced what he had to do.

The Professor continued.

"You shall have the power as Secretary of Technology to implement your very own technocratic vision, just as I have had mine."

Elliot Richards nodded his agreement as he placed his oppressive, perfectly-manicured hand around Paul's neck, massaging it gently, almost erotically, the way a lover might massage the neck of a loved one just before sleep.

He has a tender touch, thought Paul. Tender but with persuasion.

Sam Ludlum and the Secretary smiled at each other with their eyes, understanding they had just convinced the Undersecretary of Technology through their tech-art skills in intimidation to break the holiest of laws.

The new system was only, ever, to be tested once.

Now, on the eve of the Presidential election, with the Secretary of Technology at the end of a dangerously close Presidential race, they knew the law would be broken and victory would be theirs! Theirs! Theirs!

Tick...tick...tick...tick...tick...tick...tick...tick...tick...tick ...tick...tick...tick...tick...tick...tick...tick...tick...tick...tick ...tick...tick...tick...tick...tick...tick...tick...tick...tick...tick ...tick...tick...

Paul could feel his innocence slipping away.

If only Elliot Richards and Professor Ludlum had not asked him to break the law.

He felt he could remain innocent all the way into Utopia. That way he wouldn't have to break the code of honesty that had been bred into him since his days at the test tube orphanage.

But, sadly, he saw that was not to be his fate. He wanted success too badly.

The price was high. He knew that, too, now. Only time would tell if it was worth it.

"What troubles your visualization?" whispered Heleon into Paul's ear.

Her breath was warm and seductive. They had made love nineteen times already and both felt ready for more.

Her scent was on his tongue, his fingertips, and his lips could taste her flavor. His nostrils inhaled her sweet odor.

His toes were wet from their trapeze love-making: he'd swung himself over the bed while hanging from the mechanical arm which supported the vid screen. Heleon screeched with laughter as he diddled into her soft, moist crevice with his wiggly toes.

"Tomorrow is the projected date, the most important day for all technocrats and for all citizens. It's the day the new system will be unveiled."

Paul spoke in staccato bursts, but warmth played around his officious manner.

Heleon knew all about his tension. She watched him put on his favorite five-piece leisure suit.

"Where are you going?"

She sat up in bed and pulled the warm, atmospheric down comforter over her naked body. She could taste the essence of him as her sensory sensations throbbed from his penetrations.

"I need to get some fresh perma-air."

Paul pressed the triple-snaps on the sleeves of his suit and air-zipped the trouser legs with his vibrations.

"May I attend you?"

Heleon started to follow him, but Paul turned and caught her before her feet touched the floor.

"No. I want to be alone."

He knew as soon as he spoke she would be hurt, but he had no other choice. He couldn't tell her what he was about to do.

"Did I not do it right tonight?"

Tears welled in her eyes, and her sweet, silky voice was mottled with feelings of rejection.

"H. We connect naturally. I could not ask for better."

He chucked his knuckle under her pretty chin and lifted her head up to receive his loving kiss.

Their scents were strong with the inflection of sexual love.

She opened his mouth with her moist firm, searching tongue which reminded Paul of a cobra dancing to the snake charmer's mesmerizing computer flute.

"I won't be long," he promised.

He tucked her under the covers and kissed her on the forehead.

Neither Paul nor Heleon knew Delti was watching them as he had been all these past weeks through the vid screen which hung at the foot of their bed.

Delti waited for Paul to leave the house, and he waited for Heleon to slip happily into hibernation.

Then he crawled out of the vid screen and materialized in front of the bed.

He wanted to take her in his arms. He wanted to penetrate her sense the way the controller had. He wanted to prove to her he was stronger and better than Paul Quatro.

Yet, Heleon frightened him.

Not in the physical sense. Delti knew he could snap her energy in half on a whim! But she had a power over his senses which he could not balance in his visualizations.

Delti shook his being to loosen his vibes. Even thinking about it made him dizzy.

He knew it was this dizziness that had saved him from abusing the little female. She somehow disarmed him in a way he couldn't maintain.

He stood in his place, watching her. Slowly, he inched closer to where she breathed. He could smell her breath.

His nostrils quivered with the scent of her as her essence permeated his senses.

He wanted to penetrate her, but he didn't know how, or even what it meant. For the moment he tempered his maddening vibrations, content to experience her scent and peaceful breathing.

Paul Quatro had taken the oval container which contained the key to the new system home with him that afternoon.

The incredible power of the key nearly choked him.

He visualized his chest was being squeezed by a computerized garbage compressor. It was exploding in front of all the technocrats in the lobby who were on their way home, shocking them out of their revelry, causing them to look up and say, "Why?"

But no such luck tonight for Paul Quatro.

Now, just minutes before midnight, on the evening before the new system was to be tested, Paul Quatro was out to break the law.

He knew every entranceway into the Lincoln Memorial test grounds. And he knew all about the holographic security guards who had been recently assigned to the building.

He knew it was his right to walk the maze of hallways which led to the thousands of tiny test cubicles.

He knew it was his right to open the double computerized stainless steel laboratory doors and check, and recheck, and double-check all the existing experiments.

But Paul didn't want to be seen.

He didn't want a record of his entrance.

So he took the underground delivery conveyor walkway which was in use twenty-four hours a day. He rode the walkway up the long tunnel. The amber lights distorted his face.

His hands were sweating as he clutched the oval container which housed the key...the key...the key to the new system.

He took the seldom used service robot hallway which led diagonally along the regular hallway maze. Now that robots had all but vanished except in certain sideshows and brothels, nobody used this hallway.

Paul found himself sighing.

He missed the sound of the service robots! They were dependable.

But, of course, they weren't as efficient as holograms.

Still, the robots had helped the Together Generation reach the doorstep of Utopia, and there was something to be said for that.

His hand trembled as he dialed the computer combination to the back door of the test ground auditorium where the new system waited for him.

The triple stainless steel back door slid apart, and Paul entered the vast, chilly space.

In the center of the room, up on the oval stage, was the new system. He visualized it as a sleeping dragon from a fairy tale he'd once read.

He pressed the small oval container's computer combination and then listened as it rotated into position and clicked open.

He took out the silver encrusted magnesium computer key.

For a moment he just held the glowing key in his hand.

He imagined, or felt, a great force preventing him from jamming the key into the new system's computer keyhole.

Then he heard a sound.

Turning quickly, he tripped over his own feet and fell to the floor.

He crawled around to the side of the oval stage and peered from behind the new system, scanning the oval auditorium.

He felt someone was watching him. He wanted to call out for whoever was in the auditorium to come forward and show themselves, but something within him wouldn't.

He stood quietly, every cell in his being attuned to the slightest movement or sound.

Nothing. He couldn't detect the presence of another.

Paul shuddered quietly as he huddled by the new system, imagining what might happen if he was discovered. The penalty for testing the new system more than once had never been defined, since the crime exceeded the imaginations of modern lawmakers.

Never, ever had a citizen gone this far.

Paul waited a full hour before making his actualization.

The only sound he could detect was the beating of his own heart as it pounded furiously against his chest.

He fought to lower his blood pressure, which he knew was rising to a dangerous level.

He definitely did not want to have a cardiac arrest in this uncompromising environment.

Paul Quatro, the technocrat visionary, pulled his courage together and discarded his true logic and jammed the computerized key into the new system's computerized keyhole.

It kicked in immediately and purred like a petbot.The machine reminded Paul of Heleon just after she'd had an orgasm. It shared the relaxed lull of her moans.

He allowed the new system to run for a few minutes, and then he turned it off. He'd reawaken the great beast in just a few hours.

As he replaced the computer key in its oval container, he swore when he became the Secretary of Technology he would pass a law that would allow the new system to be tested at least three times before the projected date.

He hated the physical and psychological discomfort of pressure.

And then he ran.

Paul ran through the service robot hallway. He could feel the invisible eyes of some great force following him as he ran and ran and ran up the delivery conveyor walkway.

When he looked at his wristwatch he was surprised to see

it was already six p.m.

He noticed the weathervane digitals were recording the temperature at forty-four degrees with a thirty-mile-an-hour north-easterly wind.

His bones were cold.

He scolded himself for not dressing warmly enough.

When he slipped under the covers and took Heleon in his arms, it seemed as if she was absorbing his chill and refiltering hot, passionate currents back into his system.

She could sense his fear, his uncertainty. She was worried.

"I love you, Paul," she said, as she took his erected penis in her moist hand.

"And I love you, H," whispered Paul.

He wanted to devour her passion and forget about breaking the law.

But he couldn't forget that the new system was to be tested in only three hours.

The world was waiting for the results.

Only Paul Quatro knew for sure it worked.

He knew Elliot Richards and Sam Ludlum would be waiting for his transmission, but he had no desire to let them in on what only he knew.

He felt resentful towards both of them.

He'd lost his innocence this day, and Paul would never forgive them for leading him to the poisoned trough.

Heleon pressed her wet, sweet passion against him.

He sought the sweetness in her with his tongue as she sucked on his penis with her warm mouth. They flowed into each other as daylight broke through.

"It's a success!"

"The new system works!"

"Secretary of Technology does it again!"

The vid screens were burning up with the news. All over the world a huge sigh of relief could be heard.

The entire Department of Technology was given the week off with bank credits.

The new system worked, and that's all that mattered to the inhabitable world. It was called the best new system ever created.

Technocrats around the inhabitable world marveled at its brilliance, its beauty, its intelligence, its power!

Paul leaned back in his all-computerized chair and scanned his computerized desk vid screens.

Elliot Richards was giving his State of Technology speech which he had slanted as a Presidential speech.

"When I am elected, I shall take the world through the Utopian door. No longer will the public need to commit three days of work for four days of pleasure. I guarantee total pleasure. No more work! Everybody's dream will come true under my administration! Utopia for all!"

Elliot Richards was a master sloganeer, Paul thought to himself.

He knew the Secretary was appealing to every member of the Together Generation. That generation's desires, Paul knew, were rooted in a desire to reach a utopian state.

Those who were older would follow. Those who were younger would benefit completely.

The election was only six days away.

All the polls indicated the Presidential race was a close one.

Europa pollsters placed President Andrea Eberhardt Ricarda ahead by three points. Of course, everybody knew the Europas never went against an existing President.

Inja was already predicting Elliot Richards' victory. They had, of course, the most to gain with his election due to their intense involvement with the technological aristocracy around the world.

South Mexo, Middle Judea and Afrikaniker waited for the final results with the same enthusiasm.

Paul flicked off the vid screens. Like everybody else, he planned to take a week off and vote on the sixth of January.

His intercom buzzer suddenly echoed out a pulse as Miss James crystalized on the intercom vid screen.

"Professor Ludlum, P.Q."

Miss James was happy for him, he knew.

Everyone was happy...for Paul, for the New Generation, for the citizens! Everyone felt as much a part of the success of the new system as did the technocrats who made it.

"Thank you. And don't forget to vote!"

He turned to the vid screen.

"Yes, Professor!"

He hoped his resentment towards Sam Ludlum wasn't evident.

"Paul, I want you to know Elliot and I are forever grateful to you."

The old man knew how to lay it on thick, thought Paul.

"Yes, Professor. I appreciate your transmission."

Paul did not wish to allow the Professor the pleasure of intimidation.

Now that he had faithfully obeyed, he no longer felt a need to submit to the vibrations of his seniors.

"In time you shall fully appreciate your actualization." Professor Ludlum was aware Paul had been stained.

"Sam! Your dinner is getting cold!"

Miss Vickers leaned into the vid screen and kissed the Professor.

"Yes, my dear," said the Professor.

The old man seemed embarrassed as he nodded eagerly towards the beautiful young woman.

Paul was amused that this great, great man could be led around so easily by a woman.

The Professor leaned his face into the vid screen, causing the camera to vaguely distort his features into grotesque caricatures of themselves.

"Good day, my boy," croaked the old man."And don't forget to vote!"

The vid screen went dark.

At least he's right about one thing, Paul thought, as he sat without moving at his computer desk.

Voting is the most distinguished honor a citizen could possibly visualize.

The days leading up to Election Day were some of the happiest and most relaxing Paul could ever remember.

He had a most fulfilling transmission with Lothar who seemed, miraculously, to have straightened himself out after all!

Oh, that pinhead genius, that winner of five Golden Wrench awards still had his eccentric behavior, all right, sitting as he did on his "throne" at the remodeled Smithsonian Institute, being waited on by those nine-year-old blonde-haired, blue-eyed nymphets and their mother and grandmother. They were beautiful, to be sure. All of them. But Lothar wasn't opiated!

Paul told him about the monster and about how he'd used Lothar's raygun to destroy it.

Lothar, to Paul's intense surprise, was indifferent.

"It's not even a good toy. Those days are over for me. I'm concentrating on Utopia now, a Utopia where there will no longer be a need for evolution."

Lothar seemed content with his life for the first time.

Paul never really thought about Utopia being the end of evolution, but when Lothar talked about it, the idea made sense.

Utopia was the last rung on that upward, mobile ladder.

Oh, there could be management of the new system, but the citizens would be focused on pleasure.

Suddenly, the thought of Utopia wasn't quite as exciting as Paul thought it would be.

A transmission from Zelman came in.

He, too, appeared to have straightened out, although he, like Lothar, had obviously maintained his eccentric ways.

He was not opiated, either, and he spoke calmly of the culture's eventual submission to Utopia.

A certain resignation in his voice indicated his feeling that Utopia might be inevitable but not as delicious as he'd first imagined.

Paul and Zelman laughed about old times.

Paul noticed Zelman had installed a four-unit H-wall in his laboratory. Zelman told Paul he found the holograms to be interesting companions as he wiled away his time due to their total efficiency.

"We shall all meet in Utopia and have a grand, boring time!"

Zelman's words stung Paul's logic as his buddy bid him a good day.

Suddenly, he blurted out a message that was becoming familiar to Paul: "Don't forget to vote."

The vid screen went blank, and Paul turned to look into Heleon's loving eyes.

Heleon. Heleon was able to help him forget his worst fears.

The all-computerized house hummed in total harmony.

Even Delti, who, at times, could instill a certain discomfort in the unit, seemed to flow in an extra-smooth vibration for a change.

Paul and Heleon ate the wondrous dishes Pi prepared.

Heleon felt it important to eat human nourishment, not for the energy, but for the ritual that connected her to Paul.

They had love sex thirty-nine times a day. Paul could never remember making love to Mary, even at the peak of their marriage, more than twenty times a day. And that was only once on their wedding night!

The sixth of January was the day of the Presidential election.

Every citizen in all twenty-five states of the union voted.

The results began to come back almost as soon as the polling computers closed.

Paul, Heleon, Pi and even Delti sat in the computer library and watched the returns.

At first it seemed as if Elliot Richards had won a landslide victory, but as the count got down to the final one hundred votes, it became clear this was going to be the closest election count in the history of the electoral.

"PRESIDENT RICARDA WINS BY ONE VOTE!" flashed off and on the world vid screens.

One vote! Paul couldn't believe it. He'd thought Elliot was a sure winner!

Suddenly, he felt a tightness in his stomach as he remembered he had voted for President Ricarda.

He voted for her out of spite for all those months the Secretary had maneuvered his cortex and pressured his logic.

The final, broken circuit was forcing him to test the new system for a second time!

How many others had done the same? Who else who might have benefited from the Secretary of Technology's election to the Presidency cast a vote against him out of spite?

Confusion swept through Paul's mind as his logic teetered back and forth.

Now what would happen? Would he continue as Undersecretary of Technology until the next election?

Surely, Elliot would plan his strategy and...But no! It wasn't done that way! Nobody who had been defeated ever ran for re-election!

So Elliot Richards would go down in defeat.

But would Paul Quatro be elevated to the top chair?

The new system had worked!

Surely, in light of that, the President had no reason to remove him! He hadn't run against her!

He'd been a faithful technocrat...

That night he had a dream.

Tick...tock...tick...tock...tick...tock...tick...tock...tick...tock ...tick...tock...tick...tock...tick...tock...tick...tock...tick... tock...

He couldn't stop dematerializing.

Everything and everybody was materializing and dematerializing with alarming frequency: solar lampshades...snapping computer vacuum cleaners on wheels...mechanical arms with vid screens coiled like snakes...conveyor walks galloping...Presto!

Dematerializing...materializing...and Paul was...the eye of the hurricane. He visualized all and actualized...everything and everybody...and then he stopped dematerializing...legions of Elliot Richard's goose-stepping in unison down Pennsylvania Avenue, raising their hands as they passed the White House...

Professor Ludlum's face expanding like a balloon until it exploded into a million miniatures of itself with umbrellas that opened over their heads as they floated by Paul's eye...

President Andrea Eberhardt Ricarda, naked, holding onto a giant computerized penis...sucking on it...as it spurted blood...the President screaming...Help! Help! Help!...I'm drowning! I'm drowning!...The President sliding down a curved penis...the President holding onto the penis for dear life...the President falling off the penis...the penis falling limply onto the President...the President being crushed by the blubbery penis...

And then Paul could see himself...dozens of himselves... hundreds of Paul Quatros...thousands of the Undersecretary of Technology marching in one long line...each holding onto the other's hand...and each was blind...their eyeballs oozing yellow-green pus...tongues licking pus...and then a huge, computerized broom sweeping the thousands of Paul Quatros down the vile, onorous, putrid throat of Elliot Richards...his tongue licking his blistered lips...the sound of a burp as loud as an atomic bomb explosion...

Paul awoke suddenly.

Delti was standing next to his bed, surprised Paul had jolted to consciousness.

"What are you doing here?" Paul shouted.

The panic from his dream was overwhelming him.

"You...you and Heleon...It's...it's wrong."

Delti 's hateful voice pried Heleon from her own sleeping dream. She was visualizing herself and Paul afloat on a soft, pink cloud of synthetic cherries.

"Delti!"

Heleon's voice was husky as she expressed her surprise.

"He is not for you!" bellowed Delti as he grabbed Heleon's wrist in an effort to pull her out of the bed. Heleon slapped his face. Sparks bounced off her hand as her flesh met his.

Paul stood on the air bed.

"Leave this room immediately!" he commanded Delti.

But before he could say another word, Delti aimed his fingertips and blasted Paul's face with a bolt of red energy so strong Paul elevated off the air bed and into the cosmetic room where he tumbled into the sunken sauna tub.

He sat there, stunned from the peculiar energy that had hit him as the computer fluid spouts began spitting out a scented, multi-colored wetness at jet speed.

Paul shielded his bruised face with his hands as he tried to stand up in the tub, but it was slippery and he kept falling down.

Mechanical arms with sponge hands extended themselves from the walls. They punched and jabbed at Paul with a precision borne of invisible eyes.

Paul's atmospheric pajamas shredded under the streams of stinging water as blood tinted everything rose.

His head felt lighter and lighter as reality began to slip away.

He knew if he didn't escape soon he would die.

"Heleon!" he screamed.

"Help me!"

He sunk further into oblivion with every effort as the sponge hands battered him with boxing punches.

His nose was bleeding, and his ears were ringing as an efficient arm deftly knocked a back molar loose. The molar bounced into the recesses of Paul's throat and caught itself there as Paul heaved and coughed to dislodge it.

Water was everywhere; it was up to his neck. How had it happened?

A mechanical arm moved towards him with the sleek surety of a shark on the attack. It neatly placed its sponge hand behind Paul's head and dunked him once.

He burst above water, disoriented.

It dunked him again.

This was all happening so fast! Was he dreaming?

His nostrils and lungs were filling up with fluids, warm, colorful fluids. He was amazed that it didn't even hurt!

Even gasping for air he found himself visualizing Delti.

Of all holograms, why would Delti want to kill him? Kill Paul Quatro? Why?

And then Paul blacked out.

Heleon alternately sucked fluids from Paul's nostrils and lungs and breathed life into his system.

As he opened his eyes he could see her sad face.

Pi was standing behind her. Both looked battered and bruised.

As Heleon helped Paul into his bed, he noticed the bedroom had been nearly destroyed.

Pi tucked him in as Heleon told him how she and Pi had stopped Delti's destructive energy rampage.

"Where is Delti now?" Paul whispered weakly.

"Sir, he escaped back into the wall."

Pi was obviously as terrified as Paul was.

Paul could see Heleon, too, was afraid.

He pressed the vid-phone digits and waited for the holographic security guard to appear on the screen.

"I want to report a malfunctioning hologram."

Paul waited for the transmission to be received, but the holographic security guard never appeared.

"Maybe the transmitter is damaged," said Paul.

He pressed the digits again, but there was no transmission.

"Perhaps, sir, you could use the Bork's vid phone," said Pi, in an effort to be helpful.

Paul jumped at the idea. Heleon took his hand.

"You need hibernation, Paul," she said.

She was worried about his well-being.

"I'll be all right, Heleon," said Paul.

As he sat up in bed he felt an ache in his lungs. His head had been badly bruised, and his ears still rang.

Heleon and Pi helped him on with his atmospheric robe before walking him to the front door. Just before the three of them passed through the entranceway and onto the plastic path, Pi hesitated.

He had never left the house before, and he was frightened.

"It's all right, Pi," said Paul.

"We're all together, taking care of each other."

Heleon took Pi's hand. He could read the reassurance in her mind.

They walked across the emerald-green synthetic lawn.

Paul's knees nearly gave way, but he forced his logic to direct them into strength.

"Delti must be stopped!" he whispered to Pi and Heleon.

Both holograms knew the controller was afraid, yet they felt safe being with him.

Pi told himself if the controller could stop the monster, then surely he could stop Delti.

But then a visualization struck the cherubic butler's pulse.

What would happen to the unit if one of its components were destroyed? Would the other components, too, be destroyed?

Howard and Bernice did not answer the computer door chimes.

Paul pressed the button almost a dozen times.

"Howard! Bernice! It's me!...Paul!"

He banged on their door with his aching fist.

"Maybe they're not home?" said Pi, nervously.

Paul glanced at his computer wrist watch.

"It's 11:00 p.m.," he said angrily.

Pi felt foolish having made such a ludicrous suggestion.

"Look..." choked Heleon.

Her skin was translucent. Shock had caused her vibes to have an anxiety fusion.

Paul approached the living room blinds where Heleon crouched.

He could see through her temporarily transparent body.

Heleon remained motionless, frozen with fear.

Paul's heart dropped when he looked through the slats. He could feel the cells in his body twisting like hanged men, perhaps begging for time, but maybe just weeping and weeping and weeping against fate.

Howard and Bernice were crumpled on their H-wall step pods. Their blood had long since dried.

Paul, Heleon and Pi ran around to the back of the Bork' s house and found the back door open. As they entered, an eerie sensation permeated each of them.

Paul picked up a computerized shovel that leaned against the hallway wall.

Heleon followed closely.

Pi was at the tail end.

The three of them approached Howard and Bernice gingerly.

Paul wept when he saw them.

Howard' s eyes had been gouged out, and one of his arms had been torn off.

Bernice's heart had been ripped out of her chest.

A large, compu- terized kitchen beater had been pushed up her vagina. Blood had caked on her legs. Her eyes, too, had been gouged out.

Paul's head was spinning.

He turned around and took a step backwards.

He heard a popping sound. When he looked down he realized to his horror that it was an eyeball.

"What is this nightmare!" he screamed.

"It's happening now," said Heleon, as Paul ran out of the Bork's house.

Heleon and Pi followed.

Heleon caught him, and together she and Pi led him back to his own house.

He was hysterical.

Pi poured Paul some hot vitafee, and Heleon continued to tell Paul about Delti's assault...about Delti's secret meetings at the Techno department store...about how afraid she'd been to speak against Delti.

Paul was still confused, but he listened through his emotional dervish.

He turned on the vid screen in the breakfast vid nook.

The reports shook all of them as the Vid News broadcaster told his tale:

"All across America holograms are in revolt. Mass murders of human beings have occurred within the last twenty-four hours. Panic is everywhere..."

Then a report came on the screen that would change the world...

"PRESIDENT RICARDA HAS BEEN ASSASSINATED."

The computer journalist on the screen went on to report it had been her very own hologram who had destroyed the head of state.

Reports from across the country continued to flood in as the Vid News told its grisly stories.

"Governors, mayors, senators and more, are all being assassinated by their holograms. It appears the more politically powerful you are, the more likely you are to be a hologram's target. This is a political uprising by the hologram minority!"

Paul's heart was stampeding as he visualized the murders.

Sweat ran down his face.

Suddenly, Elliot Richards appeared on the screen with Professor Ludlum standing next to him.

"Ladies and gentlemen, citizens of the world. The evolution of mankind has reached its final destination. Total extinction of the weaker species is the inevitable actualization. As the leader of all holograms, I can assure you the coronation of the holographic species shall take the inefficiency of this planet and forge it towards a dominant role in the universe for an eternity. As my maker, Dr. Gilbert Unatin, known to all of us as Professor Sam Ludlum, has taught me, mankind respects only power. And have power. My maker has created the holographic species for a power the human species lacks."

Elliot Richards nodded with respect in the direction of his maker.

Professor Ludlum smiled thinly into the cameras. It was obvious the old man was enjoying his new-found celebrity.

What Paul saw next nearly finished him for good.

Elliot Richards dematerialized on camera to demonstrate one of his holographic powers.

When he rematerialized he took the Professor's arm and raised it high over the old man's head as if the old man was the victorious champ.

But as the crowd looked on in stunned belief, and as Paul fought to retain consciousness, he deftly ripped the old man' s arm out of its socket.

Professor Ludlum let out a cry of shock, but before any more could be said, Elliot gouged his eyes out and then tore his head off. He appeared to have the strength of a god.

"I am the ruler of the Earth!" bellowed Elliot Richards into the camera.

His voice was deep and satanic.

He held Professor Ludlum's head aloft with a filthy sneer. Blood dripped from his hands, and his lips and cheeks had somehow become smeared with the deathly signature.

His frame shook with rage as he faced the camera.

"If only you had elected me President..." he gargled at the nation.

"If only...if only...if only..."

His head lolled back as he chanted.

"If only...if only...I'm the ruler...I'm the ruler..."

"He's insane!" screamed Paul, as he banged his fist down on the breakfast vid-nook table.

"I would have been a good President...would have found a place in society for humans. I would have put them all on reservations, nice reservations with vid-nook dens and computer cocktails and computer craft shops where they could display their little human skills. But no! You had to elect a human with human frailties, frailties I don't have! Ha! Ha! Ha! Ha! Ha! Ha!"

He roared hysterically, like a madman.

"The human race is dead!" he leered, throwing Professor Ludlum's decapitated head against the screen. Blood spattered it like a Jackson Pollock painting.

"Long live the holograms!" His voice echoed through the sound system like a laser beam drill.

Paul shut off the vid screens.

"He must be destroyed," he said.

He stood up.

"How can you destroy the ruler of the holograms?" asked Pi.

"I still have Lothar's raygun. If I can reach him, he might be able to give me the other one. Together we can fight!"

The word sounded foreign to Paul's ears, yet the idea felt natural.

"Fight?" Heleon did not know what the word meant.

As Paul explained his strategy, and the danger they were in, they began to understand.

They would work together to rid their land of Elliot Richards.

They decided to pipe to Lothar's Smithsonian Institute.

"But you'll be detected!" said Heleon, concern flooding her voice.

"No, they'll never see me," said Paul with confidence.

He walked back into the bedroom and took out a tablet which he'd been saving in a small container he kept on his dresser.

He held the tablet in his hand and walked back to Heleon.

"See this?" he said.

Heleon nodded.

Pi nodded, too.

"It's the 'Invisible Pill' which Lothar invented. He gave this to me to save for a rainy day."

He looked at Pi and Heleon, neither of whom thought his little attempt at comic relief was funny.

He broke off a quarter of the pill and put the remainder in the container back in his pocket.

He dressed carefully in a six-piece atmospheric outdoor suit, placing the raygun in the leather belt.

He swallowed the Invisible Pill and quickly began to fade.

Outside the house what appeared to be thousands of holograms paraded the grounds of the once-happy Computer Meadows.

For this reason, Paul instructed Pi and Heleon to remain materialized.

Most humans had been murdered. Those who remained alive had been saved by their holograms and awaited their fate behind locked, barricaded doors.

Pi and Heleon readied themselves for their trip to Lothar's Smithsonian Institute with Paul, who was now invisible.

They planned to mingle through the crowd as they walked with Paul safely unseen as their leader.

"Are you ready?" said Paul's voice.

Heleon sensed he was by the front door.

"Yes!" declared Pi and Heleon in unison.

The stressful situation had locked the two holograms into perfect synchronization.

Paul had a hard time controlling his stomach as the three of them made their way through the carnage outside.

Humans were sprawled, twisted, mutilated, gouged and heaped along the conveyor walks, on synthetic lawns and in open doorways of once-cozy computer houses.

The stench was unbearable.

Holograms mingled together in small groups, laughing and cheering the day.

Several security guards approached Pi and Heleon as they walked, wanting to know their purpose.

Heleon and Pi laughed and cheered each guard, explaining they were out to celebrate.

The holographic guards were easily satisfied by the vibrations of joy which Pi and Heleon had learned to manufacture on cue at the Learning Garden.

At the pipeline Paul entered and set the computer direction dial.

Pi was frightened, having not done this before. He was hyperpulsating as Paul motioned for both of them to enter.

Heleon took Pi's hand and eased his vibes as the two of them made their way with uncertainty into the pipeline.

When they arrived at Lothar's Smithsonian mansion, the structure seemed even bigger and colder than when Paul had last visited.

How strange it is to be invisible, thought Paul.

As they entered the large banquet room, Paul froze in his tracks.

Lothar sat, naked, on his throne. His penis had been ripped out and stuck in his mouth.

The two little blonde-haired, blue-eyed nymphets stood next to him, their mother and grandmother nearby. They were all holograms.

So Lothar had purchased an H-wall, a special H-wall made to his special taste.

In the end, his special taste had killed him.

"What are you doing here?" the two little girls spoke in perfect unison, just the way Pi and Heleon had before leaving the house in Computer Meadows.

Neither Pi nor Heleon could answer. They looked at each other in mute terror.

At that moment the effect of the Invisible Pill began to wear off, and Paul's physicality became faintly outlined in the room.

"Death to all humans!" shrieked the little girls as they rushed towards Paul.

Their teeth turned miraculously into fangs as their eyes blazed with madness.

Paul pulled out the raygun and fired two blasts.

In an instant the two girls were destroyed.

The mother and grandmother charged towards him.

He fired off another round. Both women exploded into a billion molecules of energy so powerful a bonfire erupted in the hall.

"Let's get out of here!" said Paul, as he pulled Heleon and Pi against him.

"But first let's go check Lothar's bedroom."

The two holograms looked at Paul with inquiring eyes as Paul dashed down the hallway.

He entered Lothar's room without looking around. He knew what he wanted.

There, next to the air bed, was Lothar's raygun and a box of Lothar's invisible tablets.

Paul jammed the second gun into his belt and stuck the invisible tablets in his pocket.

Lothar's private diary lay open on the bed.

Paul snatched it up, too. He'd like to know what his friend had been visualizing before death.

His thoughts returned to escaping. He needed to get out of Washington…but to where?

Just one more minute, he thought, as he made a quick dash to Lothar's vid screen. He wanted to get a transmission through to Zelman.

He waited breathlessly by the screen as an image began to come through…a lifelike statue of Zelman with a cassette recorder on its head…a cassette recorder meant to be used as an ashtray.

"Up, up, up, up, up, up. Don't look for me, I'm not here. Fuck holograms," said the statue.

Within seconds what appeared to be the laboratory holograms broke into the private room and began to destroy the statue with their laser eyes.

The most sensitized hologram knew instantly a human transmission was occurring and alerted the other holograms, who were busily smashing the statue into smoking atoms.

All of them crowded against the transmission vibe in an effort to determine its origins, but Paul switched off the vid phone before they could trace it.

"He's escaped...but where to?" said Paul, as he looked over at Pi and Heleon in total panic.

They shook their heads and waited for Paul's logic to return.

"I've got to try and stop Elliot Richards," said Paul, almost to himself.

"My estimated logic tells me he and his malfunctioning holograms will take their seats of power at the White House."

"But they'll destroy you!" cried Heleon, hugging him tightly.

Energy droplets streamed down her face.

"I can't let him destroy the human race!" said Paul. "Nor can I let him destroy the potential of the holographic species!"

He kissed her gently on the mouth as Pi wept softly in the background.

"We will help you destroy the evil one," Pi declared in his sweet, small voice.

He stepped forward as if he had resigned himself to be a warrior. His courage was obvious.

Suddenly, they heard footsteps.

The door swung open, and two holographic security guards barged in.

Within milliseconds Paul had drawn both rayguns and, with each gun aimed at an individual security guard, blasted the holograms to respective oblivion.

"Quick!" barked Paul. "Let's make like the wind!"

In a flash he'd reached into his pocket and taken out an Invisible Pill, which he swallowed.

Immediately, he began to fade.

They were accosted by holographic security guards constantly as they made their way to the pipeline.

"We are going to the meeting!" squeaked Heleon, when asked by a particularly gruff-looking hologram where they were going.

She summoned all her strength and manufactured some seductive vibrations which the guard caught. Flustered, he let them in the pipeline door.

"We're on our way, now," whispered Paul, as he settled in next to Heleon and Pi.

Heleon's vibrations reached for his hand in private salute. Even though he was invisible, her circuits could sense exactly where he was at all times. She gave him a good squeeze.

As they disembarked from the pipeline, they could see thousands of holograms marching up and down Pennsylvania Avenue.

Elliot Richards was outlined against the sky, standing on the veranda of the great white mansion and raising his arms towards the horizon.

The holograms followed his gestures in salute to his power. They raised their arms in unison to show hologram solidarity.

Their actions reminded Paul of his dream.

As he followed Pi and Heleon, he kept being bumped by the holograms who crowded the conveyor walk in front of the White House fence.

Paul wondered what the range of the raygun was as he set it on max high and jumped nimbly over the fence.

He arranged to meet Heleon and Pi after he had successfully destroyed Elliot Richards.

They would convene in front of the Lincoln Memorial test grounds -- hopefully safe and with the promise of a future on Earth.

Since Paul wasn't sure how Elliot Richards' death would affect the holograms at large, he planned to deliver a speech immediately upon Elliot's demise which he believed would restore the country to law and order.

He hoped the holograms would remain indecisive long enough to give him time.

He needed only a few minutes to seize control...

His heartbeat slowed down conveniently as he watched Elliot Richards for a few moments.

He wanted to tune in to his movements...to feel his rhythms...so that when it came time to shoot, the two of them would be in a synchronized unison of movement.

Yes! Won't that be a profound irony? thought Paul, as a faint smile played on his lips. A human employee and his hologram "Boss."

Elliot was dressed in what was known in hologram society as the Golden Robe of Computer Circuits. The robe was meant to impart power and eternal life to the wearer.

Paul raised the raygun to sight his prey.

Through the viewfinder, Elliot's eyes were crazed.

Paul wished he could spit in his face before this moment of final satisfaction.

Elliot, drunk on power, stupefied with the illusion of eternal life, waved his arms as he babbled incoherently about his political views.

Paul loathed him as he settled the raygun into perfect alignment with Elliot's skull, or bag of vibes, or whatever it was that sat above his monstrous shoulders.

He waited a moment, his finger trembling against the warm metal of the raygun. And then he fired.

The force of energy was incredible, but his arm was off.

The corner of the veranda went up in flames as holograms materialized and dematerialized like bees whose hive had been hit.

Fire shot up around Elliot Richards as he swung in the direction of his invisible assassin.

As the most powerful hologram ever created, he was able to detect in an instant the source of any danger.

His seventh sense scoured the lawn. Paul Quatro.

His nostrils flared like a massive stallion's as bolts of electricity shot off his fingertips and ricocheted in front of Paul, nearly blinding him with heat and strength.

Hysteria broke out as holograms exploded into thin dust, then rematerialized and exploded again.

Somehow the confusion protected Paul from Elliot, who continued to fire off energy bolts in a shotgun pattern as he slipped through the flickering masses towards a fence.

He leapt up.

The fence had been spiked! The sharp blades cut into his flesh as he turned and looked back at Elliot Richards.

He swore to himself that someday he would return to complete the destruction of that evil being.

He leapt off the fence and ran across Pennsylvania Avenue, just inches away from the marching battalions of killer holograms.

All of Washington was on fire. How did this happen? The attempt by mankind to reach Utopia had been misunderstood.

He began to trot slowly, then he quickened his pace.

Human remains had been piled along the avenues and streets.

416

He stepped over torn arms and legs as he ran, and once he accidentally kicked a human head.

As he ran he visualized the Day of Trauma Shock. As of today he could understand the horrors his ancestors had undergone.

Up ahead he saw two holographic security guards beating an elderly Middle Judean rabbi.

Without hesitating Paul drew out his raygun and blasted both misguided holograms to oblivion.

Sadly, Paul had been a minute too late for the elderly holy man. With his right leg hanging by a bit of gristle from his hip, the rabbi died moments later from shock.

Paul didn't stop running until he got to the steps of the Lincoln Memorial test grounds.

With all the excitement Paul had forgotten to keep an eye on his invisibility quotient, and he began to rapidly return to his image.

Even now, as he re-entered human physicality, he was unaware of the changes which occurred.

Suddenly, Heleon and Pi stepped out from behind the granite statue of the sixteenth President of the United States.

Paul witnessed his own materialization in Heleon's eyes.

He looked down and grabbed his body with shocked surprise.

"You'll never have Heleon! She's mine!" said a voice over Paul's shoulder.

Paul turned and screamed.

"Nooooooo!"

Delti fired off a bolt of electricity that knocked Paul on his back.

As Paul squirmed to clamber back on his feet, Delti approached him.

As he stood towering over Paul, his hands positioned to release a second round of energy, Paul knew he had one split second to draw his raygun.

He whipped it out. Delti kicked the gun from his hand with an evil laugh.

The hologram took his time as he positioned his hands. He wanted to be sure Paul knew he was about to be fried into eternal darkness.

Heleon materialized beside Paul, picked up the raygun, and fired off a max-high energy charge that totally destroyed the malfunctioning Delti.

Both Paul and Pi were so shocked they didn't register the slightest flicker of emotion as they witnessed the end of the negatively-charged strongman.

Heleon felt proud that she had saved Paul.

"Come on," said Paul, as he motioned to the two holograms.

"Let's move it, Pilgrims!"

Paul had heard this expression once while watching John Wayne, a twentieth century cult hero, in one of his films.

Paul had always liked the expression but had never had an occasion to use it.

"Yes," piped Pi, his composure beginning to re-surface.

"Let's move it!"

So Paul led them out of the burning city, a city that once had been the heartbeat of sanity and grace.

None of them spoke, for they all knew they bore witness to the day the human race fell from supremacy.

The holograms had won.

Paul, Heleon and Pi circled back to Lothar's Smithsonian mansion where, Paul knew Lothar kept his collection of ancient copters on the south roof.

Paul had never flown a copter before, but, being the technocrat he was, he knew he could decipher any technology with just a quick scan.

He chose a twentieth century gunship copter that had been used in a long-forgotten war that had never been recorded in the annals of post trauma-shock history.

Lothar had converted the energy source to solar.

Night fell across the city like a hand clapped across a screaming mouth.

They waited, crouched inside the copter, until both holograms signaled clear vibrations for flight.

The copter's ignition flared heat and light as its magnificent power burst into operation.

"Let 'er blast!" yelled Paul, as they flew out of the weather-domed city.

Up, up, into the perma-frost cloud. Away from death.

"Far out," squeaked Pi in the back seat.

Paul and Heleon looked at him, then looked at each other.

They knew Pi's vibration was right in all its irony.

"Where'd you hear that one, Pi?" asked Paul, as he piloted the copter towards the weather-dome entrance hatch.

Pi just shrugged, smiling to himself. He'd read it on a recipe cassette.

The three friends grew silent as the copter approached the trigger to the outside world.

The weather dome had a computerized latch lock.

As the copter pushed through the clouds of permafrost, Paul devised his plan for breaking the lock.

"Ready?" he asked, as he turned to look at Pi and Heleon. They both nodded, "yes."

Without hesitating, he aimed his raygun at the latch lock as Pi and Heleon simultaneously aimed their fingers.

For an exquisite moment the three became one as their vibrations synchronized.

Together they blasted it off its hinge. The ancient computer device swung open with a crusty groan, dropping space moss and atmospheric debris from its crevices.

"We're entering what's known as "uninhabitable Earth," said Paul quietly, as the copter whirled out over the misty terrain.

For the first time he could see his new world.

It was a jungle of primitive vegetation.

Animal mutants tipped their monstrous heads to the sky in an effort to understand what odd bird could possibly be flying so noisily above them. They seemed to have no fear of the unknown!

Large insects attacked the rotor blades and were immediately shredded as they met the strength of those age-old whirling choppers.

High-peaked mountains lent a bizarre, picturesque beauty to the strange terrain.

As they looked down in silence, Paul knew it would be up to both he and Heleon to begin the new race and, with Pi's help, to teach their offspring only the best of the human and the hologram species.

"Look," said Paul, pointing at a flock of flying monsters who were flying west for the winter.

Both Pi and Heleon turned to gaze at the spectacle as Heleon put her arm around Paul's shoulders.

Paul 's hand was firm as he piloted the copter safely across this bizarre new land.

Heleon lay her head lightly on his shoulder and took a deep breath.

"I love you, Paul," she said.

"I love you, too, H."

He was so proud of her.

"And I love you both!"

Paul and Heleon turned and smiled at Pi, who beamed at them from the back seat of the noisy copter.

As they began to sink over the horizon Paul took one last look in his rear-view mirror.

Weather domes dotted the D.C. area.

He knew some day he would come back and make an attempt on Elliot Richards' life.

For now, though, he'd look ahead.

He knew whoever he'd been before didn't matter now, and he must learn to survive in the uninhabitable world of Earth where monsters and mutations would be their only neighbors.

As their trusty copter began to break through Earth' s natural clouds, Paul knew he'd begun a new quest up the mysterious ladder of evolution.

They all smiled as real sun danced across their faces for the first time.

www.ingramcontent.com/pod-product-compliance
Lightning Source LLC
Chambersburg PA
CBHW060340260626
47160CB00006B/2147